What readers are saying

KNOWING PEOPLE

and

The Val & Kit Mystery Series

FIVE STARS! "Intrigue and shenanigans! Val and Kit rank among my all-time favorite characters—yin and yang. *Knowing People* continues the adventures of this entirely relatable pair. It's the best kind of mystery—entertaining, witty and unguessable until the writers are ready to expose the secrets. No worries if you haven't read the others in the Val and Kit series—they work in any order and each mystery is its own fun!"

FIVE STARS! "Another great Val and Kit mystery! The twists and turns throughout the book, especially toward the end, kept me at the edge of my seat. Would highly recommend!"

FIVE STARS! "Another extraordinary read about Val and Kit, two friends who know each other better than they know themselves. The authors have taken us on another adventure full of suspenseful twists and turns. When the story comes to an end you feel sad it has ended, and yet excited for the next book and adventures for Val and Kit to begin."

FIVE STARS! "Love the newest Val & Kit mystery. Wit, love, mystery. And all pulled together beautifully at the end. Just might be my favorite."

FIVE STARS! "This series is a fun read. There's friendship, suspense, mystery, humor and a bit of romance for good measure."

FIVE STARS! "My favorite so far! It's easy to get lost in the story, and the characters seem real. Their dialogue is SO readable, you don't even think of it as dialogue. And best ending ever. I cannot tell you how much I loved it!!!!"

FIVE STARS! "Loved it soooo much! I couldn't put it down—family had to go without dinner! The best one yet!"

FIVE STARS! "These girls bring a sense of humor and a lot of fun . . . They always keep me guessing until the end—not only about the who but the why."

FIVE STARS! "This is my favorite series. I know I could be BFFs with Val and Kit. Characters are real. Writing is smart and funny . . . who could ask for more?? Well, I could . . . more books, please!!!"

FIVE STARS! "When meeting an old friend for coffee and a chat, do you think to yourself 'Wow, I really miss them. Why do we wait so long to catch up?' That is exactly how I feel every time I read a Val & Kit Mystery. Like I just sat down for a hilarious chat over coffee and cake followed by wine and chocolate. These girls are a hilarious mix of Laurel and Hardy with a dash of Evanovich sprinkled with Cagney & Lacey. Comedy, love and mystery: a brilliant combination."

FIVE STARS! "Easy reads, page-turners and full of fun can describe this series. Though these books aren't deep and overwrought, the characters are wonderfully developed. I can see each of them so clearly in my mind's eye. For me that's the mark of a good read. Delightful and entertaining. I can't wait for the next installment. Thanks, Roz and Patty!"

Knowing People
A Val & Kit Mystery

Rosalind Burgess
and
Patricia Obermeier Neuman

Cover by

Laura Eshelman Neuman

ISBN: 9798686867710

Blake Oliver Publishing
BlakeOliverPublishing@gmail.com
rozandpattywriters@gmail.com

Acknowledgments

We cannot adequately express our deep gratitude for our copy editor, Sarah Paschall, who parses our every word in search of mistakes and inaccuracies. We so appreciate her expertise and the gift of her time. We also would never go to print without those willing to be our beta readers: Michael Gerbino, Ella Hunt, Kerri Hunt, John Neuman, Laura Neuman, Clayton "Pete" Obermeier, Anna Lydia Tracy, Emma Tracy, and Melissa Tracy. They, too, share with us the precious commodity time, and their feedback gives us the confidence to send our book on its way to our readers (whom we also thank from the bottom of our hearts).

In memory of Bruce

Knowing People
A Val & Kit Mystery

The Val & Kit Mystery Series

CHAPTER ONE

The first time I saw my new neighbor, I was at Hannah's Nail Salon getting my twice-yearly manicure.

Hannah, whose given name is Huong, sat across from me, vigorously filing the nails on my right hand while keeping an eye on the fingers of my left, which were submerged in a bowl of green liquid.

"Is this dish soap?" I asked her. Same question I ask her twice a year.

She smiled, without looking up, and gave me her biyearly response. "No, it's an ancient Vietnamese nail-improving liquid; it's good for cuticles. It also works great for dried-on food particles." She glanced up and gave me a wink. "Do you want color today? Maybe red? Or pink?" Her eyes traveled to the station next to me, where her sister Phuong was applying a bright-red polish on another customer's nails.

"I think I'll stay with clear."

"Hmm." Hannah frowned. "Maybe you'd like to try Pink Paradise?" She stopped filing briefly and used her nail file to indicate one of the bottles of polish displayed behind her. "It's very chic," she said.

"No. Let's go with the clear."

Hannah nodded. Decision made. No point in arguing with her boring client.

Meanwhile, the customer next to me, who appeared to be in her early thirties, glanced over and gave me a weak smile.

"Your nails look beautiful," I said to her, and her weak smile got slightly stronger. But then she turned her attention back to Phuong. Oh yes, Red Nails was my new neighbor, although at the time, I didn't know it.

***

The second time I saw my new neighbor was in the parking lot of my apartment building. When I pulled in, I noticed that my favorite spot next to the dumpster was taken, and I was forced to pull in three cars down from the interloper. While I sat in my car removing the aux cord from my phone, silencing Wham! from being woken up before they could go-go, I noticed Red Nails exit from the passenger side of the brown sedan in my spot. At the same time, another woman got out from the driver's side, and the two of them proceeded to the trunk, where they removed several grocery bags.

"Hello." I waved at them as they walked past my car, their arms full.

Red Nails stopped, but her companion kept walking.

"Hi," I spoke again. "Are you moving in?" This, by the way, was a total assumption on my part since they could have been visitors, or volunteers from the local food bank, or in fact just nice people delivering groceries to the elderly (there are plenty of those in my building).

Red Nails looked hesitant before replying, keeping one eye on the other woman. "Yes," she said.

"Number 201?" I asked. "That's two doors down from me."

Red Nails gave me her feeble smile. "Nice to meet you," she said.

"Val," I offered. "Nice to meet you too."

A few seconds passed, and then she said, "Autumn Grey. I'm Autumn Grey."

Then her companion turned. "C'mon," she called. "We need to leave."

"Sorry, I have to go." Autumn looked apologetic. "Er . . . maybe we can . . ." She didn't finish her sentence, but gave me a nod and walked quickly toward her buddy.

Although I didn't have any reason to, I delayed following. If nothing else, I know when I'm not wanted. So I waited long enough for them to make it up to the second floor, and then started for my own apartment. But not before I noticed the car they had arrived in had Washington, DC, plates.

***

Since my divorce, I've lived alone in what I describe as a desirable apartment in a five-story building in a captivating neighborhood in Downers Grove, Illinois. I use adjectives like "desirable" and "captivating" every day since I work in real estate and the lingo comes naturally. But the reality is, my apartment has three rooms; the security of the building is questionable, at best; and my reserved parking space is really reserved for whoever gets there first. And, I love the place.

When I was married, I lived in a palatial house (by comparison, anyway). But it was never really desirable, and my ex-husband kept it far from captivating. So, after my divorce, moving to my current abode seemed equivalent to permanently locking myself in my bedroom. My daughter, now in her twenties and living in California with her husband, is the only thing I miss from my former life.

I threw my keys into the extra-large coffee mug emblazoned with a picture of William and Kate that I bought on a recent trip to England and now keep on my kitchen counter for such purposes. The counter serves as my dining table and separates my galley kitchen from the living room.

Next, I headed straight for my couch and perched my laptop on my knees. I logged on to Facebook and typed *Autumn Grey* in the search box. Predictably, there were too many Autumns for me to take the time to count, and I gave up just as my cell phone rang. The screen indicated a call from Kit James, my best friend of over forty years and the one person who would not find it odd for me to be checking up on my neighbor thirty minutes after meeting her.

"Val, whatcha doin'?" Kit asked.

"Well," I said, moving to the refrigerator and taking out a half-empty bottle of Diet Dr Pepper, "I have a new neighbor, and so I was just—"

"New neighbor?" Kit sounded incredulous. "Someone new moved into that place you call home?" From her own palatial house that is most definitely desirable and in a captivating neighborhood, my friend thinks any apartment building without a doorman means you are living on skid row.

"Yes, Kit, someone new moved in. And I met her in the parking lot—"

"Ha! You call that a parking lot—"

"Her name's Autumn Grey. She looks to be in her early thirties at the most. Sort of attractive. She arrived in a car driven by a friend, or at least another person, and it had Washington, DC, plates. I actually first saw her when I was getting my nails done earlier this morning—"

"Oh, did Huong seem busy? I just broke a nail, and I should go see her." Kit, who visits Hannah every ten days, insists on using our manicurist's Vietnamese name. She says it's too beautiful not to. Plus, I think she thinks it gives her an edge.

"Don't know," I answered. "Surprisingly, she didn't show me her appointment book."

"I bet she can fit *me* in." Kit paused before continuing. "Do you realize there are millions of Autumn Greys on Facebook?" She was obviously having the same idea as I was, only doing it much more thoroughly.

"How did you count that fast?"

"*Approximately*, Val. Approximately."

"It was kinda weird. When I introduced myself to her, she barely gave me her name. But when I ran into Hettie Randall—"

"The woman who smells like cheese?"

"Yes, her, but she does not smell like cheese. So, she's across the hall from this Autumn Grey, and she heard her moving in. Apparently, Autumn lives alone and is possibly from Arizona."

"Hmm, how did Cheesy come up with that?"

"She told her. Well, about living alone. I came up with the Arizona part. I was next to Autumn when she paid for her nails at Hannah's. When she opened her wallet, I saw an Arizona driver's license."

"I see six Autumn Greys from Arizona," Kit said as I quickly scrolled down the list on my own computer, finding none who resembled my neighbor. "So, anyway," Kit changed the subject, "I'm fixing jambalaya tonight. New recipe. Wanna come for dinner?"

My friend, whose many accomplishments include gourmet cooking, was hard to resist when my own meal plan was a bowl of Cheerios. "Is it a special occasion?" I asked, knowing full well she needed no such thing to cook something delectable.

"No, but I have some leftover andouille sausage in the fridge that I need to use up."

Who has leftover andouille sausage? Or leftover anything? I thought of the contents of my own refrigerator, which, since I'd removed the Diet Dr Pepper, now contained a box of Velveeta Cheese, two limes that had shriveled to the size of grapes, and an unopened bottle of a decent chardonnay. Realizing I didn't even have the milk necessary to accompany my Cheerios, I was happy to accept the invitation. "Love to." I shut down my computer. "I'll be there at seven. Can I bring something?"

"Funny." Kit laughed, and then we said good-bye.

***

Later that evening, when I was on the way to my car armed with the bottle of chardonnay, I saw Autumn Grey again. She and the other woman were standing by the trunk of the Washington, DC, vehicle. I couldn't hear their conversation, but when they saw me, it seemed like a signal for them to stop talking. I watched Autumn type something into her phone, and then they shook hands and the unknown woman got into the car and left the parking lot, driving past me. Standing alone now, Autumn wrapped her oversize cardigan tightly around her slim body and hurried by me, her head down.

"Hi," I said to her disappearing back, but she didn't hear me, or pretended not to, and then she was gone.

CHAPTER TWO

L arry," Kit said, "you want more?"

Larry James smiled across the kitchen table at his wife and rubbed his stomach. "Why's she always trying to fatten me up, eh, Val?"

I smiled at my dear friend in commiseration. I've known him almost as long as I've known Kit, and if there's been any fattening up, it looks good on his six-foot frame. The rounder cheeks he now sports enhance his amiable face and complement his balding head. We went to the same high school, same football games, and same proms. My detour was marrying David, but thank goodness I got back on the right track. "She probably has some evil plan," I said. "By the way, this is magnificent jambalaya, Kit. Best I've ever tasted."

"Thank you," Kit purred. "It is rather good, isn't it? Better than any I've tasted in New Orleans."

"Hah!" Larry winked at me. "New Orleans! What do those people down there know about Cajun food?"

"Exactly." Kit broke off a piece of her homemade French bread and used it to wipe the edge of her plate. "Hey, did I tell you, Val, that Sam might be coming home for a visit?"

"Oh, that would be great." I copied her plate-cleaning method with my own piece of French bread. "When? What's he up to?"

Kit and Larry's only son lives in Texas. A good-looking guy close in age to my daughter, Emily. He hadn't been home to Chicago for almost two years, but his parents had been down to see him—Kit more often than Larry.

"Soon" was all she said in response. "Key lime pie, anyone?"

The pie was creamy and tangy, just the way it should be. After finishing my glass of wine, I took my purse from the back of my chair and reluctantly rose from the kitchen table. "I really should go. I have work tomorrow."

Larry stood and leaned over to kiss me on the cheek. "Good to see you, Val. Tell Tom hi. How is the old buzzard?"

Tom Haskins, my boss and owner of Haskins Realty, also went to high school with us, and he and Larry remain buddies.

"He's good."

Kit rose too and busied herself filling a container with a generous amount of jambalaya and another with key lime pie. Then she put them in a Whole Foods sack and handed it to me. I rarely leave Kit's house without some delicious leftovers. When we reached the front door, my pal gave me a hug. "By the way, I can confirm there is no Autumn Grey from Arizona on Facebook who fits your description," she said, sounding a little too much like a CIA operative.

"*What?* You didn't really check—"

"Of course not; that would be a total waste of time." Kit looked pleased with herself. "I had Larry do it."

"Wait a minute; you actually asked Larry to—"

"Exactly. I told him she was my new gynecologist and I wanted to check her profile. By the way, I can also confirm there are no doctors with that name specializing in that field."

"I can't believe you made Larry do that."

"It didn't come cheap, Val. I had to promise to go with him to that blasted golf-banquet thingy next Friday."

"But still—"

"Oh, and he insisted I find a new doc."

I laughed and gave her a hug. "Thanks for dinner. And this." I held up the Whole Foods sack.

"You're welcome." She patted me on the back as I turned to leave. "You're always welcome. Oh, and I put some clementines in there, nice and juicy; don't let them dry out."

"Right." I nodded, thinking of the shriveled limes she'd given me several weeks ago.

I took a step into the night and then turned back toward her. "That's great about Sam. Is he coming on vacation or business or what?"

Her smile vanished. "Good question. I don't know. But Val, I have a feeling something's wrong. As soon as I know, you will too."

***

I'd barely gotten settled in bed, remote in hand and ready to watch a *Law & Order* episode I'd seen only a few times, when my phone rang. I considered letting it go to voice mail until I saw that it was Kit.

I'd thought about Sam as I'd driven home and then gone through my nightly routine of getting ready for bed. At first I tried to think what could possibly be wrong for the young man who had achieved great success as both a Texas ranch owner and businessman at such an early age. And then my thoughts turned to the Sam I'd watched grow up, as I worked through my four nightly tasks (when *had* I quit going to bed with makeup on and turned into my *mother*, brushing and flossing and removing makeup and putting night cream on my face and neck?).

I found myself thinking of Sam the adorable little boy who had more energy than his mother, more energy than *five* Kits. And Sam the charming teenage son of my best friend, the guy both of his parents so wanted Emily to pair up with, the kid I wanted Emily *not* to pair up with. I just didn't trust him, even though I really wanted to, and that broke my heart.

I love Larry and Kit as much as I love my brother, Buddy, and for that matter, I wanted to love Sam that much too. But I never saw him as boyfriend (let alone husband!) material for my Emily. I'd been so relieved when in spite of a few dates with Sam, including one prom and one college dance, she met Luke, and the rest, as they say, is history.

I glanced at the small bowl of ice cream on my nightstand (I know; the key lime pie should have been enough) and made a mental note to take it to the freezer if Kit and I talked more than two minutes. Then I sighed, knowing that was a given, and climbed out of bed. "Hey, girlfriend. What's up?" I answered my phone as I made my way to the kitchen with the Ben & Jerry's Chunky Monkey. This was the first bowl of the new month, one of three or four (depending on the restraint I could muster when dishing up) I would have from the one container I allowed myself to buy each month. "Did you hear from Sam already?"

"Val. You just left here."

I thought she sounded annoyed, like I feel when my mom pesters me for news of Emily's job. My daughter's a striving actress, recently back in Hollywood—or as close to it as she and Luke can afford to live—after residing in England for a year. My mother is always bugging me to find out if Emily has gotten any new parts. I always tell her, sounding like Kit did now, that if I hear anything, she'll be the first to know. But still, she calls from her home in Wisconsin almost daily to ask.

When my pal didn't continue, I filled the silence. "I know. I just thought that because you were calling—"

"I was just googling Autumn Grey. Ya know, because you said she acted kinda weird. Also because you said the car had DC plates. That's weird too."

"How is *that* weird?"

"Because Buddy lives in DC," she said, her tone adding an unspoken *duh*.

"For Pete's sake, Kit. I'm sorry I even told you about Autumn. You always make something out of nothing."

"Oh, I don't know about that. I might argue that my somethings usually amount to, well, *something*."

She had a point there.

But right now, all I wanted to think about was my Chunky Monkey and *Law & Order*. "Why *did* you call, Kit? Before we forget." I smiled as I thought of all the times we get sidetracked with our chitchat and have to phone one another back about the *real* reason for the original call. But the chuckle of acknowledgment I'd expected wasn't forthcoming.

"I didn't hear from Sam, but I did want to talk to you about him. Without Larry around."

"So you weren't really calling about Autumn Grey?" I felt relieved that my friend wasn't as desperate for something to do as I was beginning to fear. I'd been about to suggest she get a job. Which was about as likely as me quitting mine.

"Nah. I was just finding it hard to tell you what I should have told you already. About Sam."

I felt a lump form in the pit of my stomach. Kit and I tell each other *everything*. What was so bad with Sam that she hadn't been able to tell me?

"Oh, crap," I said as I heard a knocking on my door. I didn't want to be interrupted just now, but I am the worst when it comes to ignoring ringing phones or someone at my door. I'd like to think it's intense curiosity, but I know it's more likely attributable to fear. Fear that something is wrong and that someone is trying to let me know. Fear of so many things, another trait inherited from my mother.

Valerie, make sure no one follows you from the grocery store; that's how rapists get you. (I always thought rapists wanted your help to find a missing puppy. Or was that only kidnappers and serial killers?)

"What?" Kit sounded annoyed with me again.

"Just someone at my door. I'll ignore it. Go on. Tell me about Sam, Kitty Kat."

"Is it someone buzzing to get in from outside the building?" she asked, referencing the system that works only sometimes.

"No. At my apartment door."

"I'd rather talk tomorrow in person, anyway," she said, and I thought she sounded okay. "Go answer your door. Maybe it's Autumn Grey. Just don't let a rapist in." She giggled, and so I decided she really was okay. (Apparently, she doesn't know that rapists follow you from the grocery store—and I hadn't grocery shopped in about a week.)

Not surprisingly, Kit was right. As she'd said, she usually is. It *was* Autumn Grey. I would have been shocked to see her standing there, had it not been for Kit's suggestion. So instead, I was able to forego any display of astonishment and graciously invite her in.

What did surprise me—and I couldn't believe I hadn't thought this earlier, like back in the salon—was Autumn's choice of bright-red nail polish. It just didn't go with the rest of her bland, if slightly pretty, appearance and her meek demeanor. While that was registering in my mind, I used one hand to pull down on my Cubs T-shirt that served as a nightgown, to try to eke out a bit more coverage, and I motioned with the other hand for Autumn to take a seat on my couch.

I watched her travel the few feet in mincing steps and then sit down tentatively on the edge of the cushion, as if to be ready for a quick getaway, and then I told her I'd be right back. When I returned, tying my cotton bathrobe around me, I noticed she was seemingly lost in thought as she gazed at my coffee table. Which had nothing on it.

I sat down on the chair next to the couch and took in the sight of her, waiting for her to say something. But still she stared at the coffee table with her wide-set pale-blue eyes, which were matched by her pale skin and paler white-blond hair. *Both her coloring and her bearing are actually colorless,* I thought. And I found myself wondering about the relationship between her and the woman I'd seen her with, who had definitely been old enough to be her mother. The only other thing I could remember about the older woman was her aloof attitude.

I decided that Autumn's companion was no business of mine. And Autumn herself was of interest only because she was sitting in my living room. "So, are you settling in okay?" I asked.

"What? Oh yes, thank you."

"You're new to town? To Chicagoland?"

"Chicagoland? Oh yes. I'm from Arizona." She nodded her head but didn't say anything further, so I felt compelled to continue.

"And your friend? Who was helping you move? She's from DC?" So much for her companion not being my business.

"She's not really my friend. I mean, I just met her. She helped me move here."

I couldn't help but note that Autumn seemed on firmer ground speaking about her nameless acquaintance than about herself.

"So, did work bring you to Downers Grove?" It felt like I was interviewing a candidate for a job. "Or do you have family here?" *Can you start on Monday, and should we talk 401k contributions?*

She hesitated, as if deciding. And then she said, "Work."

"What do you do?"

"Um, Valerie, did you say your name was?" She brushed her bangs to the side, as if to see better, and then quickly brushed them back to the center, where they covered her forehead and her pale eyebrows. When I nodded, she hurried on, apparently deciding to question *me*. "Have you always lived in Downers Grove?" Again, she reached up with one hand and flipped her bangs to the side and then back, as if she couldn't remember to just leave them where she wanted them—obscuring her face?

"Well, yes, I'm from Downers Grove. Born and bred. Would you like something to drink? A soda, or wine, or water?" The only thing I was sure I had was the water—from my tap—so I was relieved when she shook her head no.

"Does your family still live here?" she asked.

"Well, no." I was about to go through the short list that comprises my immediate family members and then thought better of it. "Just me," I said.

She nodded and furrowed her brow. "I'm an only child too," she said.

"I didn't mean I'm an only child. I have a brother who moved away long ago. He went to the Naval Academy," I said, feeling the pride that always wells up in me when I talk about Buddy and his life of service to our country and how he settled in the Washington, DC, area when he retired from the Navy—still quite young—to teach a class at the Academy.

She nodded, and then she asked, "Does he get back here often? Do you see him much?"

"Not as much as I'd like."

"Is he older than you or younger?" She looked like she was at that very moment trying to calculate *my* age.

"Older. So, you're an only child. My daughter is an only child. It can be hard. Say, Autumn, do you think we could have this visit some other time?" I pulled out a lapel of my robe to call attention to my attire and said, "I was actually in bed when you knocked. I've had a busy day."

She looked confused and then she stood. "Yes, forgive me. I should have known not to come this late. I really just wanted to know about the garbage removal."

"We take it out to the dumpster in the parking lot; didn't they tell you when you signed your lease?"

"I probably just forgot," she said, her back to me as she scurried to my door and let herself out. I thought I heard her mumble a good-bye, but I wasn't sure.

CHAPTER THREE

The next morning, I arrived at the office at the perfect time—meaning that Billie, our twentysomething and do-everything office manager, had already made coffee. I could smell its inviting aroma as soon as I opened the door.

Haskins Realty, where I've worked since Emily started high school a decade ago, is housed in a small office with a glass front wall. Since I'd pulled in next to the only car in the area, Billie's Prius, I knew our other two staff members were not in yet. Tom and his nephew, Perry (sometimes referred to as *my pain in the butt* by his uncle).

"Hi, chickadee," I called to Billie as she headed toward my desk with a freshly poured cup of coffee.

Since I'd last seen her, she had added a purple streak to her chestnut hair, which complemented the Black Sabbath T-shirt she was wearing under her red jumpsuit. "Hey, Val," she said. "How ya doing?"

"Good. What's going on this morning?" I took the cup she handed me and sipped the tasty brew. "Mmm. Thanks." I tapped my computer keyboard with my free hand.

"Perry has a dental appointment—"

"As in teeth whitening?"

"You got it. And Tom is due here any minute. You two are meeting with the Lavender Group this morning at ten."

"Right. Let's see . . ." I scrolled down my computer screen. "Those guys are—"

"Looking to secure the top five floors of the building on Weymouth. The CEO, Mike Pardy, the guy you are meeting, is a Colts fan. He graduated from Purdue, has a daughter studying economics in London, drives a Jaguar, goes fishing once a year in Minnesota—aren't you going to say anything, Val?"

"Ha." I laughed. "Like . . . what? That you're doing a fantastic job?"

"About my hair." She looked a little sad.

"Oh, you cut it?"

She looked even sadder. "Keep going."

"Oh." I dug my glasses out of my purse. "Er . . ."

"My streak!"

"I'm kidding," I said, not putting my glasses on. "I love it."

"Cool, right?"

"Way cool," I confirmed, not quite truthfully since I personally would never have messed with her glossy locks. But that's just me.

"Good." Billie brightened. "So, back to Mike Pardy; he's a big-time Catholic, and he's slightly diabetic, so—"

"Don't bring donuts?"

She laughed. "That's the idea."

Just then the front door swung open, and Tom Haskins stormed in. "Good morning, employees." He walked right past us toward the only room with a door, his office. "Billie, coffee. Val, bring me the Lavender file."

17

Billie handed me the file, which I hadn't even noticed she was carrying, and then turned her attention to Tom's coffee.

"So," I said when I sat down and faced him across his enormous desk. "Mike Pardy is the CEO, and he's—"

"What the hell has Billie done to her hair?"

"It's a purple streak."

"No kidding, Val." He stood and took off his bespoke jacket, carefully placing it on a wooden hanger. "That much I could figure out myself."

"Then why did you ask? There's not much more to say about it, except I like it."

"Yeah." Tom took the folder I handed him. "I doubt that very much. If she wants to change her hair, why doesn't she pick a pretty color, like yours?"

Such flattery from Tom is not the norm, and I suddenly felt pleased with my blond bob—also not the norm. Usually, I feel it is too short, too frizzy, or too . . . something.

Tom settled himself in his tufted-leather wingback chair and opened the file. He was done talking about hair. "So, what do we have here? Mike Pardy—"

"Billie says he's a Catholic, possibly diabetic, follows the Colts—"

"He's a closet drunk, sucks at golf, and wears cheap suits." Tom snapped the folder shut. "So, ready, Kiddo? Let's go sell this chump some office space."

***

After a successful meeting with Mike Pardy and two lesser executives of the Lavender Group, Tom released me from joining them for lunch, and so I headed back to the office, relishing the quiet of my car.

I glanced at the clock on my console and saw that it was after one already, and so I slowed down to pull into Steak 'n Shake on Ogden Avenue. The restaurant was crowded, but I was able to secure a booth by a window that looked out onto the parking lot. A pretty, blond waitress appeared at my table, pad in hand, ready to take my order. "What can I get you to drink?" she asked, not really looking at me.

"Water. Wait, water with lemon."

Now she did look at me and smiled. "Okay, I'll be right out with that and to take your order."

"Thanks," I said. "No, wait; could you bring me a vanilla shake instead of the water?"

She gave me another smile. "Okay, no water; just a shake."

"Wait," I said again. "I'll take the water too." This was in honor of the diet I had started last Thursday, dropped out of on Saturday, and started again on Monday.

"Coming up," she said, but not before a quick glance at the ten pounds I obviously needed to shed. Okay, make that fifteen.

I thanked her and took out my reading glasses to study the menu. I quickly decided on a Royale Steakburger because the fried egg and bacon would make it a combination breakfast and lunch. As I set the menu down, I glanced out the window just as two vehicles were backing out, exposing the car at the far end of the parking lot. A man and a woman were standing by the driver's door. The man was holding his phone, and they were both looking at the screen.

The woman looked familiar. When I removed my readers, I could clearly see that it was my new neighbor, Autumn Grey. She seemed to be listening intently to the man, nodding in compliance, one hand raised to her brow to shade her eyes from the bright sun.

I put my readers back on and glanced at the dessert section of the menu, then stopped. A cold feeling swept over me. I looked out again, in time to see the man open the car door for Autumn to climb in. When he closed the door after her, he looked toward the windows of the restaurant and then up and down the parking lot. And then he headed off on foot, presumably to his own car, but I couldn't see it.

Despite the aviator sunglasses he was wearing, there was no mistaking his identity. He had on a red golf shirt and navy pants, and his white hair was a little shorter than it had been the last time I'd seen him, in California.

But there was also no mistaking his six-foot frame and his strong, square chin. And it was a safe bet that under those aviators, his eyes were as blue as if Picasso himself had painted them (during his Blue Period).

"Ready to order?"

My head snapped back to the waitress, who was placing the vanilla shake in front of me. "Huh? Oh, sorry; give me a minute, would you?"

She smiled, not seeming a bit annoyed. "I'll be back with your water."

She left the table, and I immediately turned back to my view. The car, Autumn Grey, and Detective Dennis Culotta were gone. If he was even still a detective. If he'd even been there in the first place.

CHAPTER FOUR

I wasn't thrilled to get a phone call from my mom. I'd just buckled myself in and turned the air conditioner on full blast, prepared to call Kit as I drove back to the office. But before I could press my pal's name on its screen, my phone began playing the *Law & Order* theme song.

"Hi, Mom," I spoke into the air after pushing the answer button on my steering wheel, marveling as always at the technology that allows me to talk hands-free. I don't think I'll ever take it for granted, but I also don't think it will stay the latest and greatest for long. I put the car in reverse and turned my head to look over my shoulder.

"Valerie, what's wrong?"

"What's wrong? Nothing."

"You sound so . . . strained. Have you been lifting weights or something? You know you have to be careful—"

Okay, you caught me, Mom. I'm in training for a WWE match. "No, Mother, I haven't been lifting weights. I'm—"

"Well, I'm just concerned. No need to call me *Mother.*"

Only my mother would take offense at being called *Mother*. Although if I were honest with myself, I had to admit she was right: I use that form of address only when I am irritated with her. I smiled as I realized how surprising it is that I don't call her *Mother* more often. I pushed my way into the heavy traffic of Ogden Avenue and headed toward the office.

"Anyway," my mom went on, "I just wanted to know what you think."

Well, that was a rarity. "About what?" I stopped at a red light and grabbed my lipstick out of my purse. I didn't need to glance in the mirror to know I needed to reapply some color if I wanted to look awake, or at least alive.

"About Buddy, of course."

I pulled forward when the light turned green, having applied my Rum Raisin only to my top lip and hoping I wouldn't forget to cover my bottom lip with it when I stopped at the next light. And then I decided to eliminate that worry by simply rubbing my lips together, and I tossed the lipstick tube back into my open purse. "What about Buddy, *Mom*?"

"Well, should we all get together here or in Downers Grove?" She sighed, as if I were purposely being obtuse.

"What are you talking about?" I really had no idea. Was I forgetting something we'd already discussed?

"About his visit next week. Surely you know about that, Valerie. No, William Stuckey! I'm saving those tomatoes for dinner," I heard her yell at her husband. If her tone hadn't been so tense from the get-go, I would have joked that it sounded like the honeymoon was over, the way she'd just shrieked at him. But I figured the sustained use of that tone probably meant her obvious irritation this afternoon wasn't aimed at him—or at me. She was just stressed out, something she is really good at. Or bad at. I guess *practiced at* is the best way to put it.

"No, as a matter of fact, I don't know about any such thing. He's coming to visit? Chicago or Door County?"

"Well, that's what I'm asking *you*, Valerie. Pay attention. Obviously, he'll fly into Chicago, but do you want to drive up here with him, or should we all visit you?"

I would have laughed out loud, except now *I* was feeling stressed out just picturing trying to cram even *one* visitor into what my boss calls my rabbit hutch of an apartment. My *beloved* rabbit hutch, which does not, however, have room for any more bunnies. Just me.

"Why is he coming?" I avoided choosing between two evils by not answering her question.

Oh, I love my big brother, and I hadn't seen him for over a year—probably the longest separation ever. The last time he'd come was on business, and he'd stayed at the Union League Club in downtown Chicago. We'd had a blast meeting for lunch at Restoration Hardware and dining out that night at Mia Francesca. And he'd come out the next day on the train so we could do a drive-by tour of his old haunts in Downers Grove before meeting Tom for dinner at the newest steakhouse in town. Tom had driven him back downtown that night, and I'd felt happy that the two old pals had that time alone to reminisce about their high school days together—things that were probably best for a little sister not to know about. I'd been just as happy to get home to my bed and TV.

But the thought of Buddy *staying* in my nine-hundred-square-foot apartment I call home was laughable.

"Your brother can't come to visit his family?" my mother said. "Heaven knows he doesn't do it often." I was relieved to hear her irritation transfer from me to him, although I knew the one she really blamed for his visits being too infrequent was his wife, Elaine.

"No, I'm just surprised, that's all. I'm surprised he didn't let me know. When next week?"

"Monday."

Crap. It was already Thursday. No way could I make a trip to Door County, Wisconsin, on such short notice, even though I know that August up there is heavenly.

I groaned inwardly, envisioning my stacks of paperwork on the coffee table and the pile of unfolded laundry on the half of the bed I don't sleep in, as well as everything I'd removed from underneath my bathroom sink so the plumber could access a leaky pipe last week. I'd have to deal with all that, knowing Buddy might at the very least pop into my apartment at some point.

"Well, I am fully booked with showings for the next week, Mom. That's a good thing," I hurriedly assured her. "But I'll have to stay down here. Buddy could go up there for part of the time—"

"We all have to be together eventually, Valerie." I was about to ask her *why*, even though I knew she would take offense for some reason known only to her, when she answered my unspoken question. "He says he has something important to tell us, and he wants to do it in person."

Now I *really* wondered why he hadn't called me. And I was a little worried. But not enough to forget the main thing on my mind: Dennis Culotta and Autumn Grey.

***

Normally, the busy schedule I had of showing two different couples their potential dream homes would have kept my focus on smart thermostats and newly installed faucets. But instead, I was itching to touch base with my brother. And of all times, both couples wanted to make offers.

When I finally finished the last set of paperwork and graciously (I hoped) said good-bye to the young couple who seemed in no hurry to return to the home of the wife's parents where they were temporarily living, I decided to stop at Jewel before calling Buddy. I debated which wine to add to my grocery cart that held a six-pack of Diet Dr Pepper. I settled on pinot grigio and headed to the checkout, congratulating myself on the fact that the next time I offered a visitor wine or soda, I'd actually have some.

Before pulling out of the parking lot, I decided to call Buddy while I drove home. But as fingers have a way of doing, mine took on a will of their own, and instead of punching my brother's name in my phone's contacts, I scrolled down to the next letter and pushed the name of the other man who'd been on my mind all afternoon.

"Culotta," I heard, and it took my breath away. Apparently, it also took away my ability to speak. "Dennis Culotta here," the deep voice said more insistently, as if my silence were expressing doubt that it was really him.

But I had no doubt whatsoever. Only that voice could make me feel so weak in the knees even when I was sitting down. I tightened the grip on my steering wheel as if to keep from floating out of the sunroof in spite of my seat belt. "Hello, Dennis, it's Valerie Pankowski," I said at last, in a voice that was not mine.

"Valerie Pankowski!" He sounded pleased to hear from me. No, more than pleased. He sounded downright happy. But I'd soon take care of that. "How're you doing, Val? It's been a while."

"Yes. I've been great." There was a silence, and I was out of small talk. "So, Dennis. I just saw you. Uh . . . it made me realize how long it's been since we've spoken. Uh . . ." I wanted to crawl into my glove compartment and never come out. What *had* I been thinking, to place this call? Well, that was the problem. I'd done it with no forethought whatsoever. So it wasn't really my fault (which would be small comfort even if it *were* true).

He rescued me—but only momentarily. "It's great to hear your voice," he said. "When did you see me?" Suddenly his joy seemed diminished.

I wanted to say, *I saw you with Autumn Grey. Why? Who is she?* But I knew that would obliterate his joy—and any chance I'd have of him . . . what? What *did* I want from him? A date, I supposed. A chance to pick up where I felt we'd left off—*almost* kind of dating. Certainly feeling attracted to one another, attracted enough to enjoy a passionate kiss in the hotel hallway in Palm Desert. But mainly I wanted to know why he was chatting with my neighbor, and not me.

"*Where* did you see me?" Apparently, he'd decided if I couldn't remember *when*, maybe I could remember *where*.

"Oh, I was just having breakfast, um, lunch, um . . . whatever." I giggled, but it held no mirth, only nervousness. "At Steak 'n Shake. On Ogden. I saw you in the parking lot, talking to—"

"I'm sorry, Valerie. I have to go. It was good to hear from you."

And then silence.

I felt a different kind of weakness suffuse my body. No longer that of a teenage girl, this weakness was one of defeat, of humiliation, of regret. I was in my parking lot now and could not get up to the safe haven of my apartment fast enough.

CHAPTER FIVE

I took my new bottle of pinot out of the refrigerator and poured myself a glass. I wanted to tell Kit about seeing Culotta with Autumn, as well as my calling him. That hadn't amounted to anything other than leaving me feeling like a fool, but I did want my pal's thoughts on why Autumn might be talking to him.

"You busy?" I said as soon as she picked up the call.

"I was doing a quiz on Facebook. Apparently, I have the same IQ as Einstein."

"Hah. You needed a quiz to tell you that?"

"Not really, but it all makes sense now. So, what's going on?"

"Well . . ." I hesitated.

"Val, I can't talk long now. I have a blind person coming over, and she'll be here any minute."

"Blind person? What do you mean, blind person?"

"Didn't I tell you? I'm replacing the drapes in Larry's study."

"Oh, that's nice. What are you thinking?" I expected her to tell me she was having them custom woven by Tibetan monks.

"Something simple, sort of like yours."

"Mine?" I was shocked.

"Okay, not exactly like yours. I'm going with hardwood, made in an eco-friendly forest somewhere. The color is ecru."

"So basically nothing like mine." I was over my shock, thinking of my plain-white aluminum blinds that don't quite reach the windowsill when pulled all the way down. They were most certainly manufactured in China as far away from an eco-friendly forest as you can get. Plus, I have only a vague idea what color ecru is. "Well, they sound fabulous. Lucky Larry."

"Right. Like he will even notice. So, how about lunch tomorrow?"

I heard an almost pleading in her voice and assumed she was feeling desperate to discuss Sam's situation. But the last thing I wanted to do was push her before she was ready, so I didn't probe further. Instead, I said, "Yes, lunch tomorrow would be good. You pick the place and call me in the morning. But before we hang up, there is one thing I have to quickly tell you."

"Shoot," she said.

Now *I* hesitated. Kit is no fan of Dennis Culotta. And even less of my infatuation with him. But I counted on her being as curious as I was about his parking-lot meeting with Autumn Grey. "Okay. I was having lunch today at Steak 'n Shake and—"

"*Steak 'n Shake*," Kit interrupted, as if I'd dined at a roadside taco stand.

"Yes, Steak 'n Shake. I love their milkshakes. Anyway, the point is, I was sitting by the window, and I saw Autumn Grey in the parking lot—"

"Val, everyone knows the best milkshakes are at 25 Degrees."

"Well, that place is downtown, and besides, I didn't plan on spending a week's salary on a milkshake."

"Thirteen bucks, Val, and—"

"Did you hear what I said? Forget the milkshake. I said I saw Autumn Grey in the parking lot, and she wasn't alone. Guess who she was with? It's the last person you would expect to—"

"Just tell me."

"No, guess."

"Warren Buffett?"

I sighed. "Yes, Kit. What billionaire wouldn't want to go to Steak 'n Shake—"

"Cindy Crawford, then?"

"Okay, stop guessing. It was Dennis Culotta." She was silent for a few seconds, so I continued. "Don't you think that's strange?"

More silence. "Yes," she finally said, "it's strange. I wonder what the great detective would have to say for himself."

"Well, that's just it. Not much."

"Please don't tell me you ditched your second-rate milkshake and ran out to talk to him."

"No, of course not. But they left after a few minutes. And so I called him when I got back in my car."

"Of course you did. What did the schmuck have to say?"

I felt humiliated that Culotta had ended our phone call so abruptly, but I wasn't going to admit that to Kit. "Nothing much; we just chatted for a while. I didn't mention Autumn."

"So you never found out why—"

"No."

"Would have been better if it *had* been Warren Buffett."

When we hung up, I refilled my glass. But after taking a few sips, I poured the rest down the drain.

Instead, I settled in bed and called my brother. It went straight to his voice mail, so I left a message asking him to call me in the morning. Then I turned off the lamp on my nightstand and turned on my TV, and pretty soon I was dreaming about Dennis Culotta and the cottage we lived in off the coast of Ireland. In my dream, I had flowing red hair, like Maureen O'Hara in the John Wayne movies, and I loved how it curled down to my waist.

***

Tom was already in the office when I arrived. I followed the aroma—or rather the stench—of his cigar and knocked lightly on his office door. He looked up from the pile of papers he was holding and beckoned me in.

"Morning, guvnor," I said in my best British accent, which was totally lost on him.

"Sit." He indicated the empty chair across from his desk. Tom, who always dresses in an expensive suit no matter how hot it is, had removed his jacket, revealing a gray paisley tie and red suspenders over his crisp white shirt. In the small office, sitting behind his desk, he always looks slightly too big, with his football player's body that he somehow keeps in shape. I'm not sure how he does it since I've never known him to exercise and he doesn't belong to a gym.

"How'd it go at lunch yesterday?" I asked.

He looked up again and ran a beefy hand over his bald head. "How'd you expect it to go?"

"Blimey, guvnor," I said, giving my British accent another go, "I expect you to 'ave sold the whole blooming building to the Lavender Group."

He gave me a half smile, which looked more irritated than pleased. "Why are you speaking with an Australian accent?"

"Crikey, guvnor, it's not an Aussie accent, it's—"

"Whatever the hell it is, cut it out. You sound demented. And yes, I sold them on the top six floors—"

"Good on ya, mate!"

"Valerie—"

"Sorry. Well done, Boss. Need me to do anything?"

"The usual." He returned to the stack of papers he was holding. "Go out and sell me some houses."

***

Kit called me at eleven. "Would you mind if we meet at your place instead of a restaurant?"

"No, of course not." I was puzzled. Kit considers my apartment fit for demolition and usually avoids it, and I've certainly never known her to suggest meeting there for lunch or anything else. "I don't have any food, but I can stop and pick up sandwiches."

"No need. I'll bring leftovers. I have some veal parmigiana and some gnocchi. Your oven works, right?"

"Of course it works, and that sounds good. See you in an hour." I wasn't actually sure if my oven did work, and I couldn't remember the last time I had used it. But I knew my microwave was up to the task.

I parked in my favorite spot and saw Kit's BMW pull into the space next to me as I was getting out of my car.

She was wearing a simple white linen sundress with large splashes of turquoise. Her short auburn hair was concealed under a chic panama hat adorned with a black ribbon. She looked like she should be having lunch in Monte Carlo, not schlepping leftovers, no matter how fantastic, around Downers Grove. But schlepping she was, and she handed me a couple of food carriers, one with two covered dishes and the other holding several smaller containers. I could see freshly grated Parmesan cheese, marinara sauce, and a really tiny container of something green.

She went around and opened her passenger door and took out a bottle of wine. "This is a very nice merlot. You do have a wine opener, I hope." She clicked her key fob to lock the car doors.

"Well, of course I do; I'm not an animal."

She pulled down her enormous sunglasses and gave me a look over the top, while I started rummaging around in my brain. Did I have a wine opener? Surely I did; I remembered using the spirally part at the top to dig something nasty out of the grout in my bathroom. But a wine opener isn't a necessity in my home since I generally buy wine with a screw top.

We reached my apartment, and I immediately turned the air conditioner on. Kit was soon at the oven, punching buttons on the control panel. "I just don't know how you get anything done in this kitchen," she said as she opened a cabinet door and removed two plates.

"I get plenty done," I said, for the millionth time. "But most of it doesn't involve cooking."

"You would think being in real estate, as you insist you are, that you would find something a little larger—"

"Kit, would you please stop. I love this apartment."

Then she took her sunglasses off, and I could see that her brown eyes were glassy. Filled with tears.

"Are you crying?" I asked.

"Certainly not." She roughly pulled a sheet of paper towel from the roll by the sink and began dabbing her eyes. "For crying out loud, find that damn wine opener you claim to own and pour me a glass. And Val," she continued, blowing her nose, "you really should use bamboo towels instead of this paper stuff."

I moved toward her and put an arm around her shoulders. "What is it, Kitty Kat? Tell me what's wrong." I didn't need the same IQ as Albert Einstein to know it had something to do with her son. I ushered her into the living room, where she removed her panama hat and took a seat at the end of the couch.

I hurried to the kitchen for our wineglasses, but before I could return to my friend and her problem, I heard a light tapping at my door. Surprised, I set our glasses down on the coffee table and took the three steps necessary to answer the knock.

"Hello, Valerie. I thought I saw your car." It was Hettie Randall, my rather stout neighbor, wearing a shiny silver tracksuit a few years out of date and a few sizes too small. It had an Adidas logo over her left breast. In her hand was a box with an Amazon Prime label. "I saw this by your door earlier and thought it best not to leave it there. I hope that was okay."

"Ah, the book I ordered for Billie. That was very kind of you, Hettie. I appreciate it." I took the box she handed me. "A birthday present," I said, as if I needed to explain, and began to close the door even though Hettie wasn't moving.

"Working from home today?" she asked, not even trying to be discreet as she looked over my shoulder at Kit, who was sipping her wine.

"Yes. Got a lot to do."

"Okay, I'll leave you to it."

I was forced to close the door in her face since she still had not moved, and it felt rude.

"I can smell the cheese from here," Kit said from the couch, sounding even ruder.

"Stop it. She doesn't smell," I insisted as I went to the kitchen to make sure the oven was heating our food. I returned with the plates and set them on the coffee table, since I have no actual dining room.

We were three bites into our lunch before Kit finally shared what was weighing on her mind.

"There's something going on with Sam and Leslie." She stopped and took a deep breath and put the palm of her hand on her chest. "Whew. I said it out loud and the world didn't stop spinning."

We both laughed a little, but it sounded grim on her part and worried on mine.

"What's going on?" I asked after a few seconds, when she returned to taking tiny bites out of a piece of gnocchi that was speared to the end of her fork.

"For starters," she said, putting the fork back on her plate, "I never get to speak to Leslie anymore. Whenever I call them, she's always busy, or in the pool, or out at some function or other. I haven't exchanged words with her in months. I even tried calling her cell, but it always goes to voice mail and she never calls me back."

I gave her concerns some thought. As mothers-in-law go, Leslie had it pretty good. I had never known Kit to be intrusive or meddling. She didn't demand a lot of their time and, from my point of view, was always respectful of their decisions. "Have you mentioned this to Sam?"

"Hell no. I don't want to butt in. But he's weird on the phone."

"Well, what I think you should do is ask Sam flat out if everything is all right. Can't hurt."

She nodded slowly and speared another gnocchi. "You don't think she's moved out, do you?"

"Kit, I have no way of knowing that; nor do you. That's why you have to talk to Sam."

"Yes," she agreed. But her face showed her distress, and I immediately thought of how heartbroken I would be if Emily and Luke were headed in the wrong direction. "Ya know, I was never a big fan of Leslie," Kit continued. "She's too spoiled, too flighty. But I think I did a good job of keeping my feelings to myself."

"You did, Kit. You are a great mother-in-law."

"They got married too quickly. They'd known each other only about six months, if you remember, before the idiot proposed."

"Yeah, I suppose it was a little too fast."

"I think Sam was dazzled by her family. Ya know, her father and all his money. That damn ranch that he practically handed over to Sam."

"Maybe it's not as bad as you think." I rubbed her back.

She nodded almost imperceptibly, and I knew I hadn't convinced her. So we ate in silence, and then she changed the subject and told me about her new gardener, Victor, who apparently was turning her backyard into some kind of botanical dreamland.

An hour later, I followed her to the front door and accepted her kiss on my cheek as we said good-bye. "I'll call you later," she said as she gave me another hug, an almost painfully hard squeeze. "What would I do without you, Valley Girl?"

"Don't forget to call Sam. And soon," I added.

"I think I'll wait until he comes here to talk to him. That's the best thing."

I nodded reluctantly and watched the door close behind her, and then a wave of exhaustion flooded over me. I decided the best thing for me to do was take a long nap.

***

I couldn't have been more shocked when I was awakened by my phone. I would have sworn I hadn't slept.

"H'lo," I said, not bothering to fumble in the covers for my reading glasses so I could see who the caller was. I was pretty certain it was Kit.

It was not.

"Hey, Val. How're you doin'?" It was one of the sweetest-sounding voices on earth. The only one that sounded just like my beloved and dearly missed father.

"Buddy, I'm so glad you called!" I didn't add that I was surprised he hadn't called back sooner. "Mom says you're coming to see us. That's great—"

"Uh, yeah. That's what I wanted to talk to you about. That and . . . uh . . . well, see, you have a new neighbor? Her name is Autumn—"

"Grey. Autumn Grey. Yes! How did you know?" My mind started to spin. Was I still sleeping? Was I dreaming? But then I thought of the Washington, DC, license plates on the car that had brought Autumn here, and it made a sort of weird sense.

"That's a long story. I want to explain in person. But I just want you to . . . uh . . . kind of avoid Autumn, until I get there."

"Buddy! What on earth—"

"Please, Val. I don't want to explain now. Oh. I gotta go. Elaine's home."

And he was gone. As fast a getaway as Culotta had made on the phone yesterday.

CHAPTER SIX

As soon as Buddy hung up on me, I called Kit and relayed the conversation with my brother. "What do you think?" I asked when I was finished.

"I think you should go chat with Autumn and ask her."

"Kit, I can't just go and ask her after Buddy—"

"It's the *only* thing you can do."

After we hung up, and before I could decide what to do, I took a phone call from Billie.

"Val, I'm sorry to bother you. But I have a message for you from Ridley North. He wants to make an offer on the Willmott house. I thought you'd want to know right—"

"Yes, Billie, I do. Thanks so much." The Willmott house had been empty for almost a year. The listing was as stale as the open package of wheat pasta in my cupboard, and I'd been so discouraged about it. I was only vaguely aware of my mind leaving Kit, Sam, Buddy, and Autumn Grey to focus on selling a house before Ol' Man North, as Tom called him, could change his mind.

But that night, I knocked on Autumn Grey's door. Buddy's request that I avoid her finally lost out to Kit's insistence that I don't. Plus, I was intensely curious about her connection to my brother.

My first knock on her door was unanswered. But after my second, louder, knock, the door opened a crack, still tethered by a chain. I could see one of Autumn's pale-blue eyes through the opening and also the red lipstick she wore. When she saw it was only me, she undid the lock and opened the door wider so I could enter. "Hi, Valerie," she said, as if we'd known each other forever. "Come in."

I took in the tidy, sparsely furnished apartment, knowing that if it were a home I was trying to sell, I'd have to do some major staging. I like my houses to look polished and uncluttered, but Autumn's apartment—with its utter lack of a single picture on the wall or item of interest on a tabletop—looked cold and uninviting. I immediately chastised myself for being so judgmental. She'd barely moved in, for Pete's sake.

" . . . but I do have some Coke?" I heard her saying, and wondered how long she'd been trying to offer me a drink while I was busy silently critiquing her new abode.

"Yes, that would be great." I followed her into the galley kitchen and watched as she poured us two tall glasses from a large bottle. She then added a scoop of ice and a paper straw to each drink.

I followed her again, back to the living room, and we sat down on her couch. There were no coasters for our glasses, probably because, I felt certain, the coffee and end tables were not made from anything resembling a tree. We sipped our Cokes in what I found to be an uncomfortable silence.

Pretty sure that Autumn would never start the conversation, I finally plunged ahead. "So, are you settling in?"

She nodded slightly as she took a long sip through her straw.

"So, what brought you to Chicago? Downers Grove, to be precise."

"Hmm . . ." She looked up to the ceiling, as if I'd asked her to solve a mathematical equation. "Don't you like it here?" she asked at last.

"Yes, I do, but I've lived here all my life."

"That's not a reason to like a place, or stay in one."

I found her response annoying. "So you didn't like Arizona?" I countered.

"Yes. It's lovely there. But I think I was ready for a change."

"Well, you picked a nice spot. Downers Grove is lovely too. A lot to do. Good place to raise kids. Easy access to downtown Chicago." I sounded like I worked for the Downers Grove Chamber of Commerce, but I use the spiel so many times on prospective clients, it comes easily to me.

She nodded again, seeming to agree and to give her newly chosen home a seal of approval. Then, quite suddenly, she set her glass down on the coffee table so hard some Coke sloshed out. All I could think was how she better wipe it up or it would attract ants. Then I thought wryly that maybe that would get them out of my own apartment. In Illinois, August and ants go together like July and fireworks.

She stood up, but not to fetch a paper towel, as she should have. Instead, she headed the short distance to the front door. "Valerie, I hope you don't mind me rushing you out, but I'm very tired. It's been such a long day. Would you mind—"

"Oh no, not at all . . . of course . . . we can visit another time." I hesitated. "Say, I happened to see you and . . . um . . . a detective I vaguely know . . . yesterday. I was having lunch at Steak 'n Shake on Ogden, and—"

"He's not a detective. Not exactly."

I'm sure I looked as shocked as she looked vexed. "Okaaay," I said. "Then—"

"We'll have lunch or something when I'm settled."

Obviously, I'd have to pursue that line of questioning when we next met. She already had the door open, and I could see Hettie's apartment across the hall. "I'm not a fan of neighbors calling unexpectedly, either," I said. *Well, that's true*, I thought, looking once again at Hettie's closed door. "So lunch would be great." I was in the hall now, but turned to face her. "Autumn, one thing before I go. I'm curious how you know my brother."

I barely caught her response before I found myself staring at her closed door. "I think you should ask him," she'd said. The next thing I heard was her sliding the chain lock into place.

"Everything okay?"

I turned toward the voice and found myself face-to-face with Hettie. "Oh, hi," I said. "I didn't see you there." Across her upper body was a worn leather strap attached to her purse, and I wasn't sure if she was leaving or arriving. "I was just checking . . . on our new neighbor."

"Hmm. Is she okay?"

"Yes, she's fine. Goodness, look at the time. I should get to bed. I have a busy day tomorrow." Since I wasn't wearing a watch, and the hallway doesn't have the luxury of a community clock, I had no idea what the actual time was.

"Good night, dear," Hettie said, and I could feel her eyes on me as I scrambled to my own door.

***

Even after I'd returned to my apartment and long after I'd changed into my Cubs T-shirt, brushed my teeth, and completed the skin-care steps that I hoped would stave off the aging process, my mind remained on Dennis Culotta and Autumn. I was particularly preoccupied by her declaration that Dennis Culotta was *not exactly* a detective. So what the hell was he these days?

My relationship with Culotta was complicated. Some might say it was nonexistent. When we'd first met, he was the lead detective on the murder of one Susan Reed, someone known to Kit and me. After that, we'd met a number of times and even managed several date-like dinners—before the unexpected kiss of a lifetime at our last encounter, in California. And then he'd disappeared. Since then, whenever I thought of him, it was mainly with irritation and frustration, both tempered by that damn kiss.

I searched through my TV-channel guide and my list of saved programs for something good to watch, something that would put me to sleep. I found an old *Law & Order* and settled down under the covers, adjusting the volume loud enough to still be heard but soft enough to guarantee it wouldn't keep me awake. Forty minutes into the show, I grabbed my remote, turned the volume up, and then rewound the last few scenes. Detective Olivia Benson was arguing with her captain. *WITSEC*, she spat at him, *witness protection*.

I reached for my phone and speed-dialed Kit. "Here's a crazy thought," I said. "Oh, you are awake, right?"

"Val, it's nine fifteen; why wouldn't I be awake? Everyone's awake."

"Of course," I said, remembering that this was Kit, the night owl. "So here's my thought." I hesitated, because I knew that saying it out loud, even to Kit, would sound ludicrous.

"I'm waiting patiently," she said, not sounding in the least patient.

"Okay. Autumn Grey. We can't find her anywhere on social media—"

"We probably wouldn't find my Whole Foods butcher, either."

"Yes, but he's a hundred years old. And isn't he from Ecuador?"

"Your point?"

"Maybe Autumn Grey isn't Autumn Grey. Maybe she's . . ." More hesitation.

"Still waiting."

"In the witness protection plan, program, scheme, whatever it's called."

"But aren't those people supposed to be anonymous?"

"Not anonymous, no. How can they be? Unless they are put on a desert island. They just lose their former identity. They give them a new life, and bingo—" I stopped because it truly did sound ludicrous now. "It's just an idea, but who really knows she's here, apart from you and me, and Hettie?" I didn't add *and my brother and probably Culotta*. "And even though we know she's here, we don't really know who she is."

"Buddy seems to know."

"True. And he was so . . . mysterious."

"Witness protection seems a bit far-fetched, don't you think?"

"Perhaps you're right. I was just watching an episode of *Law & Order*, and there was a character who was in WITSEC—that's what they call it."

"Okay then. Good thing you weren't watching *The Walking Dead*, or our Autumn would be a zombie, or *Game of Thrones*—"

"I get it. Funny," I said, although I didn't think it was funny at all.

"Gotta go. Larry recorded *The Great British Bake Off* for me, and I'm in the mood for boiling something."

We said good night, but it took me a long time to fall asleep.

***

I awoke early the next day. I had a couple of hours before my appointment at ten thirty with Ridley North, his wife, and their mortgage company. Selling that property was a big coup for me, and I was excited. As I got dressed, I realized I had time to kill and didn't want to go to the office, so I decided I'd go to Autumn's and offer to buy her breakfast. I felt desperate for a clue about my brother's involvement with her.

I locked my front door and headed down the hall to her apartment. I found her front door ajar, and so I gingerly pushed it with my index finger. The apartment was eerily quiet. I could see that our two glasses had been moved to the kitchen counter but had not been washed. As I took a step toward the sparse kitchen, a tall gaunt man came out of the bedroom. He did not look happy.

"Who are you?" he asked, not looking at me.

"I'm Valerie Pankowski, a neighbor of Autumn's. I was just wondering if she . . . where is she?"

"She doesn't live here anymore."

"But I was just here. Last night. Where did she—"

"She left early this morning." The man held a black garbage bag that was about two-thirds full. "You should leave now," he said, still not looking at me but instead scoping out the empty room.

"Who are *you*? And where did Autumn go?"

"I'm a friend, and I don't know where she went. Please leave." He turned away from me in a clear dismissal.

I moved about six mouse steps away from the kitchen counter to the entrance of Autumn's apartment.

"I asked you to leave," the man said again, looking at me for the first time. "Please do so."

I backed out into the empty corridor, feeling a little scared and a lot uneasy. Then I turned around and knocked on Hettie's door; surely she would know something. But there was no reply from my neighbor, and I had no choice but to leave—and stop at McDonald's for an Egg McMuffin and some of their crispy hash browns before heading to meet the Norths.

***

The appointment at the mortgage company went well, but before I could escape, LeAnn North insisted I follow them back to the Willmott house so she could measure for curtains and get my ideas for window coverings. When I was married and lived in the Big House, decor and window coverings had been a real joy for me. These days, I figure white mini blinds do the trick just as well as anything made to measure. Even Kit's eco-friendly wood blinds did not sound enticing to me now. But although I was the last person LeAnn should consult, her obvious glee at the prospect of redoing her new home was infectious, and I agreed to follow them.

By the time I got back to my apartment, the day was nearly over. I had stopped at Freddie's Deli and picked up a crab salad, a slice of cherry pie, and a bottle of Diet Dr Pepper. But first I decided to stop at Hettie's apartment. I might catch her at home and be able to discuss what she knew about Autumn's departure.

There was no response to my knocks on Hettie's door; but as I turned to leave, I noticed that Autumn's door was still slightly ajar. Once again, I used my index finger to push it open enough to see in.

"Autumn? Are you here?" I called. Once again, a spooky silence surrounded me as I stood in the open doorway, but at least the tall thin man was nowhere to be seen. "Autumn?" I said again, this time stepping into the apartment.

I couldn't believe what I was seeing.

"Oh no," I heard someone—me—say. I felt the cherry pie leave my hands, and heard it hit the carpet with a muffled splat. It had escaped from its aluminum shell and landed an inch or so from feet clad in a pair of worn Adidas.

But they didn't belong to Autumn.

The feet clearly belonged to Hettie Randall, the lady who took in my packages when I wasn't home, who made me a fruitcake at Christmas, and who brought me a chocolate-loaded basket at Easter. She was lying on the floor between the cheap couch and the cheaper coffee table. She was wearing an Adidas tracksuit, this one in maroon, which made it hard to discern the blood seeping from the bullet hole in her chest. And her eyes, wide open, seemed to stare blankly at the ceiling.

CHAPTER SEVEN

Culotta didn't come alone, and he didn't seem in charge. And something just felt off, something more than the dead woman on the floor.

He arrived with a Detective Schroeder of the Downers Grove Police Department mere minutes after I'd called 911, although it had felt like hours that I'd been in Autumn's living room with the dead Hettie. I knew it hadn't really been hours, though, because I'd had time for only a brief conversation with Kit before the two men showed up.

"Kit, she's dead!" I'd screeched into the phone. I'd thought I might be breaking some law, reporting a death to my pal before the authorities officially pronounced it, but I'd *had* to call her. I had to not feel alone with a dead woman.

"Who's dead? Autumn?"

"No, not Autumn." I heard the shock in my own voice and knew she would feel the same when I told her that innocent, cheesy Hettie was the victim.

"Just tell me who, Val."

I plunked down on the coffee table but immediately shot back up when I realized it had put me closer to the body. "Hettie. It's Hettie Randall."

"The one who—"

"Don't you dare say she smells, Kit."

"Of course not—"

"I gotta go," I'd said. Because detectives Culotta and Schroeder had arrived. Or rather Detective Schroeder and No-Longer-Detective Dennis Culotta, and they would soon confirm what Autumn had told me.

What was up with *that*? I found it as puzzling as the fact that the two men arrived even before the ambulance and the EMTs who pronounced Hettie dead. But that was not my first thought. Just the sight of Dennis Culotta, and my sudden weak knees, sent me back down to the coffee table, praying that its shoddy construction wouldn't give way. He gave me a look of recognition, but not exactly what you would call a warm greeting. As always, at the sight of him, I was filled with longing, which was replaced quickly by loathing at his cavalier attitude.

I stood up, but hung back, too shocked to move *or* speak, as they all fussed over the body. Only when Culotta trained his blue, blue eyes on me and began asking questions did I force myself to at least try uttering some words.

"What were you doing in this apartment?" Culotta repeated the question that Detective Schroeder had already asked me twice.

This time I answered. "I came to check on Hettie. No, Autumn. I mean Hettie and Autumn."

"Why were you checking on them?" Detective Schroeder asked.

"How do you know Autumn?" Culotta demanded.

"Detective Culotta," I addressed him, "I—"

"It's not Detective Culotta anymore. I'm consulting with the Downers Grove Police Department on this case, working in conjunction with them. But I don't—"

"How could they already be consulting you, when this just happened?"

"Valerie, that's none of your business," he said. But the trace of a twinkle in his eyes—which was very inappropriate, given the circumstances—told me he was remembering all the times he'd said that to me in the past. He was lucky I was even speaking to him, officially or otherwise.

"Ma'am," Detective Schroeder said in a tone that asserted his authority over the situation. And he immediately had my attention. To say he had an imposing presence is like saying Dennis Culotta is kind of attractive. Pure understatement. The hefty detective towered over Culotta's six feet something, and his pock-marked face held a threatening expression more suited to a Mafia don. His jet-black hair looked like a dye job, so I figured he was older than he looked at first glance. "We're going to need you to come to the station and give us a statement." He obviously wanted to put an end to any conversation that didn't have to do with the body that was being photographed from every angle by one of his crew now swarming the apartment.

"Could we just go to my place and do it—"

"Do what?" Dennis Culotta asked, looking innocent except for that damn sparkle in his eyes. But before I could answer, the sparkle disappeared and he shook his head almost imperceptibly, as if to shake some sense into himself.

I felt my own head nod imperceptibly in approval. He *needed* to get some sense. A woman had been murdered. A sweet, albeit slightly smelly, woman. (Yes, Kit was right, but I'd never tell her that.) "Could we go to my apartment for you to take my statement, instead of to the station?" I asked again, looking directly at Detective Schroeder and ignoring Culotta.

"No, we cannot. Dennis, take her in."

"No." Culotta's tone outdid Schroeder's in the authority department, and my head jerked in his direction. I knew I shouldn't have been surprised to note that he wasn't one bit intimidated by the large detective.

Well, I was intimidated enough for both of us. "Can I drive myself there?"

"No, I'll take you when we finish here. You wait in your apartment," the detective said. "What's your number?"

I racked my brain for a few seconds. "It's 630-555—"

"I mean your apartment number."

"It's 205," Culotta said, immediately looking slightly uncomfortable.

And indeed, Schroeder shot Culotta a quizzical look and paused briefly, as if debating whether to ask how he knew that. But instead, he looked at me and repeated, "Like I said, go back to your apartment and wait there. We'll let you know when we've finished here."

Well, at least it would give me a chance to call Kit and update her.

***

I didn't intend to fall asleep, but I did. One minute I was pacing the perimeter of my living room until I got so dizzy from the rapid turns that I had to sit down on the couch, and the next thing I knew, I was waking up, disoriented but still sitting. What woke me was Detective Schroeder on the other side of my door, pounding and hollering at me to open up.

How long had he been trying to get my attention? And would he arrest me? Was that resisting a police officer? I jumped up and rushed to the door.

I thought he looked relieved to see me. Maybe he'd thought I'd been murdered too.

"Sorry. I dozed off," I said.

"Good you can be so relaxed in the face of all this," he said, his tone sounding like he considered me an accessory after the fact. "We're ready to take your statement at the station. Let's go."

"Really, can't I drive myself and meet you there?" I had no desire to be confined in the small space of a vehicle with this overbearing man. Especially if Culotta would be joining us. And besides, I'd promised Kit I'd drive over to her house right after I gave my statement, so I wanted my car.

"Just make sure you get right there." Schroeder glared at me. "Now."

"Yes, sir," I said, and I was relieved to see he didn't seem to detect the sarcasm in my voice. Some detective.

***

When I arrived at the police station, Culotta met me at the door. "Val, I don't want you to worry." He looked over his shoulder as if he didn't want to get caught. But caught at what? Reassuring me? Consorting with the enemy?

But he did get caught. "I'll take her," Schroeder said, lunging down the hall toward us. "This way, Mrs. Pankowski." When Culotta started to follow us, the detective added, "No need, Dennis. I got this."

My heart sank. I wanted Dennis Culotta to be in charge. He really had my best interests (and maybe more?) at heart.

Didn't he?

CHAPTER EIGHT

I spent the next three hours in a room, which felt more like a cell, giving a statement to Detective Schroeder. He sat across from me at the table, which apart from two plastic chairs was the only furniture in the room. I watched as he loosened his tie and undid the top two buttons of his shirt, releasing his fleshy chin—or at least one of them.

He asked me all the questions that the person who finds a dead body should expect. This I knew from my endless hours of watching crime shows on TV. Yes, I knew the deceased. No, I was not aware of her family members or next of kin (although I thought she had once mentioned a sister in Tuscaloosa). No, I had not touched the body. And no, I did not own a gun. I told him I was at Freddie's Deli just before I found the body, and Freddie's son (Fred Junior) could confirm this since we had chatted at length about the softball team he coached.

After I answered Schroeder's questions, I shut my mouth. I'd also learned from my TV crime shows that a witness, or at least the finder of the body, should never offer too much information. But I thought my answers had sounded rehearsed, and I wished for the thousandth time that Culotta were in the room. He knew me well and knew that I was incapable of murdering anyone (except perhaps him, when he disappeared from my life).

Detective Schroeder shuffled some papers that he had taken from a manila folder in front of him. His fat fingers looked clumsy. "Okay," he said, "let's go over this again. You spent time with a LeAnn North and then stopped at this deli . . . er, Fred's—"

"Fred*die's*," I corrected, as if that made a difference to the veracity of my story.

"Fred*die's*," he repeated. "Then you headed home after your purchase—at Fred*die's*—but decided to go visit Autumn Grey first."

"No," I said. "I actually went to check on Hettie. As I told you, I had been at Autumn's apartment earlier in the day—"

"Why?"

"As I said, because I thought I might take her out for breakfast."

"Yet you claim you didn't know her well."

"Exactly. She was a new neighbor, and I was being neighborly. I had a couple of hours before an appointment. I'm in real estate, and—"

"And she wasn't home," Detective Schroeder interrupted me. Maybe he was afraid I might veer off into a rundown of my interesting career choice.

"Yes. No. She wasn't home, and neither was Hettie. But there was a man in Autumn's apartment who seemed to be clearing it out." At first I didn't offer the suggestion that maybe the Downers Grove Police Department should be investigating this guy, even though I had mentioned him several times and each time he was dismissed. But then I couldn't resist. "Do you know who that guy was?"

"No." Detective Schroeder looked up from his stack of papers. "Do you?"

"No. I told you, I've never seen him before."

"Then just forget him." He wiped his meaty paw over his forehead. "Okay, let's get back to the deceased. Tell me about the nature of your relationship."

I heaved a sigh. We'd been over this several times. There wasn't much to say. But I reiterated that she was just a neighbor, albeit a good one, who occasionally did nice things for me. We had never socialized, I couldn't remember ever having been in her apartment, and I had never even seen her outside of our building.

"So, when was the last time you saw her?"

"Hmm . . . a day or so ago, maybe. No, wait; last night when I was leaving Autumn's, Hettie was standing in the hallway at her door."

"Coming or going?"

"Not sure. We just said hello, and then I went back to my place."

"And she seemed okay?"

"Yes. She was fine."

He wriggled out of his too-small chair, closed the manila folder, and shoved it under his arm. "I'll be right back," he said. He didn't tell me not to go anywhere, but it was implied, and anyway, where the hell would I go?

I sat in silence, staring at the green wall in front of me, almost afraid to move in case my action was caught on a camera somewhere and it would be misconstrued as a sign of guilt. But guilt over what? A nice lady I knew only slightly had been murdered, and I was the unlucky person who found her. Period.

I felt myself start to cry, which turned into sobbing, and then I was consumed with sadness for Hettie, and maybe a little shame for myself. Why hadn't I taken more time to get to know her? Had Hettie been lonely? Did she know she was in danger? Was *I* in danger?

And why didn't I have any tissues in my purse, like a normal person would when being questioned by the police?

After about thirty minutes, Detective Schroeder returned, minus the manila folder. "You can go." He stood at the door and held it open for me.

"Okay." I wiped my wet cheeks with the palms of my hands. Should I thank him? Or should he be thanking *me*?

"Your alibi is good," he said as I passed him. "Mrs. North checked out, and this Freddie confirmed you were at the deli—"

"Freddie *Junior*," I felt compelled to correct him.

"Whatever."

Despite my earlier reticence, I found myself thanking him—for what, I did not know. He merely nodded and then raised a sausage finger, pointing in the direction of the exit. I walked slowly down the corridor—one I had visited in what seemed like another lifetime—looking for Culotta. But he was nowhere to be seen. Once outside, I checked the parking lot for his car, which was fruitless since I didn't even know what kind of car he was driving these days. Reluctantly, I located my own vehicle and climbed in.

It was now dark outside, and although my previous plan had been to stop by Kit's, I felt suddenly drained and definitely not up to a visit with my pal. I switched my phone on, noting there were six missed calls from her, and pressed the button to phone her back.

"Val! *Valerie!* Where have you been all this time?"

"Slow down, Kit. I've been at the police station giv—"

"Oh, that's great." Her tone was dismissive. "But I have some good news, for a change, about Sam—"

"For Pete's sake, Kit. Did you forget I just found a dead—I found Hettie today? Murdered?" I forced myself to forgive Kit's lack of empathy over my ordeal, not to mention sympathy for Hettie, and chose to blame it on her worry over her son. "So . . . tell me your good news."

"Sorry, sorry. That was unforgivable. What happened? Wait! First, I just have to tell you about Sam. *Prenup*, Val. He has a prenup, so at least that little brat won't get her hands on Sam's money." Kit's tone was now one of triumph, and I didn't want to kill her mood by reminding her that Leslie's getting her hands on Sam's so-called fortune was probably the last thing she should be worried about. And in fact, I would be willing to bet that any prenup would have been initiated by Leslie. Her parents were wealthy, extremely so, and I was pretty sure that any fortune Sam had amassed during their marriage had probably been due to his father-in-law.

"That is good news," I said.

"Yes. So, now tell me all that happened at the station."

I brought her up to date as best I could, although there wasn't much to tell.

"Did you give them your theory on Autumn Grey being in the Witness Protection Program?"

"No, I didn't." Truthfully, I had forgotten that amazing piece of deduction on my part; but upon reflection, I decided that if Autumn were in any such program, the police would know that already. "Look, Kit, I am totally whacked-out. I'm going to go home, take a shower, and go to bed. I'll come over tomorrow. Will Larry be making breakfast?"

"Of course. But I think you should stay with us tonight. I mean, you just had a murder practically next door. I don't think it's safe—"

"It's totally safe. You forget there is a security system in the building."

"Val, I hate to break it to you, but the so-called security system you've got over there in Barbie's DreamHouse wouldn't stop a two-year-old."

I laughed. It is one of our constant battles. "I promise I'll be fine. See you tomorrow."

***

"How did you get past security?" I asked Dennis Culotta after opening my apartment door.

"Hmm, it *was* tricky, but I managed to remove the newspaper that was wedged under the door."

I don't think I'd ever been so pleased to be home as when I had finally arrived back at my apartment after my phone call to Kit. This was despite the yellow crime-scene tape that had been placed over Hettie's and Autumn's doors. There was also a police officer standing at the end of the corridor, writing something on a clipboard, and he had looked up and nodded at me when I waved my door key at him. Once inside my apartment, I had gone straight to my bathroom and turned on the shower. Then I stripped and stood under the rushing water and cried once more for Hettie.

When I emerged from the bathroom, with a scrubbed face and damp hair, I put on my Cubs T-shirt and ran a comb through my wet locks. Before going to my refrigerator for something to drink, I checked my phone.

There were two messages, the first one from a neighbor I knew even less than Hettie. He was a medical student at Northwestern who lived on the third floor. I wondered how he had my number; then I recalled that when he was returning to his home in India for a visit, he'd asked me to take in his mail. I returned his call and gave him a brief rundown on what had happened.

The other message was from another neighbor I barely knew, Andy (I didn't know his last name). He had moved in on the first floor about three months earlier. He used a wheelchair, and I'd helped him bring in groceries a few times. Andy was in his late sixties, and I clearly remembered giving him my phone number just in case he ever needed help. Like me, Andy was amazed that anyone could break through the stellar security system in our building, and I did my best to calm his fears about the killer who was still on the loose.

Remembering the Diet Dr Pepper I had picked up from Freddie's earlier (although it seemed like days ago now), I grabbed it from the refrigerator and headed to bed. I was almost through the opening credits of *Law & Order: Special Victims Unit* when I heard the loud pounding at my door. Assuming it was another nervous neighbor who needed my calming influence, I headed to the living room and was forced to admit Dennis Culotta.

It wasn't that I didn't want to see him; I just didn't want to see him right now. I would have preferred to have had time to dry and style my hair, put on some makeup, lose ten or fifteen pounds, and slip into a little black dress (but I would have needed to go to the mall to buy one first).

He breezed past me as if he visited me every day and took himself to the couch, moving my pile of mail and some other undefinable junk from one end to the middle cushion. Then he sat down. "How are you?" He stretched one hand across the back of the couch and extended his long legs. I seemed to remember that he would eventually hit his knees on the coffee table, which he did.

"Excuse me a moment." I disappeared into my bedroom, closing the door behind me. I rifled through a box under my bed and found a never-worn black silk kimono Kit had given me as a present three Christmases ago. It had a pink and green dragon embroidered on the back. Then I scrambled to my dresser, swiped some Rum Raisin lipstick across my lips, and ran my fingers through my almost-dry hair. "I'm okay," I said when I returned to my guest, amazing myself at the speed with which I had transformed from a Cubs fan to a kimono-wearing diva.

"I thought I'd just stop by and check on you." He leaned forward now, his elbows on his knees, his hands clasped.

"That's nice." I sat at the other end of the couch. "It was quite a night."

"Yeah. I'm sorry I wasn't able to be in the interview room with you and Schroeder, but it's not really my case."

"Well, why were you even there? Or here? Why were you in my building?"

"Er . . ." He leaned back again and narrowed his eyes as he looked at me. He appeared to carefully guard his words as he spoke. "I was in the neighborhood when I got the call about a possible homicide in Autumn Grey's apartment, and I—"

"But Autumn Grey was no longer even there. Her place was cleaned out by some guy."

"So it seems."

Feeling annoyed, I asked, "Well, who *was* that guy? Where is Autumn? Is she okay? Was she moved, or did she leave on her own? And what is your connection?"

"Wow, this thing was actually made in Japan." He had the end of the silky kimono belt in his fingers and was reading the label. "You don't see that very often these days."

"So, you *are* still a detective," I snapped, pulling the end of the belt from his grasp.

"Look, Val," he said, "I'm sure you have some questions—"

"Yes, I just asked you at least four, and you haven't answered any of them."

His handsome face broke into a wide grin. I almost had to put my hand on my heart to calm its fluttering. Damn him for having such an effect on me. Damn him for showing up when I was makeup-free. And damn *me*, for being so pleased to see him.

"Look, Val, there's not a lot of information I can share with you, but I just came by to tell you that you are safe here. Probably safe here. Just be careful. The guy who shot your pal Hettie is probably long gone, but if you see anything unusual—"

"Do you mean if I stumble across another dead neighbor while I'm taking out the trash?"

He grinned again. "Yep, something like that. Although it's not a funny situation."

"And yet you are the one grinning like Howdy Doody. What exactly do you want, Detective?"

"I told you, I'm not currently a detective, and all I want is for you to be safe."

"Then what are you, exactly? Why are you even here?"

"I'm sort of an agent . . . for the government. That's all you need to know, really."

"Is Autumn in the Witness Protection Program? Was Hettie's killer really after Autumn? Did they move Autumn because it was unsafe here?" It was like old times, my trying to fill in what he was unable to share.

He laughed, throwing his head back a little. "Still watching *Law & Order*, I see."

I noticed he didn't deny anything. "I have one more question," I said, ready to jump to another conclusion. "Why would the witness people put Autumn in this building? And why did you meet Autumn the other day in the Steak 'n Shake parking lot?"

"Actually, that's two questions. But let me answer the first one, since it's so easy. If any *witness protection* people were looking for a safe building, this would be it because of the top-notch security you've got going on."

"Ha ha. And why did you meet her at Steak 'n Shake?"

Instead of replying, he pulled his phone out of his pocket and began scrolling through a list of numbers with his left thumb, while he held his right index finger up to indicate . . . what? That I should wait? That he was planning to make a call? Clearly, he wasn't going to answer my second question, so I stood up, irritated, pulling the Japanese belt tighter around my waist. As much as I wanted the detective-turned-agent to pull it loose, my annoyance at his lack of a response and his flippant remarks took over.

"I better get going," he said, as if reading my thoughts. "You have my number, so call me if you see or hear anything that worries you." He stood and headed toward my door. I followed him, and when we got there, he turned and took me in his arms, wrapping me in a bear hug. It wasn't quite what I wanted; it was more like the hug your drunken uncle gives you at Thanksgiving. But it would have to do, and anyway, it was over before I could properly relish it. "Take care, Val," he said.

"Humph," I muttered.

"Oh, one more thing," he said casually, opening the door and taking a step out into the hall. "Do you know a Charles Caldwell?"

My heart stopped for a second. I hadn't heard that name spoken by someone other than my family for years. "That's my dad's name. Why would you ask me that?"

"Oh, no reason. Probably a mistake. Just a name that came across my desk. I seemed to remember that Caldwell was your maiden name."

Now I took a step back to look up at him. "That's utter bullshit, Detective, or Agent, or whatever the hell you are. I never, ever told you my maiden name." I wasn't exactly sure if that was true; who knows what insignificant tidbits I might have given him in the past, especially when I was babbling nervously. But either way, it wouldn't be difficult for him to find out. "And my father passed away more than ten years ago," I said defiantly, as if I were giving my dad the perfect alibi.

"Okay," he said softly. "I'm sorry I mentioned it."

"Yes, you should be," I said as he took another step back. He was now fully in the hallway, and I was able to slam the door.

Ten minutes later, when I was back in bed sipping my Diet Dr Pepper and trying to calm down, something occurred to me. My brother, whom I had called Buddy my whole life, was in fact named for our father.

Charles.

CHAPTER NINE

My first thought was to complain to my landlord about the unacceptably lax security for my building that had allowed yet another person to appear at my apartment door without having to call ahead from the lobby to be buzzed in. My second thought was that this was Sunday, not Monday. But the only thought I expressed was pure joy at seeing my big brother on the other side of my peephole.

I undid the dead bolt that I planned to start using religiously, now that there had been a murder right in my own apartment building.

As I stood face-to-face with the most special man in my life, I forgot for just a moment about the murder and even the mystery of the Buddy-and-Autumn connection. "Buddy! You're here! You're early!" I threw my arms around his neck and clung to him. As always, I was struck by how much he looks like our father, only handsomer. Tall and slender, with his salt-and-pepper hair cut fashionably short, he was wearing slim-fitting jeans and a white golf shirt, with a leather backpack slung over one shoulder.

He returned my hug, and then he was leading me to my couch and propping me up with some throw pillows because I'd begun crying uncontrollably. It was as if all my fears were pouring out of me through my tears. The horror of finding Hettie, and the worry about what was going on with Buddy and Autumn—and Culotta.

"Val, what's wrong? Are you okay?" He was sitting with his arm around me now, patting my knee with his free hand, soothing me the way I'd seen him do with one of his twins or the other during our all-too-rare times together through the years.

If it had been anyone else, I would have asked, *Do I look okay?* But not Buddy. I knew Buddy really cared whether I was all right and asked just because he didn't know what else to say. " . . . so awful . . . so much blood . . . scary . . ." Those were the only coherent words I managed to complete through my tears as I tried to tell him what had happened and why I was crying.

"Shhh," he said. "I know. At least I know some of it. Don't worry. We'll get it all straightened out."

"Hettie? How will we straighten that out?" I found my voice in my outrage. "Who could do something like that to sweet, old Hettie? And *why?*" Thinking of old, if not sweet, I suddenly wondered if our mother knew of Buddy's early arrival. "I was expecting you tomorrow, Buddy. Does Mom know you're here early?"

"No. I wanted to check in with you first. Make sure you're all right, and—"

"How did you know about any of this?"

"Later. We'll discuss all of it later."

But that wasn't good enough; there was one major thing I had to get off my chest. "Buddy. This Autumn Grey. What is she to you? Why did you want me to stay away from her?"

"A friend. A work friend, if you like."

"And do you know where she went?"

"No."

"But—"

"Shh. Later." He actually put his index finger to his lips. I knew that one more shush from him and I would lose it. And I didn't want that. So instead, I bought us both some time. "I was just getting ready to go to Kit and Larry's for brunch. They'll be so happy to see you." I stood up.

Buddy looked uncertain, but then he rose too. "If you're sure—"

"I'm sure." I was sure Kit would know what to do next and what to ask Buddy. *That's* what I was sure of. And all I cared about right now.

***

The mingling smells of sausage and bacon greeted us along with Kit's warm welcome to Buddy. "Come in, come in." She pulled him over the threshold into a big hug that she had to stand on her tiptoes to accomplish. "How the hell long has it been, Buddy?" She stepped down from the embrace, her outstretched hands clasping his upper arms as she took in the sight of him.

"By the looks of *you*, not long at all, Katherine." Sometimes Buddy called her what our mom calls her, but with an entirely different tone. Teasing instead of critical. "You haven't aged a day."

"Okay, it's getting a little deep in here." I squeezed past them and almost bumped into Larry as he made his way to greet the guy he had so looked up to in high school.

"Buddy Frickin' Caldwell! Where've you been keeping yourself? Man, it's good to see you." He nudged his wife aside so that he could give my big brother a man hug, their right hands clasped in a handshake and their left arms around each other's shoulders as they undoubtedly competed to squeeze both hands and shoulders harder than the other could.

I found myself wondering if arm wrestling would be next on the agenda and decided I'd have to step between them if it came to that. They were both getting too old to risk injury. I felt relieved when they parted slightly to walk side by side to the kitchen.

There, Kit had an elaborately set breakfast table. "Sit down," she ordered. "Not you, Larry. You get the juice and pour some coffee."

Buddy's eyes met mine, and we both grinned at our friend's bossiness. We watched as Larry set a platter of warm waffles and pancakes in the middle of the table and then made a beeline to the refrigerator to grab the pitcher of orange juice.

"I'll get the coffee," I said. I didn't want Larry to have a heart attack doing his wife's bidding. She can be a real taskmaster, but she never expects anything from others that she doesn't give tenfold herself.

As I finished pouring the fourth cup of coffee and set the carafe down next to the orange juice, I was struck by how quiet Buddy was. He looked lost in his own thoughts as he unfolded a red-checked napkin and put it on his lap. (I love how Kit uses cloth napkins, and I am always vowing that if I ever entertain someone in my dinky apartment, I'll dig mine out instead of lazily using from my lifetime supply of the paper version. Walmart had been having a sale I couldn't resist on a package of about a million napkins for a buck. Napkins that exemplify the term *paper-thin*, napkins I always have to use at least ten of.)

"So, Buddy, Val never did tell me why you were coming," Kit got right to the point.

"Val doesn't know," I said a little too quickly and forcefully, making it clear I wasn't happy about it.

"Let's talk after breakfast," Buddy said. "We don't want to miss a minute of savoring Larry's culinary masterpiece."

"What makes you think it's his masterpiece, not mine?" Kit asked, throwing Buddy a wink.

"Oh, I thought Val said—"

Kit laughed. "I'm just yanking your chain, Bud. Breakfasts are Larry's turf when he's around. I can do them—"

"Oh, I'm sure you can," my brother said. "I've heard you're quite the gourmet cook these days. I remember when we were kids and you were making brownies at our house, and when it said stir by hand, you—"

"Yeah, I stirred by hand, all right." Kit laughed. "No utensil needed. Or so I thought."

Now we all laughed, but Buddy's and Kit's both seemed forced. And mine definitely was.

***

After finishing our scrumptious breakfast and finally having a brief conversation over one last cup of coffee, Buddy and I excused ourselves. We had to let our mother know he was in town and wanted to call her from the privacy of my apartment. We never know how she will react to anything. And as with my boss, her reaction is never helped by knowing Kit is in the vicinity.

As we drove home, Buddy listened to my inane chatter about Emily's current acting job. She had a minor role in *Streetcar Named Desire* at The Wallis in Los Angeles, and I tried unsuccessfully to temper my pride at her accomplishment. Being on the stage in LA seemed a million miles away from our Midwest upbringing.

"That's great, Val." He sounded distracted, and I noticed he was looking at his phone.

"Yes, I think it just might be. But it's an ensemble cast." I wasn't sure why I added that, or what it actually meant, but I doubted he did, either.

"Well, I can't wait to see her at the Tony Awards."

"Fingers crossed," I said. "It's a cruel business, but it's exciting too. You just never know . . ."

I had parked in my usual spot, and we were now almost to my apartment when I turned to see that he had stopped following me and instead was looking down the corridor to the two apartments with the police tape still wrapped across their doors, like giant Christmas presents. "You go ahead, Val. I need to get something from my car. I'll be right back."

"No problem. I'll wait."

"No, you go ahead; I might have to dig around a bit."

"Okay. Well, buzz me, and I'll let you in." I said this with confidence, as if certain the buzzer would actually work. Then I headed into my apartment as he headed back to his car.

I had an uneasy feeling that led me right to the window in my apartment that gave me a view of the parking lot. There I saw Buddy go past his car to the sidewalk that bordered the lot. And I saw him shake hands with a tall gaunt man. The same man I had encountered clearing out Autumn's apartment.

I called Kit immediately.

"Are you sure it's the *same* tall gaunt man, Val?" she asked after I told her I was watching Buddy talk with the guy on the sidewalk.

"Pretty sure."

"You need to ask him, ya know. As soon as he gets up to your apartment."

"Well, duh. Of course I will."

But it turned out I didn't ask him. Maybe because he outright lied to me before I even had a chance.

"What did you think about his story?" Kit asked as I watched Buddy still talking to his thin man.

What I'd been thinking about the story he'd told us after breakfast was that it was pure bullshit. "Whaddya mean?" I asked my pal now. "What's to think? He said he's here to meet with FBI agents at the Chicago Field Office, to consult with them on a case. But he didn't tell us why a retired Navy guy would be consulting with the FBI, and you asked him twice. Obviously, he's lying. At least by omission."

"He explained that," Kit reminded me. "He said he *couldn't* tell us anything yet. Not while it's an active case."

"So in other words, he didn't tell us a darn thing. Oh, gotta go. Buddy's headed this way now. Without stopping by his car." My tone was one of disgust, and the feeling in the pit of my stomach was uneasy.

"Man, it took me forever to find it in my trunk," Buddy said after I'd buzzed him up (my faith in my building's security totally restored) and met him at my apartment door.

"Find what?" I asked, glaring at his empty hands in accusation.

The flustered look on his face disappeared almost before it was formed. He put a hand in his pocket and jingled what sounded like coins. "A flash drive with some pictures I want to show you. Of the twins." He smiled the smile of a proud dad.

But was it the smile of a trustworthy brother?

CHAPTER TEN

When Buddy and I called our mom, we were hoping she would be busy with some kind of Sunday activity and unable to talk for long. Luckily, she and her husband had just finished lunch at the country club, and although she was delighted to hear from us, the planning committee for the fall festival was about to meet. Since she was the chairperson, she had no time for chitchat with her children. The children in question were grateful.

Our plan was to drive up to Door County the next morning and stay two days. That was the longest I could manage to get away from work, and Buddy had no problem returning to Chicago that soon.

I didn't bring up any of the million questions I had during the rest of our day together, satisfied that the five-hour drive to Door County the next morning, with Buddy trapped in the car, would give me ample time to press him.

My main concern that afternoon was letting my boss know I was taking a last-minute hiatus for a couple of days. I knew when I told Tom that Buddy was in town, he'd have no problem with the idea. Because they'd been such close friends as teenagers, I was sure the two of them would also want to get together.

As predicted, Tom was happy for me to leave town the next day but suggested we three all meet for a drink that night. I declined, insisting they didn't want me around for their boys' night out. Everyone was happy.

Buddy and I spent the remainder of the afternoon catching up—talking about everything except why he was really in town. We sat close together on my couch with his computer on the coffee table in front of us. His flash drive revealed what seemed like thousands of pictures of his family: his wife, Elaine, and my nieces, the twins, who are just two years older than my Emily. I love them dearly, even their squeaky voices, which they inherited from their mother (definitely not our side of the family). When Emily was younger, she and I used to call them Pip and Squeak behind their backs, until my mother overheard us and put an immediate stop to such shenanigans.

I looked at pictures of Elaine planting flowers and then showing off a cake she had baked; the twins, Penny (aka Pip) and Sandy (aka Squeak), sunbathing on their deck and playing with their dog; and several pictures of the whole family dressed up for formal occasions. Buddy reminded me that Penny was a nurse at the Virginia Hospital Center and Sandy was a physical therapist at a wellness facility in Arlington.

"You are lucky to have them both close by," I said, sounding more sorry for myself than happy for Buddy.

He put his arm around my shoulders affectionately. It was a sweet, brotherly gesture, one I had missed. "Yes, I am," he agreed. "It has to be tough for you, not living closer to Emily."

I nodded sadly. Sometimes it seems like California is on the other side of the moon. "What about their love lives?" I asked. "Any contenders?"

Buddy laughed. "Well, it's not easy for any guy who gets too close; they have to get through me first."

I was a little shocked to hear him say that. His daughters were well past the age where they should need Daddy's permission to date.

"You don't approve?" Buddy asked, reading the expression on my face.

"Well, no, not necessarily." I stared at the picture on the screen. The grown-up Pip and Squeak were water skiing, clinging to the ends of two ropes stretched out from a boat, each one with an arm extended toward the sky. I could almost hear them squealing with joy. "They are such striking . . . er . . . lovely girls . . . er, women. I'm just surprised they haven't been snatched up, that's all."

Buddy laughed again and then nodded. "Yeah, they do have to beat the guys off with a stick."

I let him have his daydream. From what I remembered—and what the pictures I was now seeing confirmed—both unfortunate girls were just an inch or two short of six feet and skinny, with their mother's frizzy red hair. Even after their buckteeth had been straightened, their high-pitched voices still had to be dealt with. At my thoughts, I literally slapped my own knee. How mean *was* I? Here were my only two nieces, and I couldn't muster up a kind thought.

Instead, a few memories flew through my head, mainly of the twins tormenting their younger cousin, Emily. Locking her in Grandma's basement for a couple of hours. Cutting three inches off her hair. Hiding her new bike in Grandma's garage. Now that I thought about it, all their evil twin misdeeds occurred while the kids were on Grandma's watch. Was *she* the real culprit? On cue, my phone rang, and it was the mastermind herself.

"Valerie, ask Buddy what kind of milk he drinks. Two percent or whole? Or does he like skim?"

I relayed the question to my brother, who answered exactly as he might have when he was sixteen. "Whatever."

"He likes two percent," I said, cutting short a conversation about dairy products that could have gone on for hours.

"What about bread? White, wheat, or does he prefer English muffins?" I suddenly pictured my mother as a waitress at Mel's Diner, licking the end of a pencil and holding an order pad.

"Wheat, Mom." I had to shut her down before she started on bacon, or how he wanted his eggs, and if he liked decaf or regular coffee. "Gotta go; Buddy and I are on our way out for an early dinner. Bye, Mom—"

"Valerie, it's three—"

"Riiiight; we want to beat the crowd. See you tomorrow. Love you."

Buddy was shaking his head and smiling as he scrolled through more photographs of his girls. "Well played, sis. Look here; this is the deck I finished last year."

"Nice." I leaned over to get a better look at Pip, or maybe Squeak, sprawled on a chaise lounge, reading a magazine. "She looks beautiful. You can see that the physical therapy stuff has paid off."

"No, that's Penny; she's the nurse, remember?"

"Oh, right; sorry. I can see that now. I love her . . . sandals." I struggled to find some meaningful story to share about the twins—something funny, some clever anecdote, perhaps—while Buddy used his fingers to scroll some more. "Remember when Penny thought she was a cat?" It was the best I could come up with.

"She was three, and it was Sandy."

"And Mom bought her some catnip? And kept a saucer of milk in the corner of the kitchen?"

"Again, she was *three*."

"Didn't she want Elaine to enter her in the local cat show?"

"Don't remember that." He was getting serious, or maybe offended.

But I kept going, remembering the time one of them stole Emily's favorite book and scribbled over the pictures inside. "She had that sweet collar, pink plastic with gigantic purple rhinestones."

"Enough, already." He snapped the cover of his laptop shut. "Enough about my obviously deranged family. Tell me what's going on with you."

"I always knew she'd grow out of it." She *had* grown out of it, I hoped.

***

After a leisurely couple of hours reminiscing about our own childhoods, Buddy got ready for his night out. He reappeared in my living room in jeans and a sweatshirt, looking comfortable and handsome. I knew that Tom would definitely be wearing a suit, no matter what type of neighborhood tavern he planned to take Buddy to. Tom doesn't do casual, and I haven't seen him in jeans since he was in his teens.

"Sure you don't want to join us?" My brother checked his back pocket for his wallet.

"Very sure. Have fun. Where are you meeting him?"

"O'Casey's. I'm kinda surprised it's still there." He checked his phone and then put it in his front pocket.

I rose from the couch and located my keys in my purse. "Here, take these. This one is for my apartment door, and this will get you in the main entrance. I'll leave blankets and a pillow on the couch. Have a wonderful time." Before he left, I gave him a hug and held him close, surprising myself.

"Hey, what's this?" He returned the hug and didn't let go for a few seconds. "You okay?"

"Yeah, I just . . . I just missed you, that's all."

He gave me his aw-shucks smile, sending me back in time to when I comforted my teenage brother. The one who had been dumped by a girlfriend or whose team had lost the state championship. "Yeah, let's get better at keeping in touch, okay?"

"Yes, sir." I saluted.

As soon as he was gone, I went to the window to watch him get in his car and drive away. I gave him a wave and blew him a kiss, even though he couldn't see it. And then, when I was sure he was out of the parking lot, I set to work going through his backpack.

***

"So, I went through my brother's backpack—"

"And?" Kit asked.

"And I didn't find a thing."

"What did you expect to find?" I could hear *The Great British Bake Off* in the background.

"Oh, I don't know. I was hoping I might find something to link him to Autumn Grey. Or perhaps Culotta."

"Have you checked his phone?" she asked.

I slapped my forehead, like one of the Three Stooges. Why hadn't I checked that while he was showering?

When Kit got no response from me, I heard her laugh. "Really, Valley Girl, you've been single too long. That's the first place any normal person checking up on a man would look—especially if she's concerned about his involvement in a murder."

"Murder! Why would you even say that? Buddy has no involvement in anyone's murder. That is just preposterous." But the question *had* popped through my head: was it just weird that he had shown up unannounced the day after Hettie's murder?

"Okay, I hope you're right." I could sense I was losing her interest. "They're just about to start working on jam roly-poly," she said, "so I have to go. Call me from Door County."

"I will, and I'll find a time to go through Buddy's phone. Enjoy your show."

***

I was awakened by the *Law & Order* theme song, which confused me because that very show was also on my television. A pretty, blond policewoman was talking to a sad little girl. The theme song stopped, and then it started again. It took me a few seconds to realize the music was actually my phone alerting me to an incoming call. Bleary-eyed, I turned down the volume on the television and peered at my phone. It told me it was Tom calling, and the time was eleven forty-three.

"Hi," I said.

"Hey, Kiddo. Let me talk to Buddy."

I sat up and switched on the nightstand lamp. "Tom?"

"Yeah, it's me. Let me speak to him."

One of the advantages of a three-room apartment is that I didn't need to search it to know my brother was not back. "He's with you. He left here hours ago. To meet you at O'Cas—"

"O'Casey's. Yeah, right."

I felt a stab of fear. "Didn't he show up? Oh, Tom, he should have been there long ago; he—"

"Calm down. He *was* here, but he left about an hour ago. And—"

"An hour? You mean he left an hour ago?"

"Er, isn't that exactly what I just said?"

"Well, where is he? That bar is ten minutes away, max. And why are you calling?"

"Because he forgot his phone; I just found it here on the bar. I got to talking with some guys, and I didn't notice it earlier."

"Well, where can he be—"

"Relax, will ya? Were you sleeping or something?"

"Yes, I was sleeping. It's nearly midnight."

"Okay, don't make a federal case out of it."

"Just tell me what happened. When he left, did he say where he was going?"

"Val, don't turn this into one of your major dramas, okay? All I'm telling you is that Buddy was here, and we had a few drinks. Then he got a phone call, and shortly after that, he said he had to leave. He dropped some cash on the bar and took off. Said he'd call me in a couple of days when he gets back to Chicago. I didn't realize he had left his phone behind. So, seeing as how he might need it, I thought I'd call, and he, or maybe you, could come pick it up."

"Me? Come pick it up?"

"Okay, maybe you could swing by the office tomorrow on your way out of town and get it then."

"No, Tom, something's wrong."

"Because a guy leaves his phone behind? Are you kidding me?"

"No, and yes, I mean something is wrong. Where is Buddy? He's not here, and he should have been back at least forty-five minutes ago."

"Unless he went somewhere else."

"Why would he do that? Where would he go?" I realized I was sounding a little hysterical, never a good tactic when talking to Tom, so I took a deep breath.

"Why don't you try calling him?"

It sounded like the logical thing to do, until I remembered Buddy didn't have his phone. "Very funny," I said, still trying to sound calm. "Do you know who called him? It was probably Elaine, or maybe one of his girls, right?"

"Nah, don't think so. Not the way he raced out of here."

"What are you saying?"

"I'm not saying nothing, other than he took a call, spoke for a few seconds, said good-bye, and left soon after."

More deep breaths. "Okay, do this. Look at the last call he received; tell me who called him."

"Whoa. No way; I'm not looking through another guy's phone."

"Just do it, Tom."

"*No.*"

"You make it sound like I'm asking you to go through his underwear drawer."

"Same thing. I won't do it."

"Please just—oh, wait, do you even know how to do it? I can tell you; it's easy. Just hit the phone icon, and—"

"I'm not going through his phone, Val. That's final. Why don't you just calm down and wait for him to get home. He obviously had a little business to take care of."

"Okay, I'll give him twenty minutes, and then I am coming down to that damn bar to get his phone."

"Okay."

"Wait. You really want me to get dressed and drive to O'Casey's?"

"I don't want you to do anything. I'm just telling you the phone is here. If you think he will want it—"

"You seriously want me to get in my car in the middle of the night?"

"Val, you're driving me nuts. Let me finish up here and I'll bring it by."

I sighed with relief and said a silent prayer that Buddy would be back by the time Tom arrived. "Thank you, Tom. And the best way to get to my place is—"

"I know. I know this town like the back of my hand. And I sure as hell know where you live. I'll be there in half an hour."

Feeling a little better, I got out of bed and put on a robe. The living room was dark, but there was one tiny orange light glowing from the coffee table. Without turning on a lamp, I walked toward it. It was the flash drive, still plugged in on the side of Buddy's laptop. I pulled it free, and the orange glow disappeared. Then I had another thought.

Maybe the Pip and Squeak collection wasn't the only thing on the drive.

CHAPTER ELEVEN

"Mom, calm down. I'm not saying we're not coming up *at all.*" *But that might be what I say in my* next *call,* I thought. "We just can't come now. We can't come yet—"

"Valerie, will you quit babbling and tell me *why.*"

"I don't have time to explain, Mom. You'll just have to take your two grown kids' word for it that something has come up that we have to deal with in Downers Grove."

"I guess William Stuckey and I will just have to come down there, then," she said, with all the decisiveness I lacked.

"No! Um, no, that's not necessary. We'll be up. Buddy really wants to visit you in Door County. You know how much he loves it." Finally, I was leveling with her, telling her a complete truth. My brother loves Door County (like everyone else who has been there—except maybe Tom). Ever since our mother moved to the Wisconsin peninsula as a widow, Buddy has claimed it's the only place on earth where he feels totally at peace.

So maybe we should be rushing *up there*, I thought, my stomach still roiling at all that had taken place overnight and my entire being craving peace. "We'll be up there, Mom," I repeated. "Just give us a day to get things—"

"I don't understand—"

"Bye, Mom." I hung up. Big mistake. I should have known better.

"You need to get back to her soon, ya know." Kit was starting a pot of coffee in my kitchen. She'd found everything she needed, which was surprising, given what little time she's spent in my tiny apartment that she says gives her claustrophobia. She's always finding someplace better that she assures me I can afford, or that she'll help me afford. But I love my apartment. It just had two too many people in it right now, never mind that they are normally two of my favorite people.

Normally.

But there was nothing normal about the fix we were in.

"If you don't get back to her, she'll be showing up at your door," Kit continued.

My pal had come, of course, the minute I'd called her the night before. Or rather, early this morning, when Buddy still hadn't come home. And after I'd found what I found on his flash drive and phone.

I'd felt disloyal and dishonest when I'd plugged it back in to see what I could see, even as I assured myself his well-being might depend on it. So while I waited for him to return or Tom to show up with the phone—not certain which I wanted to take place first as long as Buddy eventually returned safe and sound—I looked once again at the pictures he had shown me.

At first it didn't appear he had anything to hide. But then I saw, in some pictures he had *not* shared with me, a young woman bearing a striking resemblance to Autumn Grey. They were in a separate folder titled, of all the crazy things, *Uniforms*. There was a photo of Autumn nestled between Buddy's twins on a park bench, with a sour-looking Elaine accidentally photobombing under a nearby tree. And there was a photo of Buddy and Autumn, arms around each other, pulling each other close, with Buddy looking as happy as Elaine did sour.

What the hell?

Knowing I *had* to have more time to check out the contents of Buddy's flash drive, but afraid to keep looking for fear he or Tom might arrive any minute, I immediately did what had to be done. Heart pounding, I hurriedly copied the contents of Buddy's flash drive to a folder on my own computer. I titled the folder—ironically, I thought—*Recipes*. Then, because it *was* ironic, given the fact that everyone knows the only food preparation I do is pour milk over Cheerios, I quickly renamed it *Listings*. Yes, that would look less suspicious should Buddy invade my computer as I had his.

When Buddy still hadn't returned by the time Tom arrived, I tried to get rid of my boss so I could check the contents of the phone. I felt fully justified and planned to tell Buddy just that. *Of course* the only responsible thing for a sister to do was to check her missing brother's phone before calling the police.

"Got any wine?" Tom asked, heading straight to my kitchen after I'd let him in.

"No! No, I'm out." I quickly followed him, ready to tackle him if need be before he got to my refrigerator, where I knew there were three unopened bottles of chardonnay Buddy had brought.

But I wasn't close enough to tackle Tom in time. "Pankowski! Why are you holding out on me? You trying to get rid of me?" He stood at the open refrigerator and turned to give me a piercing look of disbelief.

"No, of course not. I forgot those were in there. Buddy brought them." The fact that it was partially true made it sound more natural, I thought. But Tom's suspicious look made me wonder if I'd thought wrong.

He took out a bottle and read the label. "Yeah, I guess Buddy did bring this. It looks a little upscale for you, Pankowski. You do have a corkscrew, right?"

"Yes, I have a corkscrew; of course I do. Do you think I use my teeth?"

"No, I think you normally just do this." He made a winding movement with his thumb and index finger around the top of the bottle.

"There's nothing wrong with a screw top, Tom." I watched him rifle through my kitchen drawer until he found the opener and inserted it into the bottle. "None for me," I added as he grabbed two wineglasses from my cupboard. "Do you think we should call the police?"

"No, of course not. I can think of a million reasons why he wouldn't be home yet. And since he doesn't have his phone, he can't call and tell you."

"Oh, I'm pretty sure he could find another phone." I followed Tom back to my living room, where we both sat down on my couch. He leaned back against the cushions, looking as if he could comfortably stay all night. I, on the other hand, felt bursting with the need for him to leave. I sat on the edge of the couch at the end closest to the door, unconsciously leaning toward it as if I could pull him in that direction by some magnetic force.

"I'm guessing he figures you're asleep. He'd have no sane reason to think his fiftysomething *younger* sister would decide he is in jeopardy because he's still out after midnight." Tom gave a chuckle that I found insulting. But I also found it comforting, because it made sense. I told myself I wouldn't be worried if it weren't for all the strange things going on, from Autumn to murder. Not to mention Buddy was consulting with the *FBI*.

After thirty minutes that seemed like an eternity, even though I supposed I should enjoy *me* listening to *Tom* babble for a change, he took his last sip of wine. Heaving a huge sigh, he set the empty glass down on my coffee table. "I guess I'll call it a night, Kiddo. You should too. Buddy's a big boy, and you need your beauty sleep."

"Gee, thanks."

"Not for beauty. You got plenty of that. But you have a long road trip tomorrow."

"That's sweet," I murmured.

"And I've seen you drive."

"And there it is." I stood, hoping he would follow suit. He did. And after I closed the apartment door behind him, I couldn't get to Buddy's phone fast enough.

Only to find it as dead as Hettie Randall.

Crap.

I had to fight off the feeling that I was betraying my brother. I reminded myself that I was justified in checking his phone, so why wouldn't I be justified in helping myself to the charger I'd seen in his backpack. I carefully retrieved it from among his meticulously folded clothing and plugged his phone in, feeling as if my nerve endings were going to poke through my skin any second. I decided I'd have a glass of wine, after all, while I waited for the phone to charge enough to begin examining it.

And I'd call Kit again.

Maybe I hadn't been able to convince Tom that something was gravely wrong, but it wasn't hard to draw my BFF in. Tom would no doubt attribute that to her penchant for drama, but I knew it had more to do with her keen intuition.

I was happy to learn I hadn't awakened her. She'd been too engrossed in an episode of *Ancient Aliens* on the History Channel, she assured me, to be ready to sleep yet. And she insisted she was coming right over, as soon as I told her what I'd found on Buddy's flash drive. Most of all, of course, she was enticed by the notion of combing Buddy's phone for clues.

"But what if he comes back, Kit? What reason will we give him for your being here in the middle of the night?"

"That'll be the least of our worries," my wise friend had said.

And we'd finished checking my brother's phone as well as what I'd copied to my computer from his flash drive before he finally returned. Safe and sound. That was the good news. What we'd found on his phone, not so much. The last call he had received before leaving the bar was from a number with an area code of 226. While Kit used her own phone to check what area that number covers (turned out it's Ontario, Canada), I redialed numerous times but never got an answer.

"What are you doing here, Kit?" Buddy asked after he had let himself in. We'd heard him fumbling with the key but had made no move to let him in ourselves. Instead, we sat on the couch like two mothers waiting for a truant child to return.

"Val was worried about you, so I came to keep her company." Kit always disarms me when she answers with the truth. Well, it was true as far as it went.

"Oh, I'm sorry. I would have called, but I—"

"Yeah, I know. You didn't have your phone." I pointed to the instrument in question, lying on the coffee table in front of us.

"Did Tom bring it—" He was suddenly speechless.

I didn't think I was just imagining the guilty look I saw flooding his face. And I noted how disheveled he looked. Of course, it was three in the morning, and I knew that alone could account for his pallor and his mussed hair. But why had a button-down shirt replaced the sweatshirt I was sure he'd been wearing when he left? Where did he get it, and where had his sweatshirt gone?

"It's probably dead by now?" Buddy sounded hopeful as he made his way toward his phone on the coffee table.

But my words intercepted him. "I charged it."

"Why?" he asked, and I wasn't sure if his tone was more defensive or offensive.

"I can think of several reasons," I said, "the innocent one being in case you tried to call it. I could tell you it was safe with me."

"The *innocent* one? What reason could you have that's not innocent?" By now, he'd grabbed his phone and tucked it deep in his pocket. The charger still lay on the table, coiled like a poisonous snake.

"Buddy, we need to talk," I said.

He threw a look Kit's way, as if to say, *With* her *here?*

I threw a look back to convey what my friend had told me earlier. *That's the least of your worries.*

"I'm not talking now. I'm going to sleep. I can go to a hotel . . ." He motioned toward the couch Kit and I were occupying, as if to remind me that it was supposed to be his bed for the night. He didn't sound like Buddy my brother when he said it. It was Buddy the high-ranking military officer I heard in his voice, and so I didn't argue.

Surprisingly, Kit didn't either. We rose and shuffled into my bedroom. "He better damn well be ready to talk in the morning," she said as she crawled into my bed. We hadn't discussed her sleeping over, but I figured she wouldn't be leaving my apartment—nor would either of us be sleeping much—until we had some answers.

And because we still didn't have them by the time I knew my mom was awake the next morning, the only thing I could do was postpone—if not cancel—our visit to Door County. It had shocked her, of course, but she got me back.

Less than six hours after we'd ended our phone call, my mother was, as Kit had predicted, standing at my door.

***

"Valerie, did this place shrink? It looks even smaller than the last time I was here." My mother, accompanied by her husband pulling a small suitcase, took a step into my home, and I resisted agreeing with her. But if I'd thought having two extra people had made my apartment seem crowded, adding another two made it downright suffocating. "Do you have any coffee?" she added.

"Coffee?" Kit said brightly, like this was a normal day. "What a good idea."

I saw my mom frown, and I quickly grabbed my friend's elbow and guided her into my bedroom. I knew her presence wasn't going to make whatever was about to take place with my brother, mother, and me any easier. I couldn't even believe she was still here, but I hadn't felt I could ask her to leave after she'd come over in the middle of the night to help me.

"I'm gonna suggest to Buddy that we go get Starbucks," I whispered to her now, right after I closed my bedroom door behind us.

"Great idea. We should do that—"

"No, it'll be better if it's just Buddy and I." *He's obviously not going to talk in front of you,* I thought but didn't say. "Now that my mom's here, I *have* to find out what's going on before dealing with her."

"I'm not staying here alone with your mother."

"No, of course not. Perhaps it would be better if you go home." It was what I had really wanted to say to her much earlier.

She looked upset. "Home? But I—"

"Really, Kit, it would be easier." I was taking off my Cubs T-shirt and slipping into jeans and a normal-size T-shirt with a Haskins Realty logo—a leftover from some softball tournament a few summers ago. "Do this for me."

"Okay. But you'll call me."

"Of course; when have I ever not called you?"

CHAPTER TWELVE

Getting Buddy to agree to go with me to Starbucks was easier than I'd thought it would be. Getting my mother to understand that I didn't have enough sugar or cream—or coffee, for that matter—was a lot harder.

Buddy was quiet on the short drive to the coffee shop. Once we got there, I shut off the car and turned to face him. "Okay, I think you need to tell me what's going on."

He was staring straight ahead, perfectly still, not looking at me. "Val . . ."

I kept quiet so he could finish his thought, but instead of continuing, he ran his hand over his face. "Where do I begin?" he finally said, turning his head to look out the passenger window.

"I don't know. Why don't you start at the beginning? That's always a good place."

He took some time to think about that and eventually turned sideways in his seat, leaning against the passenger door to face me. "Val, Autumn is . . . Autumn is my daughter." He switched his position to face forward again, staring out the window at a woman struggling to hold four paper cups.

I wondered idly why she didn't get one of those cup-holder trays, while my mind began to match Buddy's news with some of the cryptic text messages Kit and I had read on his phone. They referenced Autumn Grey and the fact that he had to use discretion, keep secrets. Suddenly they made sense.

"She's mine," he said softly. "Autumn Grey is my daughter," he repeated in a determined voice, like it was now easier for him to speak and breathe.

My thoughts switched from coffee-cup holders to why someone would pick Autumn for a child's name. Before Emily was born, her father favored the name Summer, but I'd dismissed it as too gimmicky, hippieish, definitely not right. I wanted something classic.

"Are you hearing me?" he asked. "Autumn is my child. Your niece."

"Yes, I heard you," I said softly. And then in a louder voice: "Are you freaking kidding me?" And then I yelled, "You're seriously telling me that you have a daughter no one knew about?"

I watched him slowly nod, his focus back on the windshield. I wanted to reach over and punch his face. I wanted to shake the daylights right out of him. I wanted to grab him by the throat and squeeze.

He turned to look at me. "It's not so bad, is it?"

I was almost speechless, but did manage to say, "It's awful, Buddy."

"Why?" he asked.

"Because . . ." Now I was totally speechless. *Why was it so bad? Could it even be a good thing? And what would our mother say?* "Does Mom know?" I asked.

"No. That's why I wanted to come see you guys. I wanted to break the news before . . . before you met her."

"Oh man." The thought of telling our mother filled my head. Just then my cell phone rang and her name appeared on the screen. "It's her. It's Mom," I told Buddy.

He smiled slightly. "Her timing is as impeccable as always. Answer it."

I hit the speaker button. "Hi, Mom. Buddy and I are just—"

"On your way to Brazil to get that coffee?"

"Funny, Mom. But there's a long line here. We shouldn't be too much longer—"

"Valerie, this soap powder you use—I've never heard of it, and it doesn't look like it would be any good. Why don't you buy Tide, like everyone else?"

"Good idea, Mom; will do, and we'll be back soon. Love you." I hit the button to end the call, and Buddy and I both laughed.

"She sounded upset about your housekeeping," Buddy said between chuckles. "Imagine how she'll take the news of her new granddaughter."

But our levity was short-lived.

I insisted that Buddy come clean. He reiterated that Autumn was indeed his daughter. He had learned this news just three months ago when a young woman approached him, at his golf club of all places, and gave him the happy news. *It's a girl!*

For his part, Buddy claimed to be absolutely blindsided. He had no knowledge of Autumn's existence, which apparently had been the result of a brief relationship about thirty years earlier, before he'd met Elaine. Autumn's mother had passed away shortly before the father/daughter reunion, and the knowledge that Buddy was her pop had become known to Autumn herself only a few months before her mother died. As Buddy spoke, he became more animated with each stage of the story, something I hadn't seen in him since he was a teenager.

My conclusion was that he was thrilled to find this young woman, or for her to have found him. "I assume

Elaine and the twins know," I said, thinking of the pictures of the happy blended family I'd seen on the flash drive.

"Yes, they were all cool with it."

Now, recalling Elaine's bitter expression, I wondered if *he* had seen the pictures.

"She's such a great girl, Val," he continued. "Don't you think?"

"Well, let's see, considering I had no idea she was actually related to me and that she disappeared leaving a dead neighbor in her apartment, all in all I'd say *yes*, she's a great gal."

"Don't be like that, Val. None of that stuff had anything to do with her. Well, okay, it had something to do with her, but she is innocent in everything that happened."

"Well, why did you want me to stay away from her?"

"Like I said, I wanted to introduce you first. Properly."

Yeah. Like anything about this whole thing is proper. "Well, why don't you tell me the rest of it."

"All in good time. There's some stuff I can't tell you; you'll just have to be patient for a while. But I promise you she is a good girl."

"So, you're planning to break this happy news to Mom?"

"Yes, of course; that's why I came to town."

"But Buddy, you say you've known this for months; why wait so long? I can tell you right now that Mom is not going to be happy."

"Val, I wanted to just digest it myself. And then you know how it is; the longer I waited, the harder it became. I didn't see a lot of Autumn at first; she lived in Arizona, but—"

"Yeah, about that—"

"There were circumstances, there *are* circumstances, that I can't get into just yet. Some of it is . . . secret."

"*Secret?* Buddy, are you twelve? That's ludicrous." He sounded like a kid who'd just discovered the identity of his Secret Santa, not at all like the retired military commander he was. That thought sparked my next questions. "Does it have something to do with the military? Or the government? Is Autumn in the Witness Protection Program?"

Buddy raised his head and gave me a hard stare. "Where did you get that idea?"

"Not a giant leap, bro. Is she?"

He threw his head back and laughed. "Val, speaking of being *twelve*. You kill me. But we should get the coffee and get back to your place."

Reluctantly, I agreed, but I wasn't nearly done yet. "Tell me one more thing, Buddy; do you know a Dennis Culotta? He's a detective, or rather he was a detective; not really sure what he is now—"

"Don't know him," Buddy answered, just a little too quickly. "C'mon, let's go."

At that precise moment, my phone rang again. Our mother advising us that she was about to organize a search party. And so thirty minutes later, we arrived home armed with coffee, both in a bag for future brewing and in cups for immediate consumption.

***

"Kit, can you talk?"

With our mom and William following, Buddy had driven to a nearby DoubleTree hotel so they could check in. I could hardly wait for them to leave my apartment, mainly because I wanted to be alone to call Kit with the astounding news Buddy had laid on me earlier. A couple of hours had passed, and I still couldn't wrap my head around it.

She listened without interruption as I tried to recall exactly what Buddy had said. "Are you still there?" I asked when I finished.

"Yes. I'm thinking."

"Well, hurry up with your thinking. Buddy will be back soon and—"

"Did he have a DNA test? Is he sure she's his kid?"

"He didn't say, and I didn't ask him. But I will."

"Ya know, if someone just waltzes up to you on the ninth hole and says *Hi, Dad*, seems like that's the first thing you would do."

"Well, yes, of course, and he probably did; we just haven't gotten around to talking about that yet." Although I didn't tell Kit, the thought of a DNA test hadn't occurred to me. But she was right, and I hoped *Buddy* had thought of it.

"Does Jean know?"

"Not yet. Buddy's going to tell her tonight at dinner—"

"He's not planning to have Autumn jump out of a cake, is he?"

That sent me into a fit of giggles, which lasted way too long. I was finally able to compose myself by thinking of the real scene to come later. "I better hang up; I don't want Buddy to find me talking to you. I'll call you as soon as I can."

"I can't wait. Just make sure you remove all the sharp knives from the table tonight."

***

At Capri, one of my favorite restaurants in Downers Grove, Buddy didn't make his announcement until dessert was served: tiramisu for Mom and me, and a mini cannoli for William. I think Buddy had lost his appetite. As I watched him swirl the remains of his wine in the bottom of his glass, and for fear he was never going to come clean, I kicked him under the table while looking at my watch. Now or never, buddy boy.

"So, Mom . . . William . . . I'm sure you are eager to know my news," he said at last.

Our mom didn't respond, but appeared busy studying her dessert, slowly mashing it with a spoon as if a prize were hidden somewhere in the ladyfingers.

Buddy continued. "So . . . it's like this, Mom . . ."

His obvious hesitation finally caused her to look up. "Will you just get on with it? You're not dying, are you?"

Buddy swirled his wine some more and then finished it off. "No. It's good news."

I nearly choked on my own wine. And then I waited for him to deliver the "good news."

At last he proceeded to tell the story of Autumn, his lost daughter, his unknown offspring, his apparent new love.

My mother interrupted him only once. "Autumn? What kind of name is that?"

"I think it's very pretty," I chimed in.

"Yes, it's lovely," William concurred.

"Continue," my mother ordered, and so Buddy did.

***

After dinner, Buddy and I drove our mom and William to the DoubleTree hotel. At the entrance, we all got out of the car so we could say good night. Our mom's hugs were cursory, detached. She hadn't said a word since she'd heard the big news. William appeared his usual jovial self, but I could sense the tension in his body as I hugged him, and I heard him whisper that I was not to worry; he would talk to his wife.

Once back in his car and headed to my apartment, Buddy visibly relaxed. "Whew, that seemed to go well." He stopped at a red light.

"You think so? Are you kidding me?" I had never seen our mother so quiet. I wasn't sure if she was planning to load her gun or knit baby booties.

"Yeah, I think so. I'm glad they agreed to stay at a hotel tonight."

"Like they had a choice? Mom asked me why I don't iron my sheets."

"Let's face it, Val. You've got a severe laundry problem." We both laughed, but it wasn't sincere merriment we were feeling. "Well, I'm bushed; can't wait to hit the sack." He feigned a yawn.

"You mean couch, and we've got a lot more to talk about."

"No, Val, please; I'm all talked out. We'll talk some more on the drive tomorrow. I promise."

"The hell we will. For all I know, you'll disappear again tonight. I'm not letting you out of my sight."

***

A couple of hours later, after we'd finished off the bottle of wine Tom had opened, we said good night. Buddy made up his bed on the couch, and I left him with his earbuds in, listening to a podcast on his iPad. I slipped into my bed, turned the TV on low, and left my bedroom door ajar so I could keep an eye on my runaway brother. Then I called Kit and, speaking in a loud whisper, gave her a recap of the evening, including what little he'd shared once we got home.

"Ya know," Kit said when I had finished, "I was thinking about Buddy returning to your place last night wearing a different shirt. Did he ever explain where he went after he left Tom?"

"He says he got a call from a friend and decided to go see him," I whispered into the phone. "Someone called Frank, a friend from the Navy. I don't know him. Apparently, while he was at this guy's house, he spilled something on his sweatshirt and this Frank gave him a clean shirt."

"Do you believe him?" Kit asked.

"Yes. No. I don't know. I've never known Buddy to lie to me—"

"Wait a minute; didn't he lie to you for about three months, by omission, about Autumn Leaves?"

"Okay, I'll grant you that. But everything else he said seems to check out. He said Autumn came from Arizona, and we know that's true because I saw her license at the nail place."

"Riiight! Because no one *ever* had a fake ID. You'd make a great bartender, Valley Girl."

I was suddenly too tired to talk anymore. I leaned over in my bed and took a quick look out to my living room. Although the back of my couch obstructed my view of Buddy, I could see the light of the iPad illuminating his space. "I'm so exhausted, I'm going to try to get some sleep now. We have a long drive tomorrow; I'll call you when we get there."

But Kit apparently wasn't ready to drop the subject. "And you didn't find out what Autumn Equinox was doing here or where she is now?"

I couldn't tell her it was a secret; that sounded so lame. "No, not yet; I'll find that out tomorrow too."

"Make sure you do."

"Can I go now?"

"Okay," she said reluctantly. "Sleep well, and we'll talk tomorrow."

"Thanks for rushing over last night, and tell Larry thanks for sharing you."

"No problem. In fact, Larry was on the phone to Sam when I left."

"So what's going on with Sam?"

I heard her sigh. "I don't know, but I told Larry to find out."

***

I checked the iPad light again, turned the volume of the TV up a notch, and settled down to sleep.

At four thirty-six, according to the digital clock on my nightstand, I woke up. I tiptoed toward the kitchen for a glass of water, passing the couch. The living room was silent, and the iPad was no longer switched on. More importantly, its owner was no longer there.

Buddy had flown the coop. Or more accurately, the couch.

Again.

CHAPTER THIRTEEN

As soon as we cleared the Chicago traffic, I deemed it safe to ask Buddy just where the hell he'd gone the night before—or rather in the wee hours of the morning.

I kept my eyes on the road while he yelled at me. We might have been free of the worst of the weavers and race-car-driver wannabes on I-94, but there were still streams of semis and smaller vehicles that needed my undying (I hoped) attention. " . . . sake, I'm a grown man. If I want to go someplace in the middle of the night, or at any hour, I don't need to report to my little sister."

"That's just it, Buddy, I'm not your *little* sister anymore; I'm a grown woman, and you're a guest in *my* house . . ." Even I knew how unreasonable I sounded. My "house" was as small as most people's pantries, and my brother was in his fifties.

"That's ridiculous, Val. Do you hear yourself?"

Because I did hear myself and did realize just how foolish I sounded—even though I still felt justified—I gave a sigh of defeat. But I didn't speak, because I didn't know what to say.

Apparently, neither did Buddy, and so we rode in silence to the Wisconsin state line. Luckily, that was only twenty minutes, because by then I was about ready to explode from the desire to know what was going on. I had so many questions for my brother, I didn't even know where to start. So I teared up with gratitude when he began to answer some of those unspoken questions.

"Val, I have a lot I need to tell you, but much of it I just cannot. Or should not."

He paused, and I wondered if I dared hope that meant he *was* going to tell me, whether he should or not. And if he did, I hoped it would include telling me where he had gone last night, because I didn't want to ask again. Then he gave a rueful laugh before continuing. "I mean, anything I tell you is like telling Kit, too, right?"

"Of course not, Buddy. You know I'd be loyal to you first." But would I? Could I? *Yes. I could and would.*

He gulped the last of his Starbucks, which we'd picked up on the way out of Downers Grove. That reminded me to take a sip of my own, which had gone largely untouched as I'd kept both hands gripped on the steering wheel to help assure we'd survive the morning traffic. I'd given thanks at least three times during the drive that my job allowed me to stay in Downers Grove and avoid this battlefront of more hectic Chicagoland traffic. I'd also asked myself why in the world we'd thought we had to leave for Door County before rush hour was over. After all, our mother was probably just now getting home.

She'd insisted we stick to the plan, albeit a day late, for Buddy and me to visit her in Door County. Because she was always up before five every morning, anyway, she and William could easily be there before us, and besides, she had all of our meals planned and partially prepared. Not to mention an agenda that would tire a person half her age, or mine.

"Well, I can't tell you everything," Buddy said. "Not now, anyway. For your own sake as well as . . ." He paused long enough that I was afraid he was going to change his mind and clam up. "But you deserve some answers, and I'm sorry I got short with you. I'm just under a lot of stress, Val."

"Because of Autumn?"

"Largely that, yes. But it's not her fault," he hastened to add, as if my face had shown my resentment toward her for doing this to my big brother.

Yes, I acknowledged, at least to myself. *I'd always be his little sister. I* wanted *to be.*

"You see, when Autumn first approached me, she was scared. That's really the reason she decided to out herself to me as my daughter." Buddy went on to explain that even though her mother had told her about him being her father, Autumn had not planned to contact him, for a number of reasons. She didn't want to disturb his life, and she just had no real yen to meet him. "She said her mom had given her a full life, and this wasn't exactly the 1950s. Not everyone thought both a mom and dad were prerequisites for happiness, and she certainly didn't suddenly need a man to protect her just because she knew of his existence. Blah blah blah." He said it affectionately, not derisively.

"Well, what made her change her mind?" I prodded when he seemed to get lost in a reverie, apparently a family trait that I'd just never noticed in him before. *So I don't have exclusive rights,* I mused. And then I threw another question at him, as soon as it popped into my head. "Buddy, that woman who drove Autumn here . . . was she related to Autumn's mother, the woman you—"

"No, she's someone I work with. But as to what made Autumn change her mind and contact me, that's where it gets a little dicey—what I can and cannot tell you. Yet," he added, but I wasn't sure if he was being honest or just wanting to keep my questions at bay. Would he *ever* be able to come completely clean with me?

"Buddy, I promise you, telling me is like telling no one. My lips will be forever sealed." I removed one hand from the steering wheel—very daring for me—and pinched my lips with my fingers to demonstrate. I immediately returned my hands to the safety of ten and two, and then I remembered reading how nine and three are now considered the best positioning and adjusted my hands accordingly.

" . . . had seen something, or rather overheard something, she shouldn't have, and she didn't know if she should go to the authorities. She was afraid for her life."

"Autumn?"

"Yes, Val." He sounded like he wondered who the heck I *thought* we were talking about. "Autumn. She was at her friend's house in New York for some kind of college reunion and overheard this friend's father on the phone talking about something illegal."

"How did she know it was illegal?"

"That's not important. Nor can I tell you. Not yet."

I decided that for now, I would settle for what he'd willingly tell me. I'd have to.

"Go on." I looked over my shoulder and then changed lanes, bracing for the Milwaukee rush-hour traffic, which sometimes is only slightly better than Chicago's. And I had stupidly chosen a departure time this morning that guaranteed we'd go through both. I never know if it will be bad because of reckless drivers zipping to and fro or if it will simply come to a standstill. Milwaukee, it seemed, was opting for a standstill this morning, largely due to construction. My shoulders relaxed. I wasn't in a hurry to get to our mother's, anyway. We could at least tell her we'd *tried* to arrive earlier. "Where did Autumn go to school?"

"She went to Arizona State. It's in Tempe—a suburb of Phoenix."

I could feel him staring at me, as if weighing once again how much he should tell me. I took my eyes off the road for one second and looked directly at him. "I won't repeat anything to Kit, Buddy."

"Okay. I believe you. I trust you. I *am* trusting you, with Autumn's life."

"Are you sure she's your daughter? I mean, did you have a—"

"DNA test?"

"Yes."

"I'm not a total idiot."

I sighed. "Good."

***

"For heaven's sake, did you oversleep?" my mother greeted us as we opened the car doors to emerge.

"Ahhh." Buddy breathed in the fresh air that was an exquisite mixture of country and lakeside. "Why don't I come here more often?"

"Humph," my mother said, which was tantamount to dittoing his remark. "Well, you're here now. Let's get you settled."

When they had married, she moved in with William at Lake View Coves Retirement Villas, a gated community of spacious one-story condos, each with a view of the swimming pool. I got settled in one of the guest rooms while our mother fussed over Buddy in the other one. She acted as if he'd never been exposed to the notion that you remove the decorative sham before laying your head on a pillow or that extra towels could be found in a bathroom linen closet. "And help yourself to these chocolates," I heard her say, and knew she had a candy dish on his bedside table identical to the one in the room I was staying in. I smiled as I thought of a similar setup in Kit's guest room, realizing once again how alike my best friend and my mother are. "Not now! I have brunch ready," I heard my mother scold.

My smile grew broader at the knowledge that Buddy would not only always be my big brother, but also her little boy.

***

That night, after dinner at Al Johnson's Swedish Restaurant (instead of lunch, my mother made sure we knew, since we'd arrived so late that the breakfast she'd prepared had to become lunch, and her lunch plans had to be moved to the dinner hour) and then ice cream cones at Wilson's, my mom and William retired early.

At last, I had Buddy to myself and a chance to ask the follow-up questions I had formulated throughout the day as I thought of little else but Autumn.

We were settled on the patio, on the other side of the house from my mom and William's bedroom window. I was having an iced tea—or sun tea, as my mom insisted we call it, no doubt wanting credit for having brewed it herself (she didn't give the sun even partial credit)—and Buddy was having a beer.

"How did Autumn happen to see this . . . um . . . illegal activity?" I asked.

"I told you, she was at a reunion at the home of her friend Gail. It was a mansion, actually. Big money, but very suspicious money, apparently."

"What exactly did she see?" I asked the question he had refused to answer in the car.

"I told you—"

"Yeah, I remember. You told me she *overheard* something. And you told me you couldn't tell me what. But I hardly see how that would hurt anything. I still wouldn't know the *who*."

He gave a huge sigh and sat up straighter on the chaise lounge he was occupying, his long legs stretched out before him and crossed at the ankles. He clicked the back of his chair into a more upright position before speaking. "I suppose I can tell you that. But I can't name names. And remember." He pinched his own lips together as I had mine earlier that day.

"I know." I pinched mine together again.

"Well, she was looking for a quiet spot in the house to use her cell to call her then-boyfriend. They were in a fight. It was the middle of the night—actually, about three in the morning, I think she said—and she went downstairs where it was all dark. But when she entered what she thought was a study, she overheard her friend's father on the phone. I'm not going to tell you precisely what she overheard; it doesn't matter. And seriously, it's better that you don't know."

I gave him a raised-eyebrows look, hoping to imply that I thought he might have been reading one too many Mario Puzo novels.

"I'm serious, Val; the less you know, the safer it is for you."

When had my brother become so dramatic? He was scaring me. I was used to the blasé guy with a nonchalant attitude, even when his Navy career had taken him to dangerous parts of the world. When he didn't continue, I spoke up. "So after Autumn witnessed, or heard, something that she shouldn't have, she contacted you."

In the dim light of the patio, I saw Buddy nod. "Yes. Not long after her mother died. She has no other family, Val. Nowhere else to turn. And she was frightened." Buddy looked away from me, toward the swimming pool. "I can tell you this. Autumn thought her friend's father saw her standing in the doorway before she ran back upstairs to the bedroom. And she was no doubt right."

I wondered if all that had something to do with why Autumn left my apartment building so abruptly.

CHAPTER FOURTEEN

Buddy said no more, or rather no more about Autumn. Instead, he launched into a story about Pip and Squeak's botched attempt to cook their parents' anniversary dinner. He apparently found it hilarious, but my thought was that the girls had inherited the noncooking gene from their aunt. When we eventually said good night forty-five minutes later, I was consumed with how much I dared tell Kit about what Buddy had told me.

After I brushed my teeth, I was wiping out the sink when my phone buzzed. Kit. Seeing her name on the screen, I steeled myself.

But luckily, she was still immersed in Sam and didn't ask a single question about Autumn. "I wish Sam and Leslie had settled somewhere other than Texas," she said.

"Do you wish they would have stayed in Illinois?"

"I never liked his dick of a father-in-law. Remember when he and Diana came to our house for dinner? How rude he was?"

"I don't remember. Was I even there?"

"Of course; I cooked an herb-crusted rack of lamb, which was quite spectacular." Since the unfortunate lamb was not ringing any bells with me, Kit continued. "With roasted butternut squash—surely you remember that?"

Even though I didn't, I acquiesced, if only to get Kit moving along. "Yes, now I remember, and it was delicious."

"Exactly. But the dick implied that the lamb was a little tough. As if."

"How awful for you, Kit."

"I know, but I'm over it." Her tone proved she was anything but.

She never did say what, specifically, was bothering her about Leslie's father right now. And I was too tired to ask. And too tired, thankfully, to even consider spilling any of Buddy's beans.

We soon said good-bye, and I slept really well that night—my best sleep in a long time, even without the aid of a television on low in the background. There was something very comforting about being under the same roof as my mother and brother. It had been a long time since we'd shared the same house.

When I awoke to a stream of bright sunlight casting its warm glow across my bed, I realized two things: the blinds on the window that I had closed last night were now wide open, and sitting on the end of my bed, with a cup of coffee in her hand, was my mother.

"Whoa." I sat up and edged as close to the headboard as I could. "Mom, this is creepy."

"Don't be silly. I brought you this cup of coffee."

I tentatively reached out and took the cup she offered. She was dressed and made-up and smiling. "What's wrong?" I asked. "Is something wrong? Has something happened?"

"Drink your coffee, Valerie. And don't be so dramatic. It's nearly seven thirty, and I assumed you didn't want to waste the day sleeping."

I took a sip of my coffee as my mother rose and picked up the jeans and T-shirt I had left crumpled on the floor last night. "You are still so messy." She shook her head and opened the closet to retrieve a hanger. "However do you manage in that tiny apartment of yours?"

"I manage just fine."

"But it's so small."

"I like it."

"You know, Valerie, I never interfered when you and David divorced."

This was a total lie. She had even hired a private detective to check out David's movements after we split.

"Mom, what has that got to do with my leaving clothes on the floor and the size of my apartment?"

"Well, if it's a question of money that keeps you in that shoebox, I can help." She had her back to me and was rearranging makeup items I had strewn across the dresser.

"Mom, it's not a question of money. I am doing quite well, and I like my home. But thank you; you are very—"

"A woman was murdered two feet away from your apartment—"

"Not exactly two feet, Mom. And besides, I like—"

"Don't split hairs. And you don't even know what you like." It was one of her favorite taunts when I was growing up, my apparent lack of knowing what I liked. She came back to the edge of the bed and sat down. "How's the coffee?"

"Good." There was something else coming, so I stopped talking to wait her out.

"Okay." She slapped her thighs. "I need you to do something for me."

I kept waiting, peering at her over the rim of my cup.

"I need you," she continued, "to make yourself scarce for a few hours this morning."

"Scarce? What does that mean?"

"It means I need you to be gone for a bit. I'm sending William Stuckey to the golf range to hit a few balls, and I think you should go to the market for me and pick up some groceries."

"Okaaaay." I thought I knew what was coming. "But why?"

"Because I need some time alone with your brother."

Several images flooded my brain, which included Buddy wearing thumb screws and my mother wearing a long black leather coat, hovering over him and shining a light in his eyes. "Mom, is it necessary for me, and William, to actually leave the house?"

"Yes. I need Buddy's full attention, with no distractions. I have to get to the bottom of his ridiculous story."

"You think it's ridiculous." It wasn't a question; on some level, I agreed with her.

"Hah! My son walks in and says, *How's the tiramisu, Mom, and oh, by the way, you have a thirty-year-old granddaughter.* Yes, I think it's ridiculous."

"So you think he's lying?"

"No, not at all. I didn't raise a liar, Valerie. But there's a lot more to it, and I mean to find out what."

"So, are you planning to beat the truth out of him?"

"Is that supposed to be funny?"

"No, not at all." I pushed back the covers and swung my legs onto the carpet. Whereas I didn't envy Buddy at all, I rather thought he deserved to be interrogated by Jean and her gestapo tactics. And maybe she'd learn some of what he wasn't telling me.

***

An hour or so later, I pulled up to the Blue Horse Cafe in Fish Creek. There I ordered my second cup of coffee, along with an egg sandwich and a fruit parfait. In my pocket was the list of grocery items my mother had sent me in search of, with an emphasis on taking my time. It seemed only logical to stop for breakfast.

I glanced at the other diners around me. Two ladies who seemed like old friends catching up. A man doing a crossword puzzle. A young woman with her laptop open before her and earbuds shutting out the rest of the world. In the corner a man sat alone, stirring a cup of coffee while he gazed my way. I was vaguely aware that he had come into the cafe a few minutes after me. But as soon as our eyes locked, he rose, picked up his cup, and stashed a newspaper under his arm. I kept the spoonful of parfait suspended in midair as he walked casually to my table.

"Culotta!" I was shocked, and yet at the same time, it seemed perfectly normal to meet him here at the Blue Horse Cafe in Fish Creek.

"Mind if I join you?" He pulled out a chair across from me and sat down.

"Should I be surprised to see you?" I laid my spoon with the uneaten bite of parfait next to the sandwich on my plate.

"I don't know; are you?"

"Why are you here? Are you following me?"

He smiled that half smile of his that drives me completely nuts. "No, Val, I'm not following you."

"Then how come . . . why are you . . . you expect me to believe you just happen to be here at the same cafe as me?"

"Okay, I'm following you a little bit. But you are not my main concern. Let's just say it's a happy coincidence that we both turned up at—" He looked around with those blasted blue eyes of his before they lit on the coffee mug he had set down before him. "The Blue Horse Cafe."

"Then who are you following? Is it my brother?"

"You know, Val, you should have considered going into law enforcement; you are really good. I bet you could teach me a lot."

"Oh noooooo," I said. "Not this time, mister. You don't get to interview me and find out stuff."

"Do you know stuff?"

"I know nothing."

"Okay, then you've got nothing to worry about."

"Worry? Why should I worry?"

"Val, I thought we just established that you don't have to—"

"I'm not in the mood for your bullshit, Culotta. Just save us both some time and tell me why you're here."

"Hmm, that's maybe not such a good idea. Why don't you tell me what you and your brother discussed during the five-hour drive from Chicago, and the cozy time you spent on your mother's patio last night."

"Good grief; you are unbelievable. You've been stalking me."

"Not really. It's routine. And if it makes you feel any better, it wasn't me who followed you. We have other people for that. I just thought that since you and I are old acquaintances, we could have coffee together." He took the spoon from the untouched place setting in front of him and helped himself to a bite of my parfait. "Delicious." He touched the napkin to his mouth.

"Why did you kiss me in Palm Desert?" I asked in a tiny voice.

For a brief second, it looked like my question had rattled him, but then his composure returned. "I couldn't help myself. I'd been wanting to do that for a long time."

"Where is Autumn Grey?" I asked, dismissing his response and finding my normal voice.

"Not sure, and not your concern."

"Is my brother safe?"

"If he doesn't break the law, he has nothing to worry about."

***

I was in the guest parking area of Lake View Coves Retirement Villas, preparing to deliver the grocery items from my trunk to my mom. Before doing so, however, I took a quick look at my phone to check for messages. There was only one missed call—from Andy, my neighbor who used a wheelchair. I punched his number. "Andy, it's Val. Everything okay?"

"Oh, hi, Val. All okay here. Just wondering where you are and if *you* are okay."

I had to remind myself that with a murder committed close by, of someone he knew, he had every reason to be a little rattled. "I'm sorry, Andy. I should have told you. I'm actually in Door County, Wisconsin, for a couple of days."

"Ah, beautiful Door County. Doing anything exciting?"

"Well, my mom just sent me to the grocery store."

"Okay, I won't keep you, but I thought I should tell someone that I saw a guy in the building that I've never seen before." I knew that Andy was able to reach up enough from his wheelchair to look out of the peephole in his door, which probably happened every time he heard the main door being opened. "He was fiddling around with Hettie's mailbox until he finally got it open."

"Oh." That shocked me. "We need to tell the police."

"Do they have any idea who did this terrible thing?" Andy asked.

"Not that they've told me," I said. "But back to the guy at the mailbox. So you don't know who he was?"

"I opened the door to ask if I could help him, but he ignored me. Rude, I'd say."

"Yes, very rude. Maybe a relative of Hettie's? I don't have any idea."

"He was bald and had a tattoo across the side of his neck, below his right ear. It looked like six numbers, crudely done. Like they do in prisons."

"Really?" I stored the information Andy had given me somewhere in my overcrowded brain. "Listen, I'll be gone for a bit, but I'm going to ask my friend Kit James to bring you over something good to eat. You know Kit, right?"

"Chanel No. 5," he replied immediately.

"Chanel—yep, that's right; she often wears Chanel."

"A classic. I used to buy my wife a bottle every Christmas."

"And listen, Andy, please call me anytime you are worried or afraid." I'd known him only a few months, but I felt very protective of him.

"I'm not afraid, but I wouldn't say no to something tasty to eat."

When we hung up, I tried Kit's phone, getting no answer, which was a relief since I wouldn't be tempted to give her any new information. But I left her a voice mail. "Kit, it's me. Remember my neighbor Andy, the one on the first floor who uses a wheelchair? If you've got any leftovers in that refrigerator of yours, please do me a favor and take him something to eat. He's a nice man. Oh, and one more thing; slap on some Chanel No. 5. He likes that." Then, just to be sure I covered all the bases, I sent her a text. *Kit, listen to your voice mail.* I knew she would definitely have some leftovers, but I also knew she'd probably prepare a three-course meal just for Andy. More than cooking, she loves a new conquest.

As I put my phone back in my pocket, my thoughts returned to the tattooed guy raiding Hettie's mailbox.

CHAPTER FIFTEEN

W hat on earth were you doing out there? Calling a boyfriend?" My mom took one of the two sacks I was carrying and began putting the avocados I'd purchased into a basket of six other avocados on the counter. Proof I'd been sent on a fool's errand.

I shook my head in disbelief as I placed the bottle of milk I'd gotten at the market next to an even bigger bottle of milk already in her refrigerator. But her remark *had* immediately conjured up an image of Culotta, and my first thought was *how does she know I saw him?* "I don't have a boyfriend, Mom." I folded the paper grocery sack I'd emptied and placed it next to the others she keeps under the sink. I watched as she did the same with hers without taking her eyes off my face.

"You're blushing, Valerie Caldwell." She grinned, and I realized *my mom* wants *me to have a boyfriend.*

"My last name is Pankowski, has been for well over a quarter of a century, and I am not blushing. Because I do not have a boyfriend."

"Don't you want one—oh, never mind. Men are useless, anyway."

"I take it your talk with Buddy was useless." *He better not have told you anything he didn't tell me*, I thought. At the same time, I hoped he had.

She sighed, sat down at the table, and took a drink from her coffee cup.

I poured some for myself and joined her. But after one sip, I knew I couldn't drink any more. Not because I'd already had so much this morning, but because I refused to waste my caffeine consumption on burned-tasting brew. I decided I would buy her a Keurig for Christmas. I was pretty sure Starbucks sold the little K-cups.

"Worse than useless," she said, setting her cup down on the table hard enough to demonstrate her frustration. "He got irritated with me. But why *wouldn't* I want to learn all I can about my granddaughter? It's bad enough that I've already missed out on thirty years. *Thirty years.* That's more than half of *your* life, Val."

"Yeah, that's a looooong time," I said, not hiding my own irritation at being reminded how very old I am. Then I softened, as I remembered my mom is even older and also that I need to be grateful that my age *is* advancing. Hettie, old as she was, would have happily lived to get even older, I felt sure. "Mom," I said, making a sudden turn in the conversation without planning to, "did Buddy say anything to you about the woman who was killed in my apartment building?"

"No. Why would he?"

"Well, I just wondered . . . never mind."

"Don't you *never mind* me, Valerie Cald—Pankowski." She began to brush nonexistent crumbs off the table, a habit I'd seen all my life whenever she was upset. "What? What were you going to say?"

I took a deep breath before answering, knowing that if I could resist giving in to my mother's demands, there was a good chance I could speak to my best friend again without divulging any of Buddy's top-secret information. "I just wondered if he told you how very upset I still am about her death. She was so sweet, Mom. She reminded me of you."

Flattery apparently will get you anywhere. My mom gave me a fond smile and then a pat on my shoulder as she rose and began taking the makings for poor-boy sandwiches out of her refrigerator. "We need to get some lunch ready for the boys," she said. "Buddy took my car to run an errand, but both he and William will be back anytime now."

I was too happy with the change of subject to point out to her that "the boys" were perfectly capable of making their own lunch.

***

I wondered if all older people slept so much, as my mom and William left Buddy and me for a nap. I beckoned my brother to follow me out to the patio, hoping I'd have better luck than our mother had.

I sipped on my sun tea as I waited for him to pop open his beer can and take a drink. I was hoping he would volunteer information about his middle-of-the-night disappearances, but apparently, he wasn't going to. So I was ready to pounce. But instead of one of the million questions I had about Autumn, I heard something else come out of my mouth. "Buddy, are you sure you don't know Dennis Culotta? Is *he* the reason you've been sneaking out at night?"

"Why would I sneak out to see *him*?"

Hmm, I thought. *Why would you ask a question like that if you don't know him?*

"And no, I do not know him," my brother added when I'd remained silent.

"Well," I said, "he seems to know you."

"He could know *of* me. I have no idea about that. Is he from Downers Grove?"

"Buddy, it's one thing if you can't tell me something, but please don't lie to me or try to deceive me."

"Val, I'd tell you *everything*, if I could be sure you wouldn't repeat it. But I'm sorry, sis, I just can't."

"Can't tell me, or can't be sure?"

"I can't tell you because I can't be sure." He gave me a sad look, and I felt bad, certain he *needed* to unload to someone. I knew I should be that someone, but I also knew he was right. It would be very hard not to tell Kit everything I knew. It was a decades-old habit.

I watched him as his sad look dissolved, replaced by one of determination. "Okay, little sis, I'm going to tell you. More, at least. But I'm trusting you. I'm reminding you that Autumn's life might depend on it. And Autumn's my *daughter*. Your niece."

Yeah, Buddy, I get how a family tree works, I thought, in my impatience for him to share what he would. But I didn't want to say anything that would risk him changing his mind. "Okay," I said softly, hoping I sounded trustworthy. Hoping I would *be* trustworthy.

I felt what he proceeded to share with me was vague enough to not risk harm to anyone. I didn't see why I couldn't repeat it to Kit, in fact. But I wouldn't.

He told me how the day after Autumn had heard Gail's father on the phone, she began to feel uneasy, knowing he'd seen her. It soon became too much pressure to bear and she'd feigned illness—complete with fake barfing noises behind the closed bathroom door—and left the gathering a day early.

She didn't tell a soul about what she knew, figuring that was the best way for it to amount to absolutely nothing. The pressure didn't start to dissipate until she located Buddy. It was only after she shared her story with her newly found father that she started to feel safe.

***

On the drive home the next morning, my phone rang and I saw it was Kit. If I answered it, Buddy would be able to hear her over the speaker, and I didn't know how to disengage it.

"Aren't you going to answer?" Buddy asked.

"Um, no. I don't like to talk and drive."

"But you're hands-free," he said, like I was someone who thought she couldn't walk and talk at the same time. "And you didn't shut up for two seconds on the drive up."

"Well, I should have. I think driving is a full-time job."

Buddy shrugged his shoulders as we drove on.

And when we stopped at the Lake Forest Oasis for a Starbucks and a potty break, I called Kit from the ladies' room. I'm actually good at multitasking.

"We're on our way back. Sorry I couldn't take your call earlier, but I didn't want Buddy to hear you on speaker; I was afraid you might mention Autumn."

"Er . . . what could I possibly mention? I don't *know* anything about her."

"Look, why don't I call you from home, after Buddy leaves. You can come over, and I'll fix us something to eat."

"Did you just say you would fix us something to *eat?*"

"Yes."

"When you say eat, do you mean food?"

"Yes. Of course."

"Not cornflakes or Rice Krispies or whatever the hell else you eat?"

"Food, Kit. Real food." I knew I was making a promise I probably couldn't keep, but I had no time now to get into an argument with Kit about our menu. "Look, I have to go. Buddy will be waiting in the car. I'll call you."

As we continued the drive home, I kept my eyes peeled for signs of Culotta or one of his minions following us. I assumed if we'd been followed on the way up to Door County, then the same would apply on the way back.

"So, what did you tell Mom?" I asked my brother when we had about an hour of driving left.

"Not much, not as much as I told you."

"Did she press you to meet Autumn?"

"Of course. I told her I'd arrange it as soon as I could."

"Well, you better, because she will hound you. And she wouldn't be wrong."

"Yeah, she was pretty worked up. The Keurig will help."

"What do you mean?" I asked. "What Keurig?"

"I borrowed her car and went and bought her one while you were grocery shopping. It was a good excuse to get out of the house since you weren't back yet. I set it on her bed before we left this morning, as a surprise thank-you gift. You do realize her coffeepot is crap, right?"

"You bought her a damn Keurig? Buddy, I was planning to get her one for Christmas."

"Christmas! That's like five months away. And don't you usually buy her a bag of tangerines or something?"

"I have sent her one or two delicious Edible Arrangements in the past. So," I changed the subject away from my lack of creativity in buying our mother gifts, "just remember, she has every right to meet her granddaughter."

"Okay, okay, I'll see that she does. Why don't we put some music on." He fiddled with my radio and located what he wanted on Sirius. I took his abrupt change of topic to mean *subject closed*. He quickly found a classic rock station, and Led Zeppelin filled the air space in my car.

After a few minutes of "Stairway to Heaven," I reached for the volume control and turned it down. "What time do you plan to leave for the airport?"

"I have a flight this afternoon at four thirty, so I'll have to leave your place as soon as we get there. I need to check my rental car in."

I waited a few seconds before replying. I knew he was lying, because I'd checked his departure time from my phone while we were still in Door County, just to be sure we allowed enough time to get back. He was booked on an eight o'clock flight from O'Hare. Why was he lying? I decided not to confront him and instead began to form my own deceitful plan.

We remained silent for a few seconds, and then I spoke. "Where is Autumn, anyway? Right now. You've never said."

"Ah." He sighed. "I just wish I knew. I'm really worried that she's not safe."

Again we were silent.

"So tell me," I said when I realized he wasn't going to offer more. "The night before we left for Door County, when you disappeared—again—in the middle of the night, where did you go?"

"Oh, I thought I told you—"

"You didn't; you know you didn't."

"It was no big deal, Val. I went to see my pal Frank again. He's having a few problems, Navy stuff. We served together. I got a call from him, and I didn't want to wake you, so I just took off. I didn't plan to be there all night."

"So what happens now, Buddy?"

"How d'you mean?"

"Don't be so obtuse. You know damn well what I mean."

"I'm not sure, Val. We just have to get this whole friggin' mess straightened out. Then I can introduce Autumn to her extended family, and we can all go on with our lives."

"Can that happen?"

"Yes, of course. We can all go back to the way we were."

I wanted to remind him that poor Hettie didn't have that luxury. But I said nothing more. Instead, I turned the volume back up on my radio just as the Eagles began singing "Hotel California."

When we reached my apartment, Buddy stuffed his few clothing items into his backpack and checked his phone for his boarding pass. "All set." He headed for the door, his backpack slung over one shoulder.

"Promise you'll call me." I hugged him.

"Of course."

"And promise you'll be careful." I felt him shake a little as he laughed. It hit me once again that he was actually enjoying the web of intrigue he had found himself in. Perhaps his retirement from active military duty had been too dull, and now something more interesting was actually going on in his life.

"Of course," he said again. "I'll be careful, and you should too. Love you, Val."

I released myself from his hug, then watched him retreat down the hall as I stood at my door. He turned around just once, and I blew him a kiss. Then I went back inside my apartment, grabbed my purse and sunglasses, and stood at the door silently counting to twenty. The idea to follow my brother had been percolating in my brain ever since he'd lied to me in the car about his departure time. And now I needed to put the plan in motion.

My only experience with tailing someone was with Kit by my side. But even though I felt the need to seek her company now, there wasn't time. Through the glass in the door that led to the parking area, I watched Buddy's car back out, and a few minutes later I backed my own car out to follow his.

Luckily for me, he wasn't driving fast. After an exhausting thirty-five minutes of following him, which included driving up and down the same quiet, tree-lined street more than once, I could see from the silhouette of his head that he seemed to be looking for an address. Finally, he pulled to a stop in front of a Victorian house that boasted a wraparound porch. I held my distance and parked four houses down from him to avoid driving past his car. Then, sitting as low in my seat as I could, I watched him leave his vehicle and run up the winding pathway to the front door and let himself in.

I had no plan in mind other than to sit and wait for something to happen, although I had no idea what that would be. I desperately wanted to call Kit, who by now would probably have disguised herself as a delivery or repair person and knocked on the door. But I lacked the sneakiness required, not to mention the courage.

My inability to come up with a plan was rendered moot fifteen minutes into my inertia. I saw some movement. The front door opened and Buddy came out, carefully closing the door behind him before taking a few steps to his left on the porch. Remaining in the shadow of the house, he removed his cell phone from his pocket and was soon engaged in a conversation. After a few minutes, he moved forward, out of the shadow and into the sun. He returned the phone to his pocket and clasped the porch rail, leaning slightly forward as he glanced up and down the street. He looked like a South American dictator about to deliver a speech to the peasants.

The front door opened again, and Buddy turned to have a conversation with someone standing there. I noticed him cock his head to one side, as if listening, and from his body movement, it looked like he was laughing. Was he visiting the elusive Frank again? I felt a jolt of astonishment when the other person moved enough that I could see it was a woman—Autumn. She held a beer bottle in her hand and, remaining in the darkened doorway, extended it toward Buddy. He moved toward her to take the beer and then stepped back inside the house, closing the door behind him.

CHAPTER SIXTEEN

Now what? I figured I'd gleaned all the information I was going to, having found out where Buddy went instead of, or before, going to the airport. I decided to leave.

Ever mindful that Culotta or his people might be following me following Buddy, I put my car in drive and headed slowly down the street, checking each parked car for occupants. They all appeared empty.

Still feeling shell-shocked, my next thought was that I needed to talk to Kit. I stopped the car long enough to text her that I would be home in fifteen minutes and really needed to see her. Her reply, which I ignored, was to ask if she should bring milk.

She arrived at my door ten minutes after me, wearing oversize sunglasses and a straw hat with a wide, floppy brim.

It felt like forever since I'd seen her, even though it had been only a couple of days. Relieved to be in her presence, I gave her an immediate hug. "It's good to see you," I said as she removed her sunglasses and hat. It was then that I noticed how tired she looked. "Are you okay?"

"I am so pissed off right now, I could scream." She roughly ran her fingers through her short auburn hair. I watched—in awe, as always—as it fell right back into place, thanks to her cut that is as expensive as it is stylish.

"Are you mad at Larry?" I asked.

"I'm mad at Larry's son," she answered.

"Okay." I sighed. "Let's hear it. What happened?"

I joined her on the couch, where she had taken a seat at one end. "So I called Sam and casually asked him why Leslie never answers the phone, or why she never seems to be home. It's been months since I've talked to that girl, and she used to always get on the phone so we could chat."

"What did Sam say?"

"He told me it was none of my damn business."

"Oh, Kit. I'm so sorry." I patted her knee. "Let me fix us something to eat." I sounded like my mother, like feeding someone could take care of any problem.

I made us tuna fish sandwiches and ignored my gourmet friend's look of disdain as I handed her a plate. She took a tiny nibble, then began chewing cautiously, as if she were afraid to swallow. But hey, she was lucky I had a can of tuna, or anything else in a can, not to mention the dollop of mayonnaise still left at the bottom of a year-old jar.

"What kind of fish is this?" she asked, taking her second mouse-sized nibble and peering under the top layer of bread to inspect it. "It is fish, right? It's not Spam, is it?"

"No, it's not Spam, but you are close. Tuna."

"Tuna!" Kit said in horror, as if I'd suggested she was eating possum. "Ya know, it needs something. Don't you have any celery?"

"No, sorry. Fresh out."

"What about garlic? Or surely you have some onion; everyone has—"

"Look, just don't eat it if it tastes bad."

"No, no, it's . . . not bad. Reminds me of the tuna sandwiches my mother used to make."

"Oh, come *on*. Your mother never made tuna sandwiches."

"Something close to it, but only when she was drunk."

We continued to sit on the couch in silence, me still eating, my pal not so much.

"Kit, I'm going to tell you something I shouldn't, and I can't believe I'm doing this."

She just looked at me with an utter lack of surprise. *Of course; you tell me everything,* her expression said.

"Well, I wouldn't be saying this, I wouldn't be breaking Buddy's confidence—" I stopped and sighed in deep regret and guilt. "But Buddy *lied* to me—"

"Wow, that's a shocker." She attempted another tentative bite of her sandwich, but changed her mind and returned it to the plate.

"Multiple times," I continued, undaunted by her tuna aversion. "Well, probably. I feel like I have to tell you so that you can help me figure things out. For *his* sake. I'm beginning to think he might be in real trouble." I shuddered. "Or maybe *causing* real trouble." I couldn't believe it, but I was honestly wondering if my brother was a victim or a culprit. How well did I know him anymore?

Whatever was going on, his deceptions made it okay— necessary, even—for me to confide in Kit. I dismissed Buddy's warning that it could put Autumn's life in jeopardy as I recalled that neither one of them had looked too concerned as they drank beer and laughed. (Yes, I had conjured up all sorts of scenarios of them relaxing together, most not very father-daughtery.)

"For crying out loud, Val, will you just spit it out already, before this sandwich takes a walk back to the can it came from."

"Okay, sorry; I will."

But before I could finish telling Kit everything, we had a visitor. Detective—or whatever—Dennis Culotta.

Well, it's about damn time, I thought. Poor Hettie had been dead for five days, and it seemed no one was even investigating her murder. Of course, for all I knew, they could have already arrested someone. But it felt like they should have kept me in their loop. *Or like Culotta was expecting Kit and me to solve the case*, I joked to myself and emitted a tiny giggle before I'd even motioned him in.

Culotta stepped into the apartment, but before he acknowledged either Kit or me, he glanced around. He even went as far as the few steps it took to peer into my bedroom. "Schroeder's not here." It was a statement, not a question.

"And good afternoon to you too," I said from my position at the front door.

Culotta looked at me quizzically. "I was supposed to meet him here; we have a few more questions. Kit James. How are you?"

I turned toward her, noting my empty plate and her tuna sandwich with only three or four nibbles taken, and watched her nod in response to his greeting. But he'd already moved on and was now staring at a print I had recently hung on the wall. "Didn't you used to have a picture of a red bus hanging here?"

"Yes." I was impressed he remembered, and a little thrilled. It had been a while.

"Where did it go?"

"Under my bed."

He moved a little closer to the framed picture of four Labradors sitting in the back of a 1950s pickup truck. Then he turned and smiled. "I like it."

"Me too. Can I get you some coffee?"

"Or a sandwich?" Kit piped up, giving me a teasing look, as if daring me to serve such fare to the handsome Culotta.

"Nothing, thanks. And we won't be long. Schroeder should be here any minute." He raised his wrist to look at his watch, and then, as if to prove what a damn good detective he was, we heard light tapping on the front door.

When I opened it, I was greeted by the enormous Detective Schroeder, who stepped inside right past me. He sounded a little out of breath as he yanked on the knot of his tie in a Rodney Dangerfield, I-don't-get-no-respect kind of way. "Sorry I'm late," he addressed only Culotta, as if Kit and I were not even in the room. "I need to speak to you, though . . . er . . . in private. Could we go outside? Something just came in. It's important."

"Excuse us a moment, ladies," Culotta said, following him out.

As soon as they closed the door behind them, I rushed to the bathroom to find my lipstick. I hadn't put on makeup before leaving Door County early that morning, and nothing I'd been through since then had improved my appearance. I was sure I looked as tired and bedraggled as I felt.

By the time I returned from the bathroom, the two men were reentering the living room. "Unfortunately, we have to leave," Culotta said, looking at his watch as soon as he saw me.

"Oh *no!*" Kit feigned dismay. "I was hoping we could catch up."

"This one's a piece of work. Who is she?" Detective Schroeder asked Culotta as he cocked a thumb toward Kit. Not waiting for a response, he turned his attention to me. "We're still investigating the murder of your neighbor Hettie Randall."

"Well, I really don't know anything I haven't already told you," I said. "She was a nice, elderly lady and a good neighbor."

"Also, she smelled like—"

I gave Kit a look, indicating she should shut up *now*. "Why? What's this about?" I gave my friend a second look for good measure.

"It's about the fact that she was murdered." Culotta spoke slowly, as if he were telling a three-year-old that rain is wet.

"Well, yes, of course," I said.

"And Autumn Grey," Culotta said abruptly, almost as if he were hoping to take me by surprise. "What do you know about Autumn Grey? Do you know where she is?"

Ah, crap. Telling Kit what I knew was one thing, but I just couldn't tell the police something that might possibly get my brother in trouble. No matter what. Or did I have to? Would I be breaking the law if I lied, even by omission? I racked my brain for information I'd gleaned on the *Law & Order* episodes I like to binge and Kit likes to make fun of me for. Was it just *federal* officers I couldn't lie to? And was Culotta now a federal officer? Well, if I didn't know, then I couldn't be doing anything illegal, regardless of what they say about ignorance of the law being no excuse. It was a good enough excuse for me. For now.

"I don't know anything about Autumn Grey," I said. "Except that she lived down the hall from me. Briefly. And she told me she came from Arizona." I ignored Kit's raised eyebrows, even though I somehow knew they had shot up. I had no doubt impressed her with my lie. She knows what a rule follower I am. Lying to authorities just isn't something I would do. Ordinarily. "And I certainly don't know where she is now."

"Hmm," Culotta said, as if he, too, realized I'd broken character.

"Why are you asking about Autumn?" Forced by nervous energy, I moved to gather Kit's and my lunch plates and was halfway to the kitchen when Schroeder spoke again.

"Look, Mrs. Pankowski, the way this goes is simple. We do the asking, you do the answering."

"And if you do anything to impede our investigation," Culotta added, "even by omission, you would be—"

"What would I be?" I glared at him as I returned from the kitchen. I knew it wasn't an idle threat he was about to make, and I didn't really want to hear it. So I kept talking. "Why wouldn't I tell you everything you want to know about Autumn Grey? She's nothing to me. Just a neighbor I barely met—"

"Are you on friendly terms with *any* of your neighbors in this building?" Schroeder interrupted me, an annoying habit of his. "It's a small building."

"Well—"

"Have you ever *met* any of your other neighbors? Apart from the victim and this Autumn woman?" he asked.

"Of course, but I wouldn't call us friends, exactly. There's a young man on the third floor whose mail I take in when he's out of the country." The name of the medical student had totally escaped me, and I prayed Schroeder wouldn't ask for it.

"Harish Chandra," he replied, saving me any more anguish over my poor memory. "Anyone else?"

"Not really. Well, yes, there's Andy, of course, on the first floor. And—" Before I could further explain how close Andy and I were, even if that would have been an exaggeration, it hit me that I didn't even know his last name.

"Yep, we've spoken to Andy."

"Did he mention the man he saw at Hettie's mailbox?"

"The one with the prison tat?"

"Yes, him. I was meaning to call you about that—"

"And yet you didn't. Fortunately, Andy did."

"I'm sorry. I really was planning to."

"Have you seen any other strangers in the building?"

"No. In fact, I didn't even see the tattoo guy; I just heard about him from—"

"Mrs. Pankowski—"

"It's *Ms.*, actually."

Detective Schroeder raised his eyes to the ceiling before continuing. "*Miiiz,*" he said, stretching it out. "We have to go now, but we might need you to come back to the station for further questioning. And like we just told you, if you do anything to impede our investigation, keep anything from us—"

Kit broke in, no doubt wanting to keep me from saying anything damaging. "My friend isn't feeling well right now. Are you, Val? Just look at how haggard her face is."

Since neither Culotta nor Schroeder seemed to disagree, her observation hung in the air.

"Right now she's going to rest." Kit stood and came over to me, using my elbow to turn me around and lead me toward my bedroom. "She probably doesn't have anything useful to offer you, anyway. Please show yourselves out," she said before closing my bedroom door behind us.

"We'll be in touch," we heard Schroeder's voice boom as we sat huddled on my bed. We weren't nearly as brave as Kit had sounded.

CHAPTER SEVENTEEN

I'd left Buddy three frantic messages before he finally returned my call. Kit and I were still lying side by side on my bed, where I had finished telling her about my surveillance.

"He just seems so thrilled to have Autumn in his life," I'd said. "What do you think?"

"Truthfully? You sound a little jealous."

I could feel myself tense up. "Why would you even think that? I have nothing against Autumn; it's Buddy I'm mad at. For not telling me, for not sharing. We used to share everything when we were kids."

"Why do you think Buddy had her move into your apartment building?"

"Well, I'm not sure it was even his decision—"

"No one moves into this building by choice—except you, of course."

"Hey, it's nice here."

"No, not really, not for a Realtor who could live anywhere. But let's not get into that right now. You apparently are making a statement, and I'm all right with that."

I didn't have a chance to question Kit's logic because now the phone lying between us began to ring. I swiped right on the screen, and then I yelled, "Buddy!"

"Val, I got your messages. Sorry. I was in the air—"

"Cut the bullshit, Buddy. I know you've been lying to me. And I know you don't fly out until tonight. You need to level with me right now. The cops are after Autumn and want to know what I know about her. I'm going to *have* to tell them—"

"You can't, Val. No. Let me talk to them. I'll talk to them. I'll go to the station now."

I started to cry, which was awkward since Kit and I were still lying side by side. I sat up abruptly. "Buddy, I don't want *you* to get in trouble. And you can't go *now*. You've been drinking!"

"I've had one beer—but how do you know I've been drinking?"

"You underestimated your little sister," Kit spoke into the phone she'd just grabbed from my hand, although I didn't know why she bothered. She'd obviously been able to hear every word Buddy had spoken, and he couldn't help but hear her. She was yelling. "Why are you lying to her?"

"It's for her own good, Katherine." Uh-oh. This time his use of her given name didn't sound so jovial. The Jean in him was coming out, which is never a good thing. "She doesn't need to be involved in all of this. And *you* definitely don't."

"All of what?" she asked.

Just as I'd also heard every word he'd spoken—a real flaw with cell phones, if you ask me—I heard his heavy sigh now. "Sit tight," he said. "Are you at Val's apartment?"

"Yes, we are." Kit's words were clipped. I wasn't sure I'd ever seen her so angry. Even at Larry. But then Larry had never put her BFF in a compromising position, and I felt certain that's what she figured Buddy had done.

"I'm going to get in touch with the police, and then I'll be right there."

"But your flight's at eight," I said loudly, just to make *sure* he could hear me. But it didn't matter, anyway.

"I'm not leaving town," I heard my brother say.

***

When I awoke the next morning, after having finally fallen asleep at some point in the night, I heard loud banging on my front door. The clock on my bedside table advised me it was five minutes after eight. I was sure it had to be Buddy because I still hadn't heard from him since our phone call. Kit had finally left, after she'd talked me out of my suggestion that we join my brother at the police station and I later talked her out of staying with me. "It will be better for Buddy and me to meet alone," I'd told her. *If he ever shows up*, I thought. "You heard him. You definitely shouldn't be involved in this."

Relieved now to think he'd finally arrived, I jumped out of bed and ran to the front door. And there was my visitor.

Not Buddy, but a good runner-up: Kit. I was glad she was back. She was wearing a simple turquoise shift dress that probably cost more than I paid in rent each month and sandals with crystals covering her toes. In her hands she held a cardboard tray containing two Starbucks cups and what looked like ham and cheese croissants.

"Morning, sunshine." She breezed past me to the kitchen. "I thought you probably didn't eat anything last night after I left, and I've tasted your coffee, sooo . . . bingo. I stopped at Starbucks. How did it go with Buddy?" she added, almost as an afterthought.

"He didn't show."

"I figured."

I wasn't surprised that she wasn't surprised. I took the latte she handed me. "You're amazing," I said, grateful for the warm cup of comfort. "Thank you so much."

"Oh, you don't even know how amazing. Hey, what time do you have to go to work?"

"I don't know when I'm going back. I told Billie I'm working from home and to cover for me with Tom."

"Good. Because I've had a brilliant idea." As she spoke, she took off her Gucci sunglasses and casually threw them on the couch. "Ya know, I noticed last night when I left here that they've removed the police tape from Hettie's door. So—"

"So what? I'm a little afraid to hear what your brilliant idea is."

"Okay, just listen. I remembered that you have a key to Hettie's apartment, right? Didn't I witness the famous key exchange ceremony on the front lawn of the White House, er, I mean in your parking lot? As I recall—"

"OMG." I plopped down onto the couch. She was right. "Yes; do you think I should turn it in to the landlord?"

"Hah." Kit sat down next to me. "The landlord, if you even have such a person, is probably in jail. No, dummy, we should go and have a look around in Hettie's place."

"Why?"

"Because . . . because we might find something. I don't know. Let's just do it."

"There are a million reasons why that is not a good idea."

Kit raised her hand in the air, palm out, indicating I should stop. "Get the key."

"Okay, first and foremost, it's not right to go into someone's home uninvited."

"Don't think we are going to get an invitation from Hettie. That ship has sailed."

"Second, what are we expecting to find? The police have been through her place and taken everything important."

"We are better than the police."

Even though I knew that wasn't, of course, true, I also knew Kit was probably just distracting herself from her son's woes, and I didn't want to quash her enthusiasm. "What are we looking for?"

"I don't know, but we might find something. Something that connects her to Autumn Showers—"

"I think the correct term is April showers. And let's just call her Autumn, okay?"

"April, Autumn, whatever."

"Why would you think there would be a connection between Hettie and Autumn?"

"Duh. Because Hettie was found dead in Autumn's apartment. Just go find that key, Valley Girl, and let's get to it."

Reluctantly, I agreed. Andy had told me that Hettie's sister would be arriving from Tuscaloosa really soon, along with two cousins, to clear out her belongings. I had made a mental note to be around when they were in the building and take them out to dinner or something. If we were going to do this, we had to *get to it*, as my friend had said, before they arrived.

Hettie's apartment was dark and tiny, and it hit me that so was mine. But I felt immediately comfortable in her space, and Kit's words about my choice of living accommodations flitted through my head.

When I was about six, we had a family dog, a lost mutt that Buddy had found and brought home. She lived with us for five years and always slept under Buddy's bed. My father explained it as her way of feeling safe. Was feeling so comfortable in my apartment the same thing? When I was married, I lived in an airy, four-bedroom house with high ceilings and large windows. Had I replaced that spaciousness with the comfort of the space under Buddy's bed?

"The smell of cheddar is overwhelming," Kit interrupted my thoughts.

"What?"

"Can you smell it?"

"Don't be absurd; it smells of . . . well, nothing. I can't smell anything."

Hettie's floor plan was the same as mine (no big surprise), and I headed to her bedroom, where Kit was standing in front of the small but perfectly adequate closet. "Hmm, she had some fairly nice things here." She flipped through several items on hangers. "Didn't she always wear a tracksuit?"

"Well, yes, whenever I saw her, but remember, I never saw a lot of her. It's not like we hung out together." I felt it was important to defend Hettie's choice of attire.

"She might have worn this to a cheese festival in Wisconsin." Kit held a hanger with a pretty summer dress up to her body.

"You are wicked." I took the hanger from her and put it back on the rack. "Look at this beautiful quilt." I had turned to admire the handmade bedspread covering Hettie's bed. It had a flock of geese flying north toward the headboard. "I wonder if she made it herself."

"Hmm," Kit said again, not looking and obviously unimpressed. She was holding up a pair of gray jogging pants, her hand in one of the pockets. "Here's something." It was a piece of paper, maybe two inches square, with some writing. Kit looked as if she'd found the Holy Grail.

"Okay, go ahead and impress me."

"I just might." Kit folded the pants carefully, respectfully. (I liked that.) "Look."

She handed me the piece of paper on which were scrawled two words: Rayjean Boxer. We both stared at it for a few seconds, hoping a light bulb would switch on in one of our heads.

"Rayjean Boxer. Is that a person's name? A relative, maybe?" Kit suggested.

"Possibly." I had never heard the name before. But I would hear it again soon enough.

CHAPTER EIGHTEEN

This is so nice of you, Val."

"Please. It's the least I can do." I reached across the table and gave Hettie's sister a pat on her hand. "I'm just so sorry. About everything."

Bree McGuire gave me a weak smile. She appeared ten or fifteen years younger than Hettie, and I found little resemblance to her sister. She was prettier and had a head full of blond curls and some nicely applied makeup. When she spoke, her voice was soft, with a charming Southern accent. I tried to remember if I had ever heard even a hint of a drawl from Hettie, but I guessed her accent had morphed into classic Midwestern many years before and any Alabama intonation had long since departed.

I had spent the day helping Bree and her cousins pack up Hettie's belongings and make arrangements for their disposal. There wasn't a lot—just two suitcases' worth for Bree to keep, and the rest was destined for Goodwill. When we were done, Kit had generously offered to drive the two cousins to the airport to catch flights back to Tuscaloosa, and I had escorted Bree to Ditka's Restaurant in Oak Brook for a late dinner. Kit would be joining us when she returned.

"I'm just so thankful Hettie had a good friend living close by." Bree took a sip of her water and glanced around the room. "This sure is a fun restaurant. Did you and Hettie come here often?"

I grabbed my own water and gulped it. Visiting restaurants together had never been on our radar. "No, we . . . er . . . never made it here."

"I thought because she was such a Bears fan, she would have loved this place."

I gulped some more. Not only had I just learned that Hettie loved football, in particular the hometown Chicago team, her sister had also made me privy to her volunteer work with the NSPCA and Chicago Veterans, her active involvement with delivering Meals on Wheels to shut-ins, and her commitment to line dancing. While it made me feel like a shut-in myself, I tried to appear as if my neighbor's good works were old news to me.

"She was an amazing lady," I managed to say before downing the rest of my water.

Bree nodded sadly. "I wish I had spent more time with her. She was twelve years older than me, you know, and moved out of our house when I was still quite young."

"Is that when she moved here?"

"Yes; she was married to Dan, a police officer. Unfortunately, he died about twenty years ago. Killed in a car accident. And Hettie just stayed on. She probably didn't talk to you about Dan. She was very private about him."

"How often did you two see each other?"

"Not a lot, not in person. But we were close. We FaceTimed at least once a week. What would we do without our cell phones, huh?"

I was impressed. Hettie had never struck me as a FaceTimer, but I sadly realized once more how little I knew my neighbor.

"I'm so glad she had you, Val."

"Well, we didn't see a lot of each other socially. We both were so busy." *Apparently, Hettie was a lot busier than I was.* "But she was a lovely lady and certainly a good neighbor," I added.

"I'm in the mood for a martini, a dirty one." Bree and I both looked up at Kit, who was pulling out a chair and seating herself between us.

"Thank you so much for taking the ladies to the airport," Bree said.

"No problem. When are you heading back to Chattanooga?"

"Tuscaloosa," I said. "Bree's leaving tomorrow afternoon."

"Oh, right. I always get those two cities mixed up. Where are you staying tonight, Bree?"

"I have a hotel in Downers Grove; it's close by."

"Pfft." Kit waved a hand in the air. "Forget that. You must stay with me. In fact, both you girls should spend the night at my place. My husband is out of town, so we'll have a girls' night in."

"If you're sure." Bree looked pleased. "I don't want to put you out—"

"Not putting me out at all; I'd love it. And just where is the waiter? Oh, here he is. Dirty martini, three olives and one onion. Please."

***

Later that evening, ensconced in Kit's living room, curled up on her two mammoth couches and comfortable in our pajamas, we drank the Baileys Irish Cream she served us.

"I'm not used to drinking so much." Bree took a sip and giggled, even though to my knowledge, it was the only alcoholic beverage she'd consumed all evening.

135

"Here's to Hettie." Kit raised her own glass in a toast. "How did it go with the police? I assume they grilled you." She looked expectantly at Bree.

"Not grilled, exactly, but they did have a lot of questions. Boy, that Detective Schroeder was tough, but the other one, the really good-looking one—"

"Culotta," I said, avoiding Kit's eyes.

"Yes, him. He was very nice. The mystery seems to be that my sister was found in that neighbor's apartment. They mainly wanted to know how well Hettie knew her and, I guess, what she was even doing there. I understand the neighbor has disappeared."

"Yes, so it seems," Kit said. "And *do* you have any idea? About why Hettie was in Autumn's apartment?"

"Good question; I don't know," Bree responded. "Maybe Autumn was having computer problems or something. My sister was somewhat of a techie, as you probably know."

"Right," I lied. *But no, I've only just come to terms with her line dancing.*

"And she was always very neighborly," Bree continued, "so maybe she was helping Autumn with her computer or tablet or whatever. She really loved that high-tech stuff. She even taught my son how to do a lot of things, although I'm probably better off not knowing exactly what he gets up to on the Internet."

Kit and I laughed a little and nodded in agreement, and then we all three sipped our drinks in silence.

***

The next day, we had a leisurely breakfast of French toast kebabs and Canadian bacon accompanied by fresh fruit. Kit was already dressed and serving Bree coffee when I entered the kitchen. I wasn't sure when she'd had time to prepare such a feast (I assumed it took a lot of time).

"This looks amazing, Kitty Kat," I said as I sat down.

"And it tastes as good as it looks." Bree slid a cube of French toast off the skewer onto her plate.

"Enjoy," Kit said, pleased, as she always is when serving something delicious to guests. "So, Bree, I was wondering," she continued, pouring herself some coffee and sitting down with us. "Do you know anything about a man, a bald man with a tattoo on his neck? A series of numbers, crudely done. He was seen in the apartment building after Hettie was—"

"No," Bree said. "Doesn't sound like anyone Hettie would know."

"Right," I agreed. "What about a Rayjean Boxer?"

"Ah, now her I do know. Wait, I take that back. I don't *know* her, personally. But I've heard of her. Hettie mentioned her, and the name was so unusual it stuck with me. She was the lady who drove that Autumn Grey to Downers Grove."

Once more I felt annoyed with my absent brother, who had described that woman as just someone he worked with who did him the favor of getting Autumn to Downers Grove safely. And he had never shared her name with me.

"How did Hettie know that?" Kit asked, as if sensing my annoyance. "Did Hettie meet her?"

"Not sure. Kit, this kebab is so clever. I would never think to cook French toast this way."

"It's nothing. I used to cook it like this for my son when he was little. Getting him to eat anything was a constant battle."

"Tell me about it. I've got a teenager at home, and if his food isn't delivered in a box and doesn't involve a tip, he won't eat it. Speaking of which, do you mind if I make a call? I should check in with the family."

"No, of course not," Kit said.

We watched Bree take her phone out of her purse and disappear into the living room. "She's so lovely, don't you think?" I said to Kit as soon as Bree was out of earshot.

"Yes. She's good people. I'm glad we got to know her."

"And thank you for being so nice to her."

Kit waved off my gratitude and sipped her coffee.

When Bree returned to the kitchen, she was holding her phone in the air. "Did you two meet this Rayjean Boxer?" She sat down and picked up her coffee cup.

"Just me. And briefly, to say the very least," I said. "We were never formally introduced."

Bree placed her phone next to her plate, then gave it a few taps. "I just googled her."

Wow, I thought. I was impressed—and more than a little chagrined. That was something Kit and I should have done—and no doubt would have, as soon as we finished with visitors and Goodwill deliveries. "What does Google have to say about her?" I asked.

Looking at her phone, Bree cleared her throat. "Seems Miz Rayjean Boxer was found dead yesterday in her home in Washington, DC . . . says here she was a private investigator, of all things." Bree was still reading from her phone. "And the police are ruling it a suspicious death."

CHAPTER NINETEEN

I was consumed with the need to get ahold of my brother. I had tried calling his phone while helping Bree and her cousins clear out Hettie's apartment. No answer. Over and over, no answer. Then, on the umpteenth time, when the last thing I expected was an answer, I'd heard my brother say, "H'lo, Val. This isn't a good time. I'll call you back." Click. Well, with a cell phone, it isn't exactly a click—rather, it's a silence that makes you wonder if anyone is still on the line or not.

When I realized he wasn't, I felt a fury that was mitigated only by the fact that at least I knew he was alive. I debated whether to call Culotta, growing more certain all the time that he knew more about my brother than he was admitting. But if he was *after* Buddy for something, as seemed more likely all the time, I didn't want to put Buddy in jeopardy. Yes, I was feeling more certain Buddy might soon be arrested.

And all because of Autumn, no doubt. I cursed the fact that she'd ever found Buddy, ever even looked for him.

Then, just as we had been about to leave Hettie's apartment for the last time, with the last load, my phone had rung. Buddy. "Val, so sorry. I did have to leave town last night, after all."

"Are you sure Autumn is your daughter?" I asked, knowing I sounded as mean as I felt. I didn't want her to be his daughter. I didn't want her to be his anything. I was sorry she'd entered his life. I was so worried about his welfare, about what she might have driven him to do. Was *that* why Culotta had been following him?

"Yes, I'm sure she's my daughter, Valerie. I already told you that."

"Are you saying you're back in DC now? You *didn't* go to the police last night? You promised you would come clean with them about Autumn because they are looking for her."

"Yes, I will. But Elaine needed me, so I decided to stick with the original plan. I'm coming back to Downers Grove, so don't worry."

I wasn't sure I even wanted him to come back, nor who he was coming back for. Me, or Autumn? If it was only to speak to the police, he could surely do that from DC.

I gritted my teeth, fury suddenly overshadowing my worry. "Let me know your flight details. I'll pick you up." It wasn't an offer. It was an order. And I right then promised myself that Buddy *would* come clean with me—or else. Or else I would go to the authorities, like he apparently had not. Let them figure out what the hell was going on. And by authorities, of course, I meant Culotta. He would at least know the *proper* authorities for me to contact. And then, after a major flood of sisterly guilt, I remembered this was Buddy I was planning to report, and I vowed that I would go with him.

But now, as I stared in shock at Bree holding her phone and looking shocked herself at the news of Rayjean Boxer's suspicious death, I thought, *Maybe Buddy killed her.* He *was* in the vicinity, after all. Was that just a coincidence?

***

Buddy didn't call me with his flight information; instead, he texted it. First, he texted that he'd get a rental car, but I shot back with the same order I'd already given him. *I'll pick you up.* We *were* going to talk. And so he sent me the details. I had to suppress a grin as I thought he might actually be a little afraid of me right now. Well, there was a first time for everything, and I rather liked the idea of seeming formidable to my big brother. I grabbed my purse and phone and headed down to my car, feeling a little more in control than I had in a long time.

As I walked toward the dumpster, an old cream-colored Volkswagen slowly headed my way and then stopped. The driver rolled down his window. It was the medical school student from the third floor.

"Hi," I said, stopping and leaning toward his handsome face. Once again, I was drawing a blank on his name, but luckily, I saw an identification badge pinned to the top pocket of his white coat. "How are you . . . Chandra?" I wasn't sure if I was addressing him by his first or last name.

He laughed. "Chandra is my last name, Harish is the first. But please, call me Harry. All my friends here do." He was kind enough not to mention that since I'd once collected three weeks' worth of his mail when he'd returned to his native India for a visit, I surely should have figured his name out.

"Harry it is." I laughed a little with him.

"Just don't tell my mother. She dislikes American abbreviations of Indian names."

"Promise," I agreed.

"So . . . I was just wondering if you have any news about our neighbor. Have the police told you anything?"

"Not a word. Nothing."

"Oh dear." His smile disappeared, along with his perfect white teeth. "What a terrible thing to have happened."

"Yes."

I watched him put his car in gear and slowly ease his foot off the brake. "Please, if you hear anything, I'd love to know. You take care, Valerie. And call me if you need anything."

"I will, Harry. You take care too."

His smile returned. "And remember, not a word to my mother." He rolled up the window and drove off. I waved at the back of his car and let myself into my own.

When I was parked in the cell phone lot at the airport, I received the next text from Buddy. I immediately but slowly made my way to the pick-up area, glad that it was summertime and still light out. The only thing worse than navigating O'Hare is doing it in the dark. I was still searching the crowd for him as I slowed to a stop, when suddenly he was hopping into my car.

"Thanks for picking me up, sis." There was an almost questioning lilt at the end of his sentence, as if he were asking me if I was mad at him. I was furious, and scared. "I'm going to stay at a hotel on Finley Road. It's—"

"Of course you are."

"Don't be mad, Val. I just think it's better this way. I do have a lot of business to take care of here."

"Starting with that visit to the police you were going to make?"

He sighed but did not answer me. I'd never seen him so preoccupied. Nor had I ever loved him more. I was reminded of the fine line that could separate love and pity and realized it could also appear between love and worry.

My mind filled with memories of my life with Buddy. In fact, I knew, I'd have no life without him. I remembered the water park we'd visited when our parents had taken us to Omaha. I couldn't remember the name, but I'd never forget going down the slide, not realizing it would deposit me in deep water. I was flailing for my six-year-old life when suddenly there was Buddy, scooping me up and getting me to the safety of the shallow water. And there was the time I was being harassed by a boy I'd broken up with, and only a threat from my big brother put a stop to Jim Connor following and phoning me.

And of course it was Buddy as much as Kit who got me through my divorce with David. Even long-distance, Buddy was my rock. He had answered every phone call I placed to him, whether it was three in the afternoon or three in the morning. No, there was no thin line separating my love for Buddy from any other feeling or emotion. I simply loved and adored him.

" . . . penny for your thoughts?" I heard him ask as I merged onto I-88 toward Downers Grove.

"Huh? Oh, Buddy. I don't know *what* to think."

***

The idea of my brother staying in a hotel instead of at my place depressed me. But he'd convinced me it was best for him. He didn't know how long he'd be in Downers Grove "cleaning up this mess," as he put it. The couch wasn't a good place for him to be sleeping, and he didn't need to "muck up" my life any more than he already had, he assured me.

"So where is your famous Autumn? Right now, I mean. Is she still in Chicago?"

"Val," he replied slowly, as we remained seated in my car in front of his hotel, "I'm this close to being able to tell you everything." To indicate just how close, he held his thumb and index finger only about an inch apart.

I watched him reach for the door handle and grabbed his arm to stop him. I wasn't letting him go just yet. I put the car in gear and drove to the closest parking space. Then I reached on the floor of the back seat for my purse before following him into the hotel.

While he checked in, I found a round table with two chairs in the far corner of the lobby and sat down, looking as determined as I could. The dim lighting coupled with the dark clouds outside did nothing to illuminate our space. But at least there was no one around to overhear us.

Buddy came toward me, putting his credit card back in his wallet, and took the chair across from me.

"Speak" was all I said.

"Autumn doesn't need long-term protection," he explained. "But she hasn't been called to testify yet. She and I both just feel better keeping her under wraps until this trial thing is over."

"Trial?"

"Yes; her friend's father."

"So she's giving testimony? Is that why there's all this moving around?"

"Yes and yes. There are some really bad people looking for her; they'll do anything to stop her testimony. I'm just trying to keep her safe."

I thought of seeing Culotta with Autumn outside of Steak 'n Shake ten days ago and wondered if I should tell Buddy that although *his* so-called police didn't know where Autumn currently was, Dennis Culotta, who was apparently still in some sort of law enforcement, might. But I simply nodded, as if I understood. I almost wanted him to stop talking. I was going to need some time to digest just this much. So I wasn't sure why I then said, "And Rayjean Boxer?"

He just stared at me. Now I cursed the poor lighting of the hotel. And I cursed myself for asking about her when I couldn't read his expression and body language clearly. So all I had to go on was his spoken response.

"What about her?" he asked.

CHAPTER TWENTY

Well, you haven't even mentioned this Rayjean Boxer," I said.

"What about her?" Buddy repeated.

"You tell me." I was growing incensed and made sure my tone of voice conveyed that.

"I thought I had. Rayjean Boxer was a friend of mine. Acquaintance, really. She retired from the Navy, but she worked for me for a while—"

"She's dead. You do know she's dead, right? You haven't even commented on that and you say she was a friend, and you don't even seem slightly upset, and—"

Before I could finish my sentence, he rose and took a walk across the hotel lobby area, with his back to me. Finally, he returned to his seat. "I'm upset, okay?"

I slumped a little in my chair, alarmed at his raised voice. I could see that he had alarmed others too. Even though we were somewhat isolated in our corner of the lobby, I saw more than one head turn. But I didn't see any lingering stares and so felt safe in pushing him further. "Can we assume Rayjean was murdered because she knew Autumn?"

"I don't know. The newspaper said it was suspicious. Why do you say *murder*?"

Was he serious? Or was he just dense? I sighed deeply and moved my chair closer to his, noting that someone had turned on some lights and the lobby had brightened just a bit. Maybe because of his outburst. "First, Hettie is murdered—"

"Your neighbor. Yes?"

I nodded. "We do know that Rayjean's name was written on a piece of paper in her pocket."

"Did the police tell you that?"

"No. Kit . . . er . . . I found it. We were in Hettie's place cleaning out stuff."

He hung his head, shaking it slowly. "It is scary about Rayjean, but—"

"No, Buddy, *Halloween III* is scary, but having a colleague who did you a big favor and then turns up dead is terrifying."

"Do the police know—"

"I don't know what the hell the police know. But Detective Schroeder is hot on the trail of Autumn, I do know that."

"And Culotta?"

"Same."

He took his cell phone out of his pocket, apparently to check the time more than to check for messages. "I guess I better get over to the police station."

"Okay. Let's go."

"No, Val. Not you. Can I take your car? I'll drop you off at home first and bring your car back in the morning. But I really don't want you there."

I was a little hurt, but also glad. Buddy and I were raised to believe the police were always the good guys and you should always tell them the truth. So of course I felt relieved that now he was going to do the right thing and come clean. I didn't have to be there; I just had to know he was going.

Before he dropped me off outside my building, I asked him one more time about Autumn's whereabouts. "What will you say if the police ask where she is?"

"The truth." He didn't look at me. "I don't know."

***

When my cell phone blurted out its familiar theme song, I closed my computer and accepted the call. "Bree?"

"Hi, Val."

"You got home safely, I hope."

"Yeah, I'm home."

She sounded a little sad, and I could hear soft music in the background. Classical, maybe Vivaldi, which for some reason surprised me. "Everything okay?"

"Yes, everything's okay. But I guess it's just now hitting me. This is when I'd normally be FaceTiming with Hettie, when it's quiet around here. Hal Jr.—he's my son—has a fencing lesson, and Hal, my husband, is playing bridge."

"Sounds like you got a couple of interesting guys, Bree."

"Yeah. I think I'll keep 'em. Anyhow, I just called to thank you again for your hospitality. You and Kit were so kind."

"It was a pleasure to get to know you. I'm just sorry for the circumstances." *Yikes. I sounded like Dr. Phil greeting a bereaved guest on his show.* "How are you doing, Bree?" I couldn't imagine losing *my* sibling.

"I still don't believe it, but going through her things somehow helps. I was just unpacking a few knickknacks and some of her books. Classics, really old. Except the one, *Discovering the Cyrillic Alphabet*—brand spanking new. In fact, the receipt was inside the cover, and it shows she'd just bought it the day before she was . . . before she died."

"Cyril—"

I heard her soft laugh. "Cyrillic. It's the alphabet they use in some Eastern European countries. Hal Jr. is planning a trip to Estonia next year, and I do believe they use it there."

"Estonia?" I asked, feeling stupid.

"Right. I had to look it up on a map. It borders Russia," she said kindly, probably to make me feel less stupid. "Y'all know how much Hettie loved all things Russian, especially the Bolshoi Ballet."

"So I heard," I said, not having heard that at all.

"Right. She went to Moscow twice to see them. And bless her heart, she went alone; I could never afford to go with her. She always said that not speaking Russian was no problem. I would have thought she'd have told me if she was suddenly planning to learn a whole new language, especially one that has its own alphabet with thirty-three letters. Anyhow, I think Hal Jr. will like to have this book that belonged to his aunt."

"Yeah. That does sound . . . difficult. The thirty-three letters, I mean." Now I felt even more stupid. But it did sort of fit that if your teenage son enjoyed fencing, then an extra seven letters in an alphabet would be no problem for him.

"I won't keep you, Val. I'm sure you've got a lot to do. But let's stay in touch. And thank you again. Tell Kit thanks too."

As soon as Bree and I said good-bye, I called Kit. "Do you know what the Cyrillic alphabet is?"

"Of course, everyone knows—"

"If you are about to say everyone knows that, I will have to kill you."

"Okay. Everyone but *you* knows that. It's what they use in Russia and other strange places."

"Okay, so I just learned that Hettie was a bit of a Russian wannabe; she'd been there twice."

"For the cheese? Ya know, I always wanted to take a cooking class in St. Petersburg; they have a marvelous—"

"For the Bolshoi Ballet, you idiot."

"Next you'll be telling me she spoke fluent Russian."

"Apparently not. She bought a Cyrillic language book the day before she was killed."

"It has thirty-three letters, ya know."

"Shut up."

***

I didn't feel my normal sleepiness as bedtime approached, so I made a big deal out of removing my makeup, going as far as putting on the pink face mask I found in the *Marie Claire* magazine I'd stolen from my dentist's office. The directions instructed me to leave it on my face for thirty minutes, avoiding the eye area, and promised it would leave me with soft and luminous skin after it had dried and been washed off thoroughly with warm water. The bubblegum-pink mixture turned to avocado green within a few seconds of application, but the instructions insisted this was normal. Maybe on the planet Zonko, but I wasn't sure about Downers Grove.

I could feel it harden as I changed into my Cubs T-shirt. I had pulled my fairly short blond hair into a teensy bun, about the size of an acorn, and a few too-short strands of hair escaped and stuck out the sides of my head. Overall, I resembled your average lunatic.

So naturally, this was the time Culotta decided to come calling. He'd certainly seen me at my worst, many times, but I don't think he'd ever seen me looking my most unhinged. If I'd been wearing a Valentino gown and Kim Kardashian had done my makeup, he would have been on the other side of the world doing heaven knows what.

After looking through my peephole and seeing Culotta standing with his hands in his pockets and looking down at his shoes, I raced to the bathroom sink and began splashing my face with water and trying to rub the mask off. I heard him knock a second time and peeked in the mirror. The mask hadn't budged. I picked up a washcloth in hopes of speeding up the process. But the cloth remained too white—and my face too avocado green—to have been worth the effort. Then I thought, *What the hell do I care? It's not like our relationship is going anywhere.* I returned to the front door and opened it.

He looked up from his shoes and smiled, not saying a word about my avocado face. "Got a few minutes?" He stepped inside.

I gave him a weak smile, the best I could manage with a green vegetable fermenting on my face. "Is affocado a fruit or a veshable?" I asked, sounding and looking like a bad ventriloquist.

"I guess that depends on whether you're eating it or wearing it."

"Funny," I replied, only it came out sounding like *bunny.*

"Is your brother here?" He did his usual quick glance around the apartment.

"No. He's gone to see the pleesh."

"Pleesh?"

"Police," I enunciated, feeling cracks form on either side of my face. "Damn you, Culotta, you've ruined a very expensive face mask." Leaving him in the living room, I rushed to my bathroom, where I eventually managed to scrape the green off.

When I returned, he was sitting on the couch. "You hardly need a face mask," he said.

"Well, we'll never know now, will we?" I was annoyed.

"I already know. You have beautiful skin. You don't need any fruit—or vegetable."

Although it was far from the truth, it was enough to make me release my poor excuse for a bun and run my fingers through my hair, returning it to as close to normal as I could manage without the benefit of a mirror. "So why are you here?" I asked, sitting next to him.

"Why am I ever here? To see you."

I felt like my heart was beating a little too hard, and was afraid he would hear it. "So, is this like a date? If so, your dating etiquette sucks. You're supposed to call a girl first and see if she is available."

"Okay, are you available?"

"Do I look available? Cut to the chase, Culotta. What do you want?" As I said it, it occurred to me that it was probably the first time I had ever used the actual words *cut to the chase*.

"I want . . . your brother, and I want Autumn Grey. Either one will do."

"So, not me?"

"You, I'll get to later, when all this bullshit is over."

Was that supposed to make me happy? Was I supposed to be elated even though I was third on the list after my brain-dead brother and some psycho runaway who was apparently related to me?

Strangely, I was.

CHAPTER TWENTY-ONE

Maybe it was my elation at the thought that Dennis Culotta might become something more permanent in my life than a periodic flirtation that led me to confide in him. Or maybe it was my almost-crippling fear that my brother was in over his head—in *what* I didn't know, but I felt certain it wasn't good—that made me share everything with Culotta.

Now, as I lay in bed reliving the rest of my conversation with him, my concern over it was interrupted by a call from my best friend.

"Hey, Kit," I answered, not really wanting to. I wanted to continue my mental sorting of the accumulating—and increasingly ominous—facts. But then I was relieved that she called. Nothing helps me sort better—or make better decisions—than running things by my pal. "I'm glad you called. I have to tell you what I did. And you have to tell me it was the right thing."

"Only if it *was* the right thing," she assured me. And I knew that was the truth. Kit loves me to pieces. No doubt about it. But she is a straight shooter. And I love *her* for that, and so much more. "But first I have to tell you about my call with Sam. Yours can wait, right?"

I had no choice but to agree with my friend. I could tell by the stress in her voice that she would be useless to me until she unloaded. And what were a few more minutes to my dilemma?

Well, the few minutes turned into almost an hour, and I was beginning to wonder how Kit could go on—and on and on—without saying anything new. But I realized how often I had assaulted her ears with the same old shit during my marriage and divorce from David while she listened patiently.

Her report went something like this: Leslie seemed to have emotionally checked out of the marriage. According to Kit, she was a rotten wife, unwilling to compromise in any way.

As Kit droned on about Leslie's selfishness, I had to remind myself that she was talking about her daughter-in-law and *not* her son. To me, her description sounded more like my memories of Sam. Leslie had seemed very likeable to me, a quiet girl who was willing to let her husband bask in the limelight. But that had given me an uneasy feeling. I feared Sam would grow tired of her and soon want a shiny new toy to play with.

I flashed back to their wedding. A breathtakingly beautiful bride and a handsome groom. I had attended without a plus-one by my side and found myself sipping too much champagne while watching the groom dance just a little too closely with several young female guests. At one point, as he and Emily had swayed to a slow song, I watched his hand run up and down her bare back until she extricated herself from his arms and moved off the dance floor.

"Maybe they should leave Texas and start again somewhere else," Kit was saying now. "It can't be easy for

Sam, living in his in-laws' pockets. It has to be tough for him."

I doubted it would be tough for Sam. Everything came too easily for that boy. He probably had wife number two in his sights already. Relating more to Leslie than Sam, I wished *I'd* had the gumption and brains to get out of my marriage when it was still in its infancy, instead of throwing away decades feeling lonely and unhappy.

" . . . even hearing me, Val?"

"Yes, of course I am. You just cut out on me for a second."

"Quit your daydreaming and listen up. Here's the crux of the problem."

OMG, I thought. *It's been more than forty minutes, and we still haven't gotten to the crux?*

"Leslie is planning to file for divorce." Kit sounded heartsick.

"Divorce? Are you sure?"

"Of course I'm sure. You think I made it up? I'm certain she's seeing someone."

"Do you know that for a fact?"

"Sam doesn't want me to go down there," she continued, not answering my question.

Well, of course not, I almost said, but stopped myself in time. "You don't have to be there, Kit. *Sam* doesn't even have to be there if he isn't contesting it. I mean, he'll be thirty in—"

"I know how old my son is, Val. But he's a lamb, really. And I need to be sure he's not led to the slaughter by that despicable family."

I put my hand over my mouth to stop myself from laughing. A lamb was the last animal Sam could be likened to, and if there was any slaughtering to be done, I suspected Sam was organizing it and selling tickets.

But I knew my job wasn't to argue with Kit. It was to listen to her vent. Just as she had done for me through the years. And so I proceeded to sprinkle a sympathetic *uh-huh* here and there as I waited for her to wear herself out. But it was growing harder and harder to fight off my impatience to share *my* worries with *her*. And at last I broke.

"Kit, I really have to tell you what I told Culotta."

"Culotta? Oh no."

"Yes. And thanks for the vote of confidence. But I just felt so scared. For Buddy. And Dennis was here."

"*Dennis?*" Her tone was teasing.

"This isn't the time, Kit."

"Okay, so what did you tell him?"

"Pretty much everything. Everything I could remember or think of. Which I think was everything. I mean, he's really a good detective. He knew all the questions to ask to make sure I didn't leave anything out."

"How would you know? I mean, if you didn't remember something, then you wouldn't remember—"

"Kit!"

"I'm just sayin'—oh, forget it. So what did he say? Did he have any advice or any answers?"

"That's the thing, Kitty Kat. I'm pretty sure he knows something he's not telling me."

"Like what?"

"Well, I don't know. If I knew, then—"

"Yeah, yeah. I get it. So. Can he be of any help?" Her tone of voice said she was certain he could not. Or would not.

But she was wrong.

"Yes, Kit, he's about to be a very big help." I stopped to let her put *that* in her pipe and smoke it.

"Go on."

I told Kit everything about my visit with Culotta earlier that evening. Everything except the elation part. And the part where I'd broken down crying as I'd sat on the couch with him. And how he'd pulled me into his arms and let me cry briefly before urging me to tell him why I was crying. I wasn't ready to share that much with her just yet; my hopes had been dashed too often in the past. I felt too vulnerable.

But I did tell her the gist of what I felt I'd accomplished. Which was a lot.

When I had revealed to Culotta that our elusive Autumn was actually my brother's daughter, he had started to laugh. Like I'd just told him a really funny joke. I knew it was my agony over the situation that made him get himself under quick control. "Uh, I don't think so, Val." He let go of my hand that he'd had in his and sat up straight, as if realizing it was time for him to get down to business.

"No, I'm serious, Dennis. She's Buddy's daughter that he didn't know he had, from some long-ago—"

"Val, you don't have proof of this. You can't."

"Buddy had a DNA test to prove it."

"No, he didn't."

"Yes, he did."

"Trust me, he didn't."

The assurance he displayed was making me angry, and I was beginning to regret I'd shared anything with him. But a tiny part of me, somewhere deep inside, hoped he was right. "Well, why don't *you*, then?" I asked him.

"Why would I get a DNA test? I know she's not my daughter, either." He grinned, but his gallows humor reminded me that if Culotta was right, then my brother had lied to me about Autumn, again. I had to shake my head, like a wet dog, to get the thought out of my mind.

"You know what I mean. Surely you have some DNA from her apartment you could test."

"Test against what?"

"Well, against Buddy's, of course. Or even mine, as a close relative. Just to confirm what I already know is true."

"It should be Buddy's. Are you offering to get me a sample?"

Sure, I can do your job for you, I thought. But instead, I said, "Well, I can."

"You do that. But don't be disappointed when you find out she is not his daughter." He sounded genuinely concerned for me as he rose to leave, but I didn't appreciate it. If I were totally honest with myself, I really didn't want Autumn to be my niece, but I also didn't want proof that my brother had been duped.

It was a no-win situation, and I wished I'd never heard of Autumn. "I'll call you tomorrow. And I'll deliver my brother's DNA," I said with confidence.

"Great," he replied. "And meanwhile, I'll go to the big building where we keep DNA and look in the file under T, for toothbrushes."

"You're kidding, right?"

"Yes, of course I am. But I'll check with the lab again. Who knows, maybe Autumn did forget to grab her toothbrush before she fled." He was chuckling as he went out the door.

When Kit and I got off the phone later that night, I left a message for my brother to return my car early the next morning. And to bring me an Egg McMuffin. "And come early," I repeated. "It's urgent."

And it was.

CHAPTER TWENTY-TWO

H ere, knock yourself out."

"You used to love Egg McMuffins," I said when I saw the look of disdain on Buddy's face as he handed me a paper sack. Apparently, my choice of breakfast food was not to his liking. "Remember when Dad used to take us to McDonald's on Saturday mornings so Mom could get rid of us while she was vacuuming?"

"I was ten."

"Oh, so now you're all grown up and too sophisticated for the McMuffin?"

"Frankly, yes."

I laughed, and it sounded fake, even to me. But I could see Buddy was not happy, and I wanted him in a good mood. "Go sit on the couch, and I'll get us some coffee. Did you get hash browns?" I asked.

"No, sorry, they weren't ready."

"Ah, right, because who serves breakfast potatoes at eight fifteen in the morning? Did you get some orange juice, at least?" I was really disappointed. McDonald's hash browns are one of my favorites.

"Again, sorry. I guess I assumed you would have orange juice already."

"Nope. But hey, I've got some orange Gatorade. I think." Why did I think that? I'd never bought Gatorade in my life. I wasn't even sure what it was.

He was sitting on the couch, wearing the same clothes he had worn the day before, and he looked tired. But I probably did, too, which I blamed on Culotta for interrupting my face mask partway through the skin-illuminating process. Buddy picked up his sandwich, took a quick look under the top muffin, and then tossed it back down on the table.

"So, how did it go at the police station?" I asked from my kitchen, where I was pouring us both coffee.

"I didn't go."

I wasn't surprised, but I did manage to spill some coffee. "But you said that was where you—"

"I didn't go, Val. And I think you already knew that." He said it with some force this time, and I spilled a little more coffee as I put his cup before him on the table.

"Well, then where in the heck were you last night?" I sat down on the other end of the couch.

"Why don't you ask your pal Culotta?"

"Culotta? Why would I—"

"I had stuff to take care of. Can we please just leave it at that?"

"Well—"

"When I found out that Ray had been killed . . ." He spoke quietly and without any emotion, as if he were telling me his McMuffin was cold. And then I realized he wasn't so much in a *bad* mood as a *sad* one. He picked up his coffee cup and took a long swig.

"Ray?" I said softly. "You mean Rayjean?"

"No, Ray Charles. Yes, of course Rayjean. Rayjean Boxer. A good woman I put in danger for no damn good reason."

"Do the police know who did it?" I asked after a few seconds.

He gave me an incredulous look. "The police? Are you fucking kidding me? It's beyond the police, Val."

"Okaaay then, but do *you* know? You sound like you do."

"Yes, I know. Of course I know, and so does your pal Culotta."

"Okay, then tell *me*. Who was it?"

"If only I could. But right now, my prime concern is Autumn's safety. And yours. If I told you anything more than I have, you would be too vulnerable to . . . some very bad people."

"Is Autumn really your daughter?"

He stood up, looking angry, something I had rarely seen. "Yes, she's my damn daughter. Why is it so hard for you to believe me?"

"I'm sorry. I do believe you. Please sit; eat your sandwich."

He reached down for his McMuffin, took a huge bite, and ran the napkin that had come with it over his mouth. Then he scrunched up the napkin and threw it on the coffee table. "Sorry, Val. I am not in the mood to be questioned by you. I have to take care of a few things. I'll call you later."

"Okay, that would be good. Oh, and my car—"

"Would it be okay if I kept it a little longer? I haven't had time to arrange a rental, but—"

"Oh, no worries. I just—"

But he was gone before I could finish my sentence. As soon as the front door closed, I eyed the napkin lying on the table next to the partly eaten sandwich. Surely that would have enough of my brother on it to satisfy Culotta. I just hoped he was as good at collecting evidence as I was.

***

"What's this?" Culotta took the box I handed him.

"It's a cigar box. Open it." I had helped myself to the wooden box from my boss's desk years before because I liked the name *Romeo y Julieta*, plus it was handy for storing paper clips and other junk.

Culotta sighed deeply, as if I had just handed him a child's toy. "Okay." He took a seat on the couch. "But you know I don't smoke cigars."

I nodded, indicating I knew that; but in reality, he could have been smoking opium all night for all I really knew about him. I had a sudden, brief hesitation about my decision to trust him, but it passed before I could change my mind. I watched him take a blue latex glove out of his pocket and deftly shove his right hand into it. Then he opened the box carefully and used the tip of his latexed finger to move the Egg McMuffin around a little. "Did you go to cooking school or something?"

I chose to ignore his remark. "Buddy was here this morning and took a bite. So there must be some DNA on it, right? And there's more." I rose and went to the kitchen to retrieve two gallon-size baggies. The napkin Buddy had used to wipe his mouth was in the first one I handed him, and the coffee cup he had taken a sip from was in the other. "These should be enough, don't you think?"

Very gently, Culotta placed the items on the coffee table. He leaned forward in a familiar pose, his elbows on his knees, his hands clasped together, and he seemed to be debating something. When he looked up at me, his face was as earnest as I'd ever seen it. "Val, sit down." He patted the seat next to him. "Yes, these will be enough, more than enough, but if, and it's a big if, I get something from this Autumn, I promise you it will not be a match."

"Because you know who Autumn really is, right?"

"Not exactly. If I had an Egg McMuffin that she'd wrapped her lips around, then I could be positive. But I don't. Her place was cleaned out thoroughly, and I don't have any other way to get something on her."

"Geez, you make her sound like she's an assassin or something." He didn't respond, so I continued. "Right! An assassin who gets her nails done at Hannah's. I don't think so. What about the car she rode to Chicago in, with Rayjean? You do know about Rayjean Boxer, right?"

He nodded in response.

"So, wouldn't that reveal—"

"That car is long gone." His tone had a sinister ring to it, and I was once again filled with desperation to prove that Buddy was not lying to me. "Val, are you aware of what your brother does?"

"What do you mean, *what he does*? He's a retired Navy officer. He does what most retirees do—plays golf, cooks out, goes to baseball games . . . wears dad pants, and washes his car on Sundays."

I was trying to think just what it was my brother did with his time. His girls were out of the house, and to my knowledge, he *didn't* play golf *or* follow a sports team. He had told me he taught a class at the Naval Academy; but when I questioned him, he *had* been uncharacteristically vague, I realized now.

Culotta laughed, but it had no humor. "He does a lot more than that."

"What are you talking about? Does he have a job of some kind?"

"That's for him to tell you. Not me."

I started to cry, which was ridiculous; but I couldn't stop. Once again, Culotta put his arms around me, but this time I shrugged him off. "He's not a bad guy, Dennis," I managed to say between sniffles.

"No. I never said he was." He reached for the cigar box and the baggies and stood up. "Let me see what the lab can come up with. I'll get back to you as soon as I know something."

I followed him to the door, wiping my wet cheeks with the palms of my hands. "If you can't tell me what Buddy does, can you at least tell me what *you* do?"

He turned and walked back to the couch. "Okay. I work for a special branch of—"

"Are you gonna say the FBI?"

"The FBI. Yes. Kinda."

"Kinda? So, what? If you tell me, you'll have to kill me?"

"Probably *you'd* have to kill *me*." He grinned.

"And I suppose now you're going to tell me that Buddy works for the KGB."

He laughed. "No. They broke up in 1991. Plus, your brother is a good American. He and I are on the same side."

"*Whew!* That's so good to know. Although I'll miss spending my summers visiting him in Moscow." I was *pretending* to feign relief with my dramatics, but the truth was, I *did* feel great relief.

"It's not a joke, Val. Do me a favor. Just ask him; not that he can tell you."

He returned to the front door and was gone before I could respond. I went into my kitchen, opened the refrigerator, and amazingly found an unopened bottle of orange juice way at the back. Unfortunately, the use-by date was two days ago.

***

Without my car, I was, of course, stuck at home. It would have been a good time to catch up on some housework, or more importantly, some paperwork for the office. I debated calling Kit, but I preferred to wait until Culotta got back to me with some news. So instead, I poured myself a glass of the outdated orange juice and found a movie to watch.

I was about halfway through whatever it was I was watching—something silly about a girl in Scotland on the eve of her wedding, but obviously to the wrong guy—when I heard a loud tapping on my door. It was Kit. She held a bottle of wine and was waving it back and forth in front of me as if she were trying to hypnotize me.

"Santa Margherita," she said proudly, as if I had any idea what that meant. "Your favorite pinot."

"It is? I didn't know I had a favorite."

"Val, your lack of knowledge about good wine is troubling. You'd never make it as a sommelier." She entered the apartment and went straight to the kitchen.

"Would I even want to?" I was only vaguely aware of what a sommelier does.

"I'm guessing Buddy still has your car, right?" she said, searching for two wineglasses and finding only one.

"Yes. And here's my other wineglass." I retrieved it from the coffee table and tossed out the remains of my orange juice.

"So, you gave Culotta the stuff you had?" She turned on the faucet and ran the glass under the stream of water.

"Yes, I gave him the McMuffin sandwich—"

"Please don't call it a sandwich."

"Well, he took it and is going to run it through his database or whatever. He said he'd let me know what he finds—"

"I can tell you right now what he'll find. Zilch."

I ignored Kit's interruption and continued as if I hadn't heard her. "But the problem is, we still don't have any DNA from Autumn to compare it to."

"Hmm." She poured her fancy wine into the two glasses. "Let's think about that."

"Cheers." I raised my glass to her, feeling much better. If anyone could come up with a good idea, it would be Kit. Even though she had never actually clapped eyes on the elusive Autumn.

We changed TV channels, or rather Kit did, discarding the doomed wedding in Scotland and settling on a rerun of *Cake Boss*. As we sipped wine that conjured up the flavor of golden delicious apples, I realized she might have been right: perhaps it is my favorite.

When my phone rang an hour later, I saw Buddy's name appear on the screen. "It's Buddy," I announced unnecessarily, since Kit could see his name as clearly as I did. I picked up my phone, filled with guilt that I'd sent Culotta off with my brother's DNA.

"Come down to the parking lot," he said before I could even say hello.

"What? Can't you just come up here—"

"Val. Just do it. I don't have a lot of time."

Kit and I both rose, and I grabbed the keys to my apartment. When we got outside, I saw my car sitting in its usual place by the dumpster. But there was another car parked behind mine with its engine running and pointed in the direction of the exit to the street. Buddy was at the wheel, and when he saw me, he opened the door and got out. There was a passenger in the car. A woman with short brown hair, cut like a boy's, long on the top with the sides shaved.

Buddy came toward me, waving my keys in the air. "Kit. I didn't know you were here." He looked uncomfortable at seeing her with me, but he'd just have to get over it.

"Yeah, we were just having a glass of wine," I said. "Wanna come up and join us?" I glanced at the other person sitting in the unfamiliar car.

"No time." He handed me my keys. "And thanks for letting me use your car; we rented this one—"

"We?"

"Autumn and I. Come say hello. Kit, I don't think you've met my daughter."

We all walked toward the passenger side, and Autumn, with her blond hair gone, rolled down the window. "Hello, Val," she said.

"Hello," I said back. "This is my friend Kit James."

Autumn gave the briefest of nods in Kit's direction. "Your hair," I said, truly amazed at the difference it made in her appearance, not quite sure if it was good or bad.

"I love it," Kit said. She pushed me aside a little as she reached in and swiped a hand over the top of Autumn's head, ruffling her hair, as those styles seem to require. "Sorry," Kit said when Autumn gave a little yelp. "I think my watch got caught in your hair. But really, I love it."

"Thank you." Autumn gave a little laugh. "Time to switch it up." She ran her own hand over the top of her head and then patted the side, running her fingers over the bristles. "Radical change, huh?"

"Yes," I agreed. "So, you two are . . . what? Going somewhere? Leaving—"

"Yes," Buddy said from his position right behind me.

"Wait! You can't just leave; we have to talk." I returned my attention to Autumn, but she was looking down at her hands folded neatly in her lap. "Autumn. We are family. We need to—" I looked back at Buddy. "I'm guessing you never made it to the police station."

"We need to get out of Illinois," he replied quickly, ignoring my question. "I'll be in touch. Don't worry. Everything is going to be okay."

I heard myself laugh. "You have got to be kidding—"

"Not kidding, Val. It's not safe for Autumn here. I have to do all I can to protect my kid." He looked at Kit. "I'm sure Val has filled you in—"

"She hasn't said a word; what's going on?"

I had to hand it to Kit; her face was now one of pure innocence. But I was positive Buddy knew better.

He turned and began walking around the car to the driver's side. "We have to get on the road. I'll call you later. Love you." He climbed into the driver's seat.

And then he and his punk daughter were gone.

Kit and I stood in the parking lot for a few minutes, watching the car drive out of sight.

"Do you think he believed you?" I asked. "About you not knowing what's going on?"

"No, not for a second. He knows how smart I am."

"Kit, sometimes you are just—"

"What? Brilliant?"

She linked her arm through mine, and we headed back toward the entrance to my apartment building. "You might want to hang on to this." She took her free hand out of her pocket and held up a strand of hair.

"That's not Autumn's, is it?" I asked, knowing full well it was and silently concurring that my friend is indeed brilliant.

"It ain't k.d. lang's."

CHAPTER TWENTY-THREE

I had placed the strand of Autumn's hair in a baggie (my last one; I'd have to remember to pick up some more) and put that in between two pages of a *People* magazine with Julia Roberts on the cover. I'd sent Kit home and was now making my way to Steak 'n Shake to meet Culotta. He was waiting outside, and when he saw my car pull into the parking lot, he strode quickly toward me.

"What kind of car are they driving?" he asked as I opened the door.

"A Toyota. It was dark blue. Maybe black. A sedan. And Autumn, my niece, has cut and colored her hair. It's dark brown. Shaved on the sides and long on the top."

"Sounds fabulous," he said.

"Well, it is a popular look right now—"

"Never mind that; just give me what you've got."

I gingerly lifted the *People* magazine from the floor of the car and handed it to him. "I hope it's enough."

"It's more than we have so far." From nowhere, he pulled out a brown paper sack and gently dropped the baggie inside. I noticed he was wearing blue disposable gloves again. "Should I ask how you got this, Val?"

"I wish I could take credit, but actually it was Kit—"

"Okay, I *won't* ask." Then he turned and walked to his own car.

"See ya!" I yelled to his back.

He turned slightly in my direction. "Tell Kit well done. You too. I just wish I could give you the news you want."

I was so pleased with myself as I drove back to my apartment, I was overcome with a fit of super energy. I vacuumed, stripped my bed, and cleaned out my refrigerator, emptying and throwing away the bottle of orange juice.

A couple of hours later, when I was compiling an extensive grocery list, including more baggies, my phone rang. "Dennis!" I said.

"You sound happy."

"Well . . . yeah. Give me the news."

"Okay; we got a good match. But it's not to Buddy."

"What do you mean?" There was a silence on the other end of the line. "Culotta, are you still there?"

"Yep," he said.

"Okay, you're making me nervous."

"Val. I have a name for you. And it ain't pretty."

"Okay. Just say it."

"Oxana Kusnetsov."

On the contrary, I thought it was a very pretty name. But I sank back into the couch, feeling at first defeated, and then terrified.

"Val, are you still there?"

"Yes, sorry, I guess I'm . . . shocked. That's all."

I heard Culotta take a sharp breath. He spoke slowly, and carefully. "You're shocked because the woman with your brother is not his kid? I think I told you that already. It's not news; I don't see—"

"Culotta, I'm shocked and scared. Scared for my brother. I'm almost afraid to ask you who this Oxana person is."

Now Culotta took no time at all to answer. "She's an operative. An undercover agent, working *against* our country, whose DNA was in the system."

"A spy?" I asked it as casually as if I were asking him if this person was a long-distance runner or a good bowler. But my heart was beating hard.

"Anyone can be a spy. An agent, or operative, is usually employed by a foreign government or organization. They adopt a false identity and—"

"Okay, assuming what you say is true—"

"Assuming?"

"Work with me here, please. Assuming this woman is not Autumn but actually . . . well, who you say she is, what does she want with my brother?"

"I can't tell you that."

"You don't know?"

"Not one hundred percent certain." The tone of his voice made me think he was not being truthful. "What you should do is contact Buddy," he continued. "Just call him, find out where he is, tell him to come in."

"Come in? Like *The Spy Who Came in from the Cold*? Buddy has not done anything wrong—foolish, maybe, but not wrong. He's driving around the country with a . . . foreign agent?" It sounded too fantastic to be true. "All he knows is that this woman is his daughter. He just wants to protect her."

"Val, you must try to reach Buddy."

"To tell him his travel companion isn't his daughter? And what about poor Hettie? What's her involvement in this? Was she a spy . . . agent . . . whatever you call them? And let's not forget Rayjean Boxer. What about her?"

Again, silence for a while. Then, "Just try to reach him, tell him to contact me. I can help him."

***

After my phone call with Culotta, I was more terrified than ever for Buddy's safety. But I also felt guilty. Buddy was obviously in way over his head, but still, I had given Culotta information that I had sworn I would keep to myself.

I immediately tried calling Buddy, and during the rest of the night, I left five messages on his voice mail, starting with *please call me* and ending with *call me, dammit!* With no response from him, and none the next morning, I was actually glad to go to the office and concentrate on something other than my brother running around the country with—well, I couldn't bear to give her a name, although she apparently had two.

"I remember giving you a couple of days off, but what the hell, Val," my boss greeted me when he arrived.

"I was working, Tom; I just wasn't in the office for a few days." I glanced at the clock on the wall, as if to point out that he wasn't exactly setting any records for getting to work early.

Kit isn't the only one who is good at reading my thoughts. "I'm the boss, remember?" he said. "And you haven't been here for over a week."

"Yeah, but you knew I was driving up to Door County—"

"How'd you go there—via Florida?" He paused at the doorway to his office, surprising me. Usually when he asks a question, he doesn't wait for an answer. Unfortunately, this was not one of those times.

I sighed and pushed my chair back from my desk, ready to try to tell him what I'd been going through without really telling him anything. But luckily, his typical disinterest kicked in. "And where are Billie and Perry?" He waved an arm in the direction of their desks and scowled.

"Oh, they were here earlier. Billie had to go out for supplies, and Perry—"

"Yeah, don't even tell me. I don't wanna hear about his latest beauty treatment." It was unfortunate for Perry that his uncle didn't appreciate the metrosexual his nephew had morphed into.

"Tom, you're too hard on him. And actually—"

"Yeah, yeah." He sounded irritated. "But when you're not here, Pankowski, we don't seem to make any progress."

"So you're saying you missed me."

"Hell no, I'm not saying that."

"*Think you are*," I singsonged as he entered his office and slammed the door.

He was done talking about his nephew, or me—or anything else. Much to my relief.

I returned to my computer, finished up the price change on a listing, and then picked up the phone on my desk. Time—past time—to get back to the business of selling houses, even though I had no heart for it right now. I had a cool, if not cold, call I needed to make, following up on a lead from a friend of a friend (all right, someone known to a mere acquaintance of mine whom I'd run into at Walgreens).

Just as the call was growing warm with the feel of an impending listing, Perry interrupted my flow. I shouldn't have been surprised; after all, I knew his appointment was at LensCrafters. But still, I was taken aback at seeing him in black-framed, large-lensed glasses. Most shocking of all was that he was as movie-star handsome as ever in them. I gave him a thumbs-up and returned my attention to Pamela Martin. "When would be a good time for me to meet with both you and your husband?" I asked.

Happy that she gave a date later in the week—maybe things with Buddy and Autumn and Culotta (and Hettie!) would be solved by then—I was winding up the call just as Billie walked in. I waved to her as I told Pamela I was looking forward to working with her.

"Oooh, sounds like someone just scored," Billie said when I hung up. She plunked a pile of papers down on her desk and pulled out her chair, heaving a sigh as she sat down in it.

"Sounds like someone's having a rough morning," I said, thinking *my* rough patch could top hers any day.

"Not really. But I didn't sleep that well last night. I'm just—"

Before I could decide whether to vocalize the thought that *my* sleepless nights were far more sleepless than hers, Perry cleared his throat, and it had its intended consequence: Billie and I both turned in his direction, our focus now on his new spectacles.

"Perry!" Billie said. "Since when did you start wearing glasses?"

He picked up his phone from the corner of his desk and appeared to be checking the time. "About an hour ago. You like?"

"Very much," Billie said. "They're really handsome on you." And they were. Their bold black color provided the perfect accent for his deep tan, snow-white teeth, and blond highlights.

"What kind of mood is Uncle Tom in?" Perry nodded toward his uncle's closed door. It always makes me smile when Perry refers to Tom as his uncle, and it's even more delicious when Perry actually addresses him that way. Although it's true, Perry is Tom's nephew, I perversely enjoy how it makes Tom squirm just a little.

"He's fine," I said.

"Hmm; I should warn you, Val, he isn't pleased about all the time you've taken off lately."

"Really?" I pulled out a desk drawer and rummaged through the folders. "He seemed okay to me. In fact, he was wondering why I didn't take longer."

Perry removed his glasses, leaned back in his chair, and swung around to face me. "So where'd you go, anyway? Somewhere nice?"

"Door County. My brother was in town, and we took a road trip—"

"Door County! I thought you had gone somewhere really special, the way you hightailed it out of here so suddenly—"

"I just told you, my brother was in town, and it was a last-minute thing. And by the way, Door County is *plenty* special. Have you ever even been there?"

"Hardly." He swung his chair back around to face his computer and put his glasses back on. "I don't do local, Val."

"It's awesome," Billie called from her end of the room. "You are so lucky your mom moved there."

"All I know," Perry continued, "is that I have a heavy workload when you suddenly disappear. Uncle Tom and I had to hold the fort together."

"You mean hold down the fort. Did you sell any properties?"

"I have a few pokers in the fire."

"I think you mean irons."

"Whatever, Val. And if you'll excuse me, I have work to do now."

"Well, don't let me stop you, for heaven's sake."

After a few seconds, Perry turned to face me again. "You didn't say anything about my glasses."

Before I could think of something not too nice to say, Tom emerged from his office. He scowled at his nephew and for the second time that morning said, "What the hell."

"Want me to fix you some coffee?" Billie asked from her corner of the room. She said it like she was talking to a baby: *want me to get your Binky?*

"Yeah, and make it quick." He looked my way and pointed his index finger at me. "Val, in my office—now. And bring the Patel file with you."

I rummaged through the folders in my desk drawer again and located what he wanted. When I entered his office, he was removing his jacket and carefully placing it on the oak coatrack in the corner of the room.

"Why are you in such a bad mood?" I took a seat.

"I'm in a great mood." He pulled a cigar out of a long aluminum case. "I've got my top salesperson back. *Billie!* Where's that coffee?"

"It's right here." She entered the room and carefully placed a mug on his desk.

"Good. Thanks. And do me a favor. Remind Mr. Magoo out there about his appointment with Trinity Title this morning."

She nodded and turned back toward the office door, raising her eyebrows at me and mouthing *good luck* as I slid the Patel file across Tom's desk. "You wanted this," I said.

"Yeah." He picked up the mug and took a sip. "I want to go over the financials."

"Okay; let me know if you need anything from me." I rose from the chair, but he indicated with his hand for me to sit back down.

Then, unusual for Tom, he actually got up and walked around the desk to close the office door himself. "How was your visit with Buddy?" He took his seat again.

I switched my gaze from his face to the map of Chicago on the wall behind him. "It was great."

"You sure? For someone who's just taken a nine-day vacation—"

"I already told you, I was working from home for some of that time. Furthermore, I have a new sale all but closed." I crossed my fingers in my lap, both for good luck and because it was a little white lie.

"Riiiight. So Buddy was good?"

"Yeah," I said, way too jovially, now switching my gaze from the Chicago map to the baseball encased in a glass cube on his desk. I was filled with agony that I couldn't share with Tom, one of Buddy's oldest friends, the fear I had for my brother. "How did he seem to you when you guys went out?" I asked.

"Off," he answered immediately. "Is something going on with him?"

"Nah, he's great," I said too quickly, waving a hand in the air. "Loving life." *Loving life?* Where did that come from? I moved my gaze from the baseball to Tom's face. "Did you guys talk?"

"*Talk?* What do you mean, talk? Like did we share our feelings? Yes, Val, we talked for *such* a long time, and then we gave each other manicures."

I gave a little laugh, even though Tom's sarcasm was not funny. "Okay, so what I'm asking is, did you two catch up?"

"Catch up?"

"I mean, did you have fun?"

"Fun?"

"Are you just going to repeat everything I say? You said he was off. Why didn't you tell me sooner, like that night? And what does that mean, *off?* How was he acting?"

"Kinda like the way you're acting now. Is something going on with *you?*"

"No. I've just been really busy."

"Bus—?" he started to repeat, but then stopped himself. "You've just been on vacation for about a month, but I'm really more concerned about your brother."

"For heaven's sake, it wasn't a month. And as for Buddy, well, yes, he's busy too."

"I thought he was retired."

"He is, of course, but he's got stuff to do." Well, at least I didn't say he was *loving life* again.

Tom leaned back in his chair and clasped his hands over the top of his bald head. His look was concentrated on me, his eyes squinting as if he didn't believe a word I was saying. But I felt pleased—and amazed—with myself for not blurting out the whole horrifying mess. Instead, I found myself staring at the safety of the baseball again.

"Okay," he said after about a minute, bringing his hands down and shifting his body so he was upright in his chair. "Get outta here, Val. But just remember, if there is anything, anything at all, I can do for you or Buddy, just say the word. I know a few people I can call."

I stared at him in surprise. What was he suggesting? And whatever his "people" could do, the last thing I wanted was Tom involved in my brother's mess. "Thank you," I said, meaning it. Then I rose from the chair again.

"Here, take this back." He slid the Patel file toward me.

"Oh, I thought you—"

"Nope. Don't need it."

I took the file and left his office, closing the door behind me, but not before I heard him flick his lighter over the end of the cigar, breaking the Smoke-free Illinois Act of 2008. Something he does several times a day.

CHAPTER TWENTY-FOUR

By the time Kit called me just before noon, I was—to my pleasant surprise—completely immersed in all things real estate.

"Wanna do lunch?" she asked.

"Oh, Kitty Kat. I'm really going to town here—finally. I think I should just keep at it. After being gone so long—"

"You gotta eat."

She had a point there. "Well . . ."

"And I gotta talk," she said. "Meet me at The Cellar Door—in a half hour?"

She was right. I had to eat. And I could never not let her talk when she needed to. "I'll be there in twenty minutes," I said, my mind already going over the menu and debating between a BLT and a pizza.

Kit was there when I arrived. She wore a look of fury I knew couldn't be directed at me. "Diana called," she greeted me as I sat down. She scooted her chair closer to me. In spite of her obvious anger, her beauty was on full display: perfect makeup, silky-smooth hair, and a Ralph Lauren floral wrap dress complemented by jewelry one could buy only at a jewelry store.

"Diana?" I had no idea who she was talking about.

Before she could enlighten me, our waitress appeared. Kit ordered pinot; I asked for water with a lemon slice. "I'm still working," I answered my pal's raised eyebrows.

But she didn't have time to care about that. The waitress was still assuring us she'd be right back when Kit started pouring out her story. After reminding me that Diana was Leslie's mom, her son's mother-in-law, she told me about their phone conversation.

"That self-righteous biddy had the gall to blame Sam. That, after she pretended we moms should help them reconcile. Hah."

"You want to start from the beginning?" I realized that might have been a poor choice of words and feared she'd start replaying the tense period of wedding preparations a few years earlier. I'd actually felt all the tension at that time was between the moms, not the couple. I was grateful when Kit began with today's phone call.

"For starters, she took me by surprise. I didn't recognize the number calling me and almost didn't answer."

I believed that. In fact, I'd never known Kit to answer an unknown caller and always marveled at how she could resist.

"What made you answer?"

"Texas area code. And she started out saying she really thought they loved each other, but Leslie couldn't possibly ignore Sam's bad behavior, blah, blah, blah."

"Well, what bad behavior is she referring to? Did she say?"

"No, she didn't. And she'd be lying if she did. Sam's treated Leslie like a princess from the day he met her. I don't have to tell you that, Val."

I was saved from responding by the pinot and water the waitress set down before us. If anyone would be lying, it would be me, not Diana, if I agreed with Kit's statement.

And the last thing Kit wanted to hear was how much Sam reminded me of my ex-husband. In my mind, they both had that same look of searching for the next conquest. I gave the waitress my order, hoping Kit would change the subject after she left. My friend seemed almost delirious with anger at Diana and Leslie, so I pushed the pinot closer to her.

"I'll just eat some of hers," she said after I'd requested the sunflower bruschetta pizza.

In a further attempt to change the direction our conversation had been headed, I took charge as soon as the waitress departed. "What do you think is going to happen next?" I asked. "Do you think they'll end up getting a divorce?"

"No. Maybe I should suggest they see a marriage counselor."

I didn't respond, because I was puzzled. I knew she had never believed in any kind of therapy, especially the marriage kind. This came from her being married to a solid and faithful man.

"You and David went, didn't you?" She sounded desperate. "Okay, it didn't work in your case, but David was a special kind of moron."

"Oh yes. I did drag him there once, if you will recall, even against your advice. He spent the whole time flirting with the counselor, which pissed me off; and when we left our first, and last, session, I could tell the therapist thought poor David was married to a bitch."

"It will be different with Sam, although I doubt Leslie will be honest." She stared off into space for a few seconds, and I could almost hear her thoughts: *make sure to tell Sam to get a female counselor.*

"Kit, there's something else we need to discuss. It's serious."

"Good, because I'm sick of talking about Sam and Leslie and the whole damn mess." She swirled the pinot grigio in her wineglass and then took a sip.

I began by taking a deep breath. "Well, to start with, Culotta called me last night. He has the results of the DNA taken from Ox—Autumn's hair."

"What? Why didn't you call me?"

"Sorry; it was late, and I—"

"Was it past eight o'clock, which I know would be very late for you?"

"Kit, I don't know what time it was, but would you shut up and let me talk?" I took a tissue from my purse and blew my nose, hoping I wouldn't start crying.

"Oh, Val, I'm sorry. Why did you let me ramble on about Sam?"

"Well, Sam and Leslie are important."

"Oh, enough about them. Tell me about the DNA stuff."

I filled her in, trying to make it sound as if it were an everyday occurrence to have your brother fooled into thinking he had a child, when in fact all he really had was a foreign operative.

"So . . . Buddy obviously did *not* have a DNA test to prove that this Oxana chick was his daughter," she concluded after I stopped talking.

"Kit, that's the troubling part; I just can't believe he lied to me. Maybe Oxana faked her DNA—"

"Get a grip, Val. He lied. He lied multiple times." She paused, frowning in concentration before continuing. "Maybe he just took her word for it, which doesn't really sound like Buddy."

I remained quiet for a moment, thinking how wrong I'd been about him actually enjoying the whole exercise. "Culotta hinted—well, more than hinted—that Buddy isn't quite the retired Navy dude I thought he was. He says Buddy is involved in something . . . else. But my biggest fear is that my brother is unwittingly transporting an agent . . . spy . . . whatever . . . around the country, and he still thinks she's his child."

Kit raised her glass to her lips, drained her wine, and then looked at me. "Am I going to need another one of these? You said 'to start with,' so I'm guessing there's more?"

I sipped from my lemon water, taking a few seconds to debate how much more I should tell her.

"So," she said when I didn't speak, "if Oxana—I love that name, don't you?—if she is not Autumn, where is the real Autumn? If there even is a real Autumn."

Now she had my full attention. But I had just gotten used to the idea of an impostor in our family. The idea that there might also be a *real* Autumn out there was too much to think about.

"And what does this Oxana want with Buddy?" she continued. "Why is she clinging to him like a leech? I think we could tell by her haircut that she's not all there."

I laughed a little as she twirled her index finger at the side of her head. Strangely, her gesture gave me a little hope. Perhaps Oxana was really mentally deranged. Of course my hope vanished when I considered how that might make her even more dangerous. "Good question. So far, he's provided an excellent taxi service for her," I said.

"Hmm . . . I kinda think that if she's indeed a superspy, the KGB probably already has Uber on speed dial. They don't use American citizens for transportation."

I didn't point out that the KGB actually no longer exists. But I was struck at the absurdity of us having this conversation. Buddy! My brother who taught me to swim and to drive and who brought home stray animals.

"Another thing," Kit went on. "Didn't he give a birth announcement to your mom and William up in Door County? So he must really believe she's his daughter."

She was right. Why would he go to such an extreme if he knew Autumn was not his child? This confirmed to me that Buddy had no idea he was being deceived. It also reinforced my fear for his safety, my fear of what Oxana's intentions were. "What I've got to do now is get ahold of

Buddy and let him know that the woman he is traveling with is an impostor."

"Riiight," she said, "and while you're at it, why don't you clue him in about Santa Claus."

***

When I got back to the office, I was feeling both relieved that Kit knew the full story and disgusted with myself for blabbing. Only Billie was still there, sitting at her desk. Perry appeared to have made his appointment with the title company and had not returned, and Tom had taken a late lunch and was still not back.

"Boy, Tom was such a grump all morning. I'm glad he had a lunch date," Billie called across the room to me.

"Yes, he was . . . well, I think he had something on his mind."

She rose and slowly walked to my desk. Under the cute brown vest she was wearing, I could see an Aerosmith T-shirt. "He worries about you, Val. You know that, right?"

"Oh, he's just being silly. He worries about all of us— okay, maybe not so much about Perry. But he's got a kind heart; we know that."

She nodded. "Val, is everything all right—with you, I mean?"

I reached for her hand and clasped it in mine. "Yes, Billie. *Yes.* Everything is okay—perfect."

She squeezed my fingers. "Good." She sounded relieved. "Because you know we're one big happy family here; we look out for each other . . ." She didn't finish her sentence immediately, but instead her face broke into a wide grin. " . . . except for Perry, maybe." She laughed.

I laughed along with her, perhaps the first genuine laugh in many days. "Except for Perry," I echoed.

***

"Valerie! What have you done with your brother?"

Crap! The last person I needed to talk to right now was my mother. But I had stupidly not checked who the incoming call was from as I backed my car out of the parking area of the office. "I'm driving, Mom. Can I call you later?"

"No, you may not. I need to reach him. It's time to set up a meeting with this long-lost granddaughter he claims I have."

"Well, I know he's busy right now—"

"We're all busy, Valerie; he doesn't have exclusive rights to being busy. I don't care what his job is, he doesn't just show up and drop a bombshell on his family and—"

"Whoa! Hold it right there. What job are you talking about? He's retired. Can you not remember his retirement party?"

"Valerie, don't be so rude. Of course I remember; how could I forget spending the weekend with those—the twins, Jump and Shout."

"You mean Pip and Squeak. And I thought we weren't supposed to call them that. But tell me why you think Buddy has a job."

"Elaine told me, a few years ago. Something to do with submarines. I don't remember exactly."

"What *about* submarines? Mom, what is his job?" I demanded.

"I told you, I don't remember. Really, I think that's all Elaine said."

"Why didn't Buddy tell me? And why didn't you?"

"Elaine told me she had spoken out of turn and asked me not to mention it. So when you speak to him, don't say anything, okay?"

"Fine, Mom. Look, I have to go now. I'll call you later. Bye-eee."

"Just tell Buddy to call me. I think he left a pair of socks here, and I need to know if I should mail them back to him."

Socks. Right, I thought. *She should mail them to* me, *so I can use them to wring her son's neck.*

CHAPTER TWENTY-FIVE

As I pulled into my parking lot, I found myself searching, albeit with little hope, for the car I'd last seen Buddy—and Autumn, er, Oxana—in. Maybe he had come back.

But no; there were only a half dozen or so cars parked there, and none matched my memory of the one they'd been in. Luckily, my favorite spot next to the dumpster was vacant, and I deftly maneuvered my car into it.

I made my way up the stairs to my apartment, where I found, to my great shock, my neighbor hunched over in his wheelchair in front of my door. "Andy, hi!"

"Hi, Val. I was just trying to check on you. I was worried."

I'd never seen Andy on my floor of the building; and even though we did have an elevator, to my knowledge, no one ever used it. "Why didn't you call?" I asked, sounding a little edgy and immediately regretting it.

"I did. You didn't answer." He rolled his chair back a little so that I could get to the door and unlock it with my key.

I got it in the slot and left it hanging there while I looked at my phone. Sure enough, there were four missed calls from Andy. I'd forgotten to turn the volume back on after silencing it at the restaurant with Kit. "I'm so sorry, Andy. I forgot to take my phone off mute."

"No problem," he said, but his voice sounded a little hurt.

I promised myself that as soon as this mess was cleared up, I'd spend more time with him. I had noticed a chess set in his apartment when I was helping him with groceries once, so perhaps I could ask him to teach me how to play.

"I was just wondering if you had heard anything from the police yet," he continued. "About Hettie."

"No, Andy, I still haven't heard anything. Just the usual stuff about them continuing with their inquiries. They told me they'd spoken to you about the man you saw at Hettie's mailbox."

"Yes, that and a lot of other stuff. None of it very important or interesting. I doubt I was able to give them much help."

I held the door and watched him wheel in ahead of me and park himself by the end of my sofa, really the only empty space in my living room. He looked tired, no doubt from the energy he had to exert to move around, and I wondered why he didn't have one of those electric wheelchairs.

"Did I tell you I'm getting an upgrade?" he asked, as if reading my thoughts.

"No, you didn't. A chair with a motor?"

A smile appeared on his face, and he nodded. "There'll be no stopping me then, eh?"

For a second, I was filled with sadness for this sweet man, and then fear because of his vulnerability, no doubt brought on by Hettie's demise. But I forced myself to match his smile. I knew he had an ancient TV with a tiny screen in his living room, where he liked to watch old Hollywood movies. Humphrey Bogart seemed to be his favorite. I'd often heard sounds coming from his apartment when I was in the hall passing his door. I vowed to buy him a flat-screen TV—they are ridiculously cheap nowadays—on my next visit to Walmart. I was convinced that would change his life, and surely Kit would know how to set it up.

I closed my front door and set my purse and keys down on the counter as I entered the kitchen. "Would you like a glass of wine? And some cheese and crackers?" I knew Buddy had brought a variety of snacks and left them untouched.

"That would be wonderful." Andy sounded like a kid accepting an invitation to a birthday party as he rubbed his hands together.

"It's nice to have you here," I said when I returned with two wineglasses and set them on the coffee table within his reach. Then I returned to the kitchen for the cheese plate I'd made that contained cubes of cheese, of course; crackers; and a small pile of garlic-stuffed olives that Buddy loves. I can't stand the way they make my mouth taste and assume my breath smells even worse. I figured Andy was past worrying about such things. I, on the other hand, have to be vigilant since I never know when Culotta might stop by.

"So, you don't know anything," he reiterated as I took a seat on the end of the couch. He looked disappointed, and I thought I noticed the light in his eyes diminish a little. I wanted to share with him that he would soon be viewing his beloved Bogie and *The Maltese Falcon*, along with some other great old movies, on a forty-five-inch screen. But surely the element of surprise would be better.

"Right. I don't know anything." I popped a piece of cheese into my mouth. Then something occurred to me. "You haven't seen my brother around here today, have you?" A feeling of hope began to form in the pit of my stomach.

"No, I haven't. But who was that woman in the car with him yesterday?"

"Oh, Andy, you don't miss a thing, do you?" I felt tender toward him, but I also felt there could be *something* he'd seen that would provide a clue—to *something*. But I didn't even know what questions to ask to make good use of my human surveillance camera. "She is a colleague of his."

I pecked away at some more cheese and a cracker while gulping my wine thirstily. Andy barely sipped his, but chowed down robustly on the meager food offerings. I worried whether he had enough groceries in his apartment. As small as he was, he surely didn't eat this ravenously all the time; maybe he was starving. I made yet another mental note that a trip to the grocery store would be our first joint outing.

"I miss Hettie, don't you?" He brushed some cracker crumbs from the front of his shirt.

"Very much."

"She used to make the most delicious meat loaf." His eyes sparkled at the memory as he spoke. "Whenever she did, she would bring me some. She was a very kind and interesting lady."

"She sure was." I sipped at my wine now.

"And oh, how she loved the Bears. We watched a couple of games together. Of course I had to go up to her apartment to do so; my television is not the best. And did I ever tell you I heard her on her phone in the hall once, when she was on her way out somewhere, speaking a foreign language? She sounded quite fluent." His eyes grew huge, as huge as his heavy lids would allow. "And she could . . . line dance, I think it's called? Who would have thought our Hettie was so accomplished?"

"What do you think it was, Andy?"

"I'm not really sure what line dancing is." He looked confused.

"No, I mean the foreign language. What do you think it was?"

"Not sure. It wasn't Polish. I know Polish; my wife and I used to have several Polish friends. But it was similar. One of those Eastern European languages."

"Well, I know her nephew is taking up a foreign language, so perhaps she wanted a connection with him, something they could talk about and do together," I said.

I could see Andy thinking hard. "That sounds like Hettie. Of course I wanted to ask her about it, but . . ." He stopped talking, lost in thought, looking sad.

And just then my phone rang. It was my sister-in-law, Elaine. "I'm so sorry, Andy. I have to take this. And I'll likely be a while. Family," I said, by way of explanation.

"No problem." He chewed on his cracker, not making any indication that he planned to leave.

"If you don't mind, I'll take this in my bedroom. Help yourself to more cheese and wine. Elaine, hi." Before heading to my bedroom, I crossed over to the small TV I keep in the living room and turned it on. I chuckled as Judge Judy appeared on the screen. "There, that should keep you busy," I said to Andy.

"Yes, don't worry about me," I heard him say as I closed my bedroom door.

"Sorry about that, Elaine—"

"Val! Do you know where Buddy is?" She sounded desperate.

"No, Elaine, I do not." I was at a loss as to how much to tell her or ask her. Since my mother had indicated Elaine knew *something*—quite likely more than I did—I was sorely tempted to ask her to tell me everything, and then I'd be willing to do the same in return. But with Buddy either on the run or *missing*, I just didn't want to take the chance of putting him in further jeopardy.

"We talk every day, Val, and I haven't heard from him for *two* days now. Something is wrong. Very, very wrong."

"Have you notified anyone?"

"Who would I notify?" she shrieked. "Just tell me who I should notify." Now she was crying; I was sure of it. But it sounded like she was trying not to, and I respected her for that. And felt all the more sorry for her.

"His boss? The police?"

"He's retired, Val." So she wasn't going to level with me about what she knew. "And I don't think I should call the police."

"Why not?"

"I can't explain right now. I just wondered if *you* knew where he was. You were the last one he was with."

Was she *accusing* me? The sympathy I'd been feeling for her leaked completely out of me, but then filled back in when she said, "Oh, I just want to do what's best for Buddy."

CHAPTER TWENTY-SIX

S omeone's been in my apartment," I said.

"Where are you now?" Culotta asked.

"I'm sitting in my car in the parking lot."

"Good. Don't go back in. Meet me at . . . er . . . meet me at Steak 'n Shake. I can be there in ten minutes."

"Okay," I said, feeling disappointed that I wasn't really hungry enough to fully enjoy a trip to Steak 'n Shake. I'd had a late lunch.

"*Are* you okay?"

"I'm a little . . . upset, I guess you could call it."

"Just get to Steak 'n Shake. Drive slowly. I'll see you in a few." He hung up.

When I pulled into the Steak 'n Shake parking lot, he was already there, standing by his vehicle with his hands in his pockets. He ambled toward my car and opened the door. He didn't look worried; in fact, he had a smile on his gorgeous face. "You'll be okay," he said, taking my hand and helping me out of my SUV. When my feet touched the ground, I felt my legs buckle, and he put his arm around my waist to steady me. "C'mon; let's get you a vanilla shake. I seem to remember that's your favorite."

After we'd gotten settled in a booth, he spoke again. "Okay, so tell me why you think someone was in your apartment," he said.

I took a sip of the creamy vanilla shake. Even though I'd been terrified knowing someone had been in my home, I was feeling pretty good now. Culotta's blue eyes were scrutinizing me across the table, and I felt safe with him. "Well, I took some trash to the dumpster last night—"

"Is this dumpster inside or outside the building?"

"It's outside; you know it is. Where I park my car."

"Right. So continue."

"As I turned around to go back to my building, I thought I saw someone standing in the shadows. I couldn't quite make it out, but it looked like a man, and he sort of disappeared among the cars." I stopped and took another sip of my milkshake.

Culotta was drinking coffee, the sleeves of his light-blue shirt rolled up to the elbows, revealing fine blond hairs on his forearms. He raised the mug to his lips and nodded his head for me to continue.

"So . . . well, it just sort of unnerved me. I ran back upstairs, and for the rest of the night, I felt spooked."

"Is that it?"

"No, that's not it. Before I went to work this morning, I left my bedroom closet door open. Six inches. I measured. But when I returned late this afternoon, the opening measured eight and three-quarters. So you see, someone must have been in there, probably going through my things."

"So you think this person in the shadows waited all night for you to leave?"

"I don't know. What I know is what I just told you: someone opened my closet door and then didn't leave it as I had left it. Six inches."

"Where did you learn to leave it open like that?"

"Ninja Safekeeping. On YouTube. It's a whole thing."

"Hmm. Pretty clever, Val." I couldn't tell if he really thought Ninja Safekeeping was clever, or if he thought I was just an idiot. "Did anything else unusual happen last night?" he continued.

"Apart from—"

"Yes, apart from the dude at the dumpster." The way he said it made it sound like a horror flick. *The Dude at the Dumpster.* "Did you speak to anyone in the building? Anything out of the ordinary happen?"

I thought about it for a moment. "No, not really. I had a visit from Andy. My neighbor. That was a little bit unusual, I guess."

"The guy who uses a wheelchair?"

"Yes. Apparently, he had called me several times and was worried when he couldn't reach me."

"Why couldn't he reach you?"

"My phone was on mu ... um, not picking up the signal, I guess. Anyhow, when I came home from work yesterday, he was at my door."

"How'd he get up the stairs?"

"The elevator."

"You got an elevator in that place?" He said it with disbelief.

"Yes. It's way down at the end of the hall. I've never used it; in fact, I didn't think it worked."

Culotta sighed and pushed a menu toward me. "You want something to eat?"

"Good heavens, no. I couldn't eat a thing."

"Sure?"

"Yes, I'm sure." But on the laminated cover was a picture of cheese fries, looking deliciously gooey, so it seemed silly not to succumb. "Well, maybe I could force something down. Want to share these?" I pointed at the menu.

"Nope. But you go right ahead."

"Okay, but maybe just a small order. Or medium."

Later, with a large order of cheese fries devoured, I listened as Culotta mapped out a plan for the problem I'd called him about.

"Okay, here's what we're gonna do. I'll follow you home and check out your place."

"Please don't tell me it's not safe. I couldn't bear it if I had to move."

"No need to move. It's probably as safe as anywhere. If someone was in your apartment, you caught them with your Ninja Safekeeping." He laughed. "Good job, by the way." He called for the check and took out his wallet, and within a few minutes, I was back in my car with Culotta following.

***

"What are you doing?"

"Checking for bugs."

"Are you going to call in your people to do a sweep?"

Culotta was bent at the knees, running his hand along the baseboard of my living room. He looked up as he spoke. "I could do that. Or I could just use the app on my phone."

"Okay, then do it," I urged from my seat on the couch.

I watched as he stood up, took his phone out of his back pocket, and for several minutes swiped the screen and punched in a few numbers. Then he walked slowly around the living room and into my bedroom and bathroom. I was getting afraid again. And why shouldn't I? How often do you have a good-looking guy, who may or may not be an agent for the government, sweeping your tiny home for a covert listening device? It was all too crazy.

After several minutes, Culotta came out of my bedroom, shut off his phone, and joined me on the couch. "There's nothing here, Val."

"Are you sure? Because if that's true, why would someone be in my apartment, and—"

"Here's what I'm thinking." He had leaned forward and placed his elbows on his knees, clasping his hands together.

195

"Someone possibly planted a listening device in this place sometime in the last ten days or so."

"Before I discovered Ninja Safekeeping!"

"Right. So, if someone was in your apartment today, my guess is they came to retrieve the device they had already planted. It makes sense because Buddy is now gone. He is gone, right?"

I nodded grimly. "So, what? They were listening to his conversations when he was here?"

"Yep. I think so. Why don't you take a good look around and see if anything is missing. Anything important."

I walked slowly through the three rooms—four, counting the bathroom. I found nothing missing, nothing amiss. My engagement ring from David, easily the most expensive item I own, was safely ensconced in my jewelry box (a gift from my mother for my eleventh birthday). For good measure, I gave the mechanism on the side of the jewelry box one turn, and the ballerina that is perched on the lid twirled daintily to the metallic strains of Tchaikovsky.

"I'm not sure what I should be looking for," I said, coming back to sit by him on the couch, where he was reading something on his phone. "I don't see anything disturbed or missing."

"That's good. I'm pretty sure whoever was in here wasn't looking to steal. You don't have anything belonging to Buddy, do you?"

"No. He traveled light and left nothing behind."

Culotta shut off his phone and stuffed it in his pocket. "Val, you were right to call me, but I am positive you are not in danger. These people want your brother, not you."

"So I can stay here safely?"

"Yep, with the help of Ninja Safekeeping, you are in good shape."

"Thank you so much, Dennis." I put a hand on his forearm. "I'm so glad I had you to call."

My hand fell away from him when he stood up. "If you hear from Buddy, have him contact me," he said.

"Okay. But why won't you tell me what your connection to my brother is?"

"Gotta go."

***

When I was tucked in bed that night, the TV on mute, I called Kit and relayed the whole story to her. She listened as I filled her in on the intruder, my Ninja solution, and Culotta giving my place the all clear.

"Are you still there?" I asked twenty minutes later, after I'd finished my story with no interruptions from her.

"Yes, I'm here."

"Well, what do you think about my place maybe being bugged?"

I heard her sigh deeply. "I think it's scary stuff, Valley Girl. But that's very likely the reason your place was broken into. I mean, you don't really have anything that's worth stealing—"

"Kit—"

"No, I mean that as a good thing." She paused for a second. "Val, why don't you pack a bag and come spend the night here?"

"No, thank you. I'm okay, really. I'm not scared. Any danger has passed."

"I could send Larry to fetch you; he won't mind."

"I know. But really, there is no need. I'm tired, and I'll fall asleep fast."

"Okay. If you're sure. But call me if you need anything."

"I will. Love you."

"Love you too."

***

Since I'd thought about it all night long, it seemed only logical that I place the call as soon as I got out of bed the next morning.

I was shaking a little as I located my phone's list of recent calls. And there he was, number two, right after Kit. I pushed on Culotta's name to initiate the call, relieved when I heard the ringing that indicated I'd made a connection, in spite of my shaking.

"H'lo." Only when I heard the grogginess in his voice did I realize that it was five o'clock and that most people do not awaken that early. If not for caller ID, I would have hung up for sure. But that is no longer a choice, for most people, most times. Ah, for the good ol' days of anonymity.

Since he knew it was me, I forged ahead. Besides, he deserved to be rousted out of bed early. He had a job to do. Which is what I proceeded to tell him.

"Val? Why are you calling me so early?"

"Dennis, I'm really worried."

"About?"

"About Buddy, of course! I want to file a missing person report."

"Valerie, Valerie, Valerie. What are we going to do with you."

"What? Why would you say that? It's going on three days—"

"First of all, Valerie, I don't take missing person reports. I'm not with the Downers Grove Police Department anymore, officially, and even if I were—"

"Fine. Then I'll call them—"

"Wait. Valerie, don't make a fool of yourself."

"What on earth do you mean by that?" My shaking was now from anger, not fear, and I found that preferable. "Why wouldn't I report Buddy missing? It's been—"

"I can think of several reasons why you shouldn't report him missing."

To my great shock, I felt calmer, less worried. But I would never let Culotta know that. So instead, I said, "Please do enlighten me."

"Your brother is a big boy; he can take care of himself. And if he chooses to . . . go off the grid for a few days, he shouldn't have to ask his little sister. Shouldn't it be his wife, anyway, who would report him missing?"

"Well, she's concerned too. I can have her file the report if it will make you feel better," I said, but I remembered the reluctance Elaine had expressed. *Would* she file one? And why *wouldn't* she?

"Whoa. It would *not* make me feel better," he said. "I'm feeling just fine. And I can assure you, neither you nor Buddy's wife needs to file a report. No one does."

"Okay, Mr. Smarty-Pants, if no one needs to report my brother missing, then where is he?"

"Look, Val, I have a meeting to go to in . . ." He paused, as if checking the time. " . . . in an hour and a half. I'll come to your place after that. I think I might have some good news for you then."

Well, now we're getting somewhere, I thought as we said good-bye, and I prepared to wait.

But it was the longest few hours of my life.

I showered and dressed for the day. And I was only slightly dismayed when I realized I'd dressed better than usual. I quickly gave up trying to convince myself that it had nothing to do with Culotta's imminent visit. It was supposed to be a hot day, so it only made sense that I'd donned my flimsiest, sheerest sundress. The billowing, lightweight fabric hid all my not-so-lightweight parts, and when I topped it with my navy-blue linen blazer, it was plenty conservative for a real estate office. The fact that the dress's tangerine floral print offset my blond hair and tan legs was what made it such a brilliant choice. I hoped that would not escape his notice.

I called the office to tell Billie I'd be in late. No, I didn't know how late. And no, I couldn't tell her a good excuse to give Tom. "Say whatever you think best, Bill, like you've been doing. I'll explain later."

Oh, I hoped that would be true.

Soon, feeling hot and sticky in spite of my cool attire and half expecting to see the flowers on my dress wilt, I lay down on my couch. The humidity seemed to have crept into my apartment in spite of the air conditioning, and I could feel my shiny, sleek bob frizzing up. I was exhausted both physically and mentally.

I'd had no intention of sleeping—that would ruin my mascara, for sure. But when I heard the buzzer, I had to rouse myself from a dream that had been making no sense. I hoped the buzzing hadn't been going on for long and rushed to the wall by my door to press it into silence. "Yes?" I said into the speaker.

"Val, I'm here," I heard Culotta say. "Open up."

With shaky fingers, I hit the buzzer and then opened my door. A couple of minutes later, I almost collapsed with relief when I saw two figures coming down the corridor. Culotta was no surprise, of course—I'd been expecting him. But walking in tandem with him was another guy.

Buddy.

CHAPTER TWENTY-SEVEN

Culotta and Buddy came into my apartment and headed for opposite ends of the couch. They looked tired, and neither of them spoke immediately.

"What are you guys doing—I mean, *together*?" It sounded like an accusation, like I'd just caught them planning a bank robbery.

"What do you mean?" Buddy asked.

"I think she means she thought I was after you—that you and I are at odds," Culotta answered for me.

"No, I did not think that," I said. But of course that *was* one of the scenarios I'd envisioned. "You told me—"

"Sit down, Val," my brother said. "Your friend Dennis here and I—we're on the same side. All right, a little competitive, maybe, but on the same side." He shot a grin toward my "friend Dennis."

I thought of all the TV shows that had me yelling at the screen to the characters from different law enforcement agencies, *You're on the same side. Who cares who catches the crook first?* I shook my head at the immaturity of my brother and my . . . whatever he was. "You want something to drink? Or eat?" I was suddenly the perfect hostess. Well, it was better than being the duped sister and . . . whatever *I* was.

Luckily, they both waved off my offer. So, since the couch was taken up, I walked over and perched on the chair. "Buddy," I said gently, "I don't know if Culotta has told you, but you have a right to know." I steeled myself to deliver the blow. "Autumn is not your daughter. In fact—"

"Stop right there, Val. I know who Autumn really is."

"Good." I sighed in relief. "I was hoping Culotta had told you because I know you never doubted her for a moment, and I never doubted you, but the fact remains—"

"I always knew," Buddy said.

I looked at his passive expression and then at Culotta, who was slowly shaking his bent head.

"But if you knew, how could you . . . I mean, why did you have those pictures of her— And what was all that bullshit up in Door County, telling Mom and William about her—"

"Your brother has been working undercover." Culotta said it simply, as if that explained everything; but before I could protest that it didn't even come close, Buddy spoke again.

"Autumn's real name is Oxana Kusnetsov. She is an operative for a foreign entity," he said. "I was targeted by her because of my Navy connections, but I knew all along who she really was."

"You knew?" I was still dumbfounded.

"Yes."

"But why did you go into all that stuff about her to Mom? Why even bring Mom into it? I don't understand—"

"Val, it was very important that Oxana, and the people she was working for, believed I fell for her deceit. Her cover story to me was that she had overheard a conversation about a crime being committed, and as a result, she counted on me for her safety. Her plan was always to get me away from any

American authorities. And her own people were keeping us in their sights, following us in a million ways you can't even believe. It was vital to the mission that I appeared to accept her as my own child. Hence, the trip to Door County and the story to Mom and William."

"So . . . when this . . . this person approached you on the golf course—"

"I knew who she really was. In fact, I had been fully briefed, and I was expecting her."

I let that sink in. My first thought was that it was no wonder the traffic up to Door County had been so heavy. I knew Culotta and his crew had tailed us, but now I was learning they probably weren't the only ones. My next thought was that the waiter who served us dinner at Capri, the night Buddy revealed his secret, seemed totally suspicious. He definitely had an accent of some kind, which in itself is not unusual in Chicago, and I recalled his slight limp as he headed to our table with a heavy tray held high in his right hand.

I shook my head to clear it of foreign agents posing as waiters with disabilities. "So there is no Autumn?" Suddenly and inexplicably, I missed my niece and didn't want to know that she never existed.

"No."

I let everything he'd said sink in for a couple of seconds. "And the whole business with what this person had overheard, the crime, the upcoming trial, her being a witness—"

"All fake. Part of her legend. There was no trial, no overheard telephone conversation. They did a pretty good job," he added, with a hint of admiration.

"Legend?"

"Yeah, it means her fake background, the false identity she assumed, her cover story."

"Oh, Buddy," I said. I was pretty sure I should be mourning our family loss, but the whole thing was too fantastic. "But if this woman was not your daughter, and she has now . . . gone, what happened to her?" I stopped speaking. I had so many more questions, but there was one part of this crazy nightmare that did seem the most important. "Where is Oxana now?"

I watched Buddy turn his head toward Culotta, as if he were looking for permission to speak. Culotta gave a slight nod. "Val, she's probably back in her home country, or more likely, she's dead," my brother said. "She never did get what she was commissioned to get from me. Either way, we'll never hear from her again."

"And just what was it she wanted from you?"

"You got anything to drink? A beer would go down well," Culotta cut in.

"So you can't tell me?" I looked at Buddy and then at Culotta. It was clear from both their blank faces that they couldn't. So I moved on. "And what about Hettie? What does she have to do with all this? Was she killed because of Autumn? Did *Autumn* kill her?"

"That's still being . . . we're not sure yet," Culotta said. "We know she was involved somehow—"

"Duh. She was found dead in Autumn's apartment. Obviously, she's involved—"

"We're not sure *how* she was connected, but as you say, it seems she was; it seems she knew something."

I wasn't sure Culotta was being honest with me— maybe he knew more about Hettie's murder than he could tell me. Or maybe he really was as clueless as he sounded. "Well, when *will* you know?" I asked, my irritation clear in the rhetorical question.

As soon as they left my apartment, I called Kit. I felt I wouldn't breathe until I shared with her what I'd learned.

***

"Do you have children?"

I looked to my left at the woman who had spoken, a fellow Target shopper. She was holding up a child's dress.

"No," I lied, but I wasn't sure why.

"Oh, sorry. I'm buying something for my niece's birthday; she's nine, and I never know what size will fit her. She's tall for her age and quite slim. Do you have any idea?" *So* that's *why I lied*, I thought. *So I'd have an* excuse *for having no idea.*

"No. Sorry. Are you British?" I asked. Her clipped pronunciation made me certain she was.

She smiled, a charming smile that complemented her accent. "Yes. Is it obvious? I've been in America for fifteen years now, and I still get asked if I'm a Brit. Sometimes an Aussie, or even South African."

"Well, you haven't lost your accent. It definitely sounds British. I love your country, by the way. I was there not that long ago, visiting—" I stopped myself just as I was about to say *my daughter.* "It was heavenly. Whereabouts are you from?"

"Surrey. Banstead, to be exact. On the outskirts of London."

I reached into the neckline of the dress she was holding. "Says here it's a medium." I racked my brain for how big Emily was at nine. "You should get someone from this department to help you."

The woman's smile turned into a laugh. "Easier said than done." We both looked around the store, and I realized she was probably right. There was no one else in sight, not even another customer. "Maybe I'll just forget the dress and get her a bag. Girls like bags, right?"

"A purse?"

"Yes." She returned the dress to the rack and eyed the purse I was getting ready to purchase for Tom's latest girlfriend's daughter—a favor I was doing as his *friend*, not his employee. *And what was he doing dating someone young enough to have a ten-year-old daughter, anyway?*

"Girls like purses," I said. "We all do. You can never have too many." I said it with authority, although the truth is, I always use the same one until it's falling apart.

"My niece lives in London," the woman continued.

"Really? Do you live in Downers Grove?" I asked.

"Not yet, but planning to move here. Relocating from San Francisco. Say, do you happen to know of any good Realtors? We want to buy and—"

Before she had even finished her sentence, I dug into my own purse (the zipper was broken, so it was permanently open) and pulled out a business card. I triumphantly handed it to her. "This could be your lucky day. I'm a Realtor, very familiar with this area. I'd be happy to help you find something."

The woman took my card and studied it. She had pretty, red hair cut into a bob that was flattering to her oval face and a sprinkling of freckles across her nose and cheeks. Her dark-brown eyes were somewhat concealed by thick-framed glasses, but they gave her a studious look. "Thank you so much," she said. "We're in a hotel right now, so I'd like to find something quickly."

"We? Do you have a family?"

"I have a husband and a fifteen-year-old son. So I need to check out schools."

"Yes, and do you need to consider proximity to work for you or your husband?" Standard Realtor questioning to give me an idea of their income.

"My husband is a psychiatrist in private practice, and I'm a family doctor. I'll be working out of Good Samaritan. Do you know it?"

"Yes, very well. I think I'll be able to find you something close by."

She smiled a twinkling smile and held out her hand to shake mine.

I noted the glittering diamond on her ring finger. A good sign for me. I also took in the posh sheath dress she was wearing and the expensive shoes.

"I don't suppose . . ." She hesitated.

"What?"

"I don't suppose I could buy you a cup of coffee right now, could I? Oh, you're probably busy; I'll call your office and—"

"No, right now would be fine. We can look over some of the listings I have. They're all on our website." For good measure, I took my phone out of my purse and waved it at her. I was almost giddy at the thought that a couple of rich doctors might put me back in Tom's good graces.

"Great," the woman said. "That is so kind of you. I'm thrilled I ran into you."

"Valerie Pankowski," I said, holding out my hand again to shake hers one more time.

"Kendra Heathcote." She gave a warm chuckle.

"Okay, Dr. Heathcote, let's go find us some coffee."

***

"I can't, Kit. I've had a *beyond*-exhausting day. I—"

"Val, you have to."

I sighed. My pal wanted me to come to dinner, normally something you couldn't *keep* me from doing. Especially with the promised coq au vin, one of my favorites. But I truly was exhausted, from my meeting with Culotta and Buddy, and then my shopping expedition and coffee with my new client, and finally a couple of hours of research on potential houses for her. Plus, I was to meet with Dr. Heathcote first thing in the morning to take her through the places I'd found. I had to be fresh for that. All I wanted to do was eat a bowl of cereal, finish scheduling homeowners to be out of their houses at the correct times tomorrow, and get to bed early. Really early. (I needed my *Law & Order* viewing time before sleep set in, after all.)

But Kit had told me Sam was going to be at dinner, and she needed me there in case the conversation got heated. And so even as I argued that I couldn't, I knew I would.

"Why is he suddenly coming, anyway?"

"*Suddenly?*" my pal rose to her son's defense. "I told you a couple of weeks ago that he was coming soon."

"Yeah, well, with all that's happened . . . with all we've learned about him and Leslie since then . . . well, I just thought the visit was no longer on."

"It's on, and he'll be here in an hour. Puh-leeze, Val."

"But why do you need me?"

"Because, obviously, you are my only divorced *real* friend."

"It's not a cult, Kit. We are allowed out in the general population. And besides, millions of couples divorce. He'll be fine."

"Yes, of course he will, if it comes to that. But yours was so painful, so gruesome; you can advise Sam and tell him how awful it will be."

"Oh great." I didn't have the time or energy to remind her that my divorce had been far from painful or gruesome. Those adjectives described only my marriage. "Why are you just now telling me this?"

"Because I just now found out. You know Sam."

Yeah, that was the problem. I knew Sam. After a few more arguments from me, each one weaker than the last, I assured her I'd be there. "I just have to make a couple of more calls," I said. "Then I'll head over." I didn't need to fake the tiredness in my voice.

"Attagirl. I owe you."

"Yes, you do. You owe me." But I knew that was not in the least true.

Glad I hadn't changed out of my work clothes yet, I made my phone calls and then grabbed my keys—just as my phone rang. I had to leave for Kit's right away; I couldn't let her down. But it was Buddy, so I also had to answer my phone. *Let this be nothing urgent,* I prayed. "H'lo," I said into my phone as I was locking my apartment door.

And as I was *un*locking my car door, I spoke again, having listened to his plea that I get over to his hotel as soon as I could. No, he didn't want to tell me why, other than that he wanted to say good-bye. He was going home in the morning. "And I have something important to discuss with you," he said. "In person."

"I'll get away from Kit's as soon as I can."

"Thanks, sis." He sounded relieved.

And that made me nervous.

CHAPTER TWENTY-EIGHT

Kit opened her front door before I had even rung the bell, as if she'd been standing in her foyer waiting for me. She instantly grabbed my arm and pulled me inside. "Thank goodness you're here. Now listen, Sam seems really upset, so don't say anything that will make it worse—"

"Wait a minute. Wasn't I supposed to remind him that divorce puts you on the road to hell, and you'd be better off in a leper colony—"

"Yes. Exactly. But say it in a nice way—but don't make it sound fun." She put her hand on the small of my back and pushed me into the dining room, where Larry and Sam were already seated. Both guys rose as I entered, and dutifully came to kiss me on the cheek.

"Nice to see you, Auntie Val." Sam led me to an empty chair and pulled it out for me to sit down. "You sure look great."

"Thank you, Sam." I took my seat and unfolded the linen napkin by my plate. "How are you? It's been a long time."

"I'm good. How's Emily?"

"She's great," Kit replied for me, removing the lid from a covered dish. "Happily married. She and Luke, her *husband*, are doing wonderful things in California. Val, pass me your plate."

Sam gave an exaggerated look of surprise, and I was forced to suppress a giggle. "Glad to hear it," he said.

But Kit wasn't done. "Not all Californians get a divorce every five minutes. Nor does that happen anywhere, for that matter." She finished spooning a large portion of chicken onto my plate and held out her hand for Sam's. "Look, Sam, all I'm saying is that we all know Leslie is no great prize, and no one would blame you if . . ." She shook her head in disgust. "You could have done much better, ya know, than—"

"You think I married down?" Sam finished his mother's thought. He looked angry now and made no move to hand his mother his plate.

"I think that maybe you had good reasons for . . . whatever the hell it is you did. But I'm just asking— no, I'm just suggesting—that you give your marriage another try. Divorce is ugly. Tell him, Val. Tell him what a nightmare it is."

Before I had a chance to answer, Larry, who had so far remained silent, threw his napkin down on his empty plate. "Kit! Would you please give it a rest. If our son wants a divorce, that's his choice. Whatever he's done, or has not done, is his business. Not ours." Then slowly and carefully he placed his napkin back on his lap. "Son," he addressed Sam, "you do what you have to do. Your mother and I will support whatever decision you make. End of subject. Kit, please pass the damn chicken."

"Coq au vin."

"Whatever the hell you're calling it, just *pass* it."

211

As I took the dish Kit handed me and gave it to Larry, I found my voice. "Sam, no matter what your mother may tell you, divorce is not the end of the world. Not always. In fact, in my case, it was the beginning of a whole new life, a much better one."

"Yes," Kit said. "But, Val, you were married to such a prick."

My friend was right, of course, but I suddenly wished we could at least get Leslie's opinion on who had married the prickiest man. For my money, it was probably an even bet.

"Sam has been an exemplary husband, haven't you, darling?" Kit went on. "But we all make mistakes." She reached across and took Sam's plate. "Whatever it is that went on between you two—"

"Mom, if you don't drop it, I'm leaving." His face still looked angry, angry enough that Kit immediately changed the subject.

"How's Texas, anyway? I don't know how you can stand the heat down there," she said.

"It's not much hotter there than it is here in the summer," Larry offered.

"Right. And isn't everything air-conditioned?" Kit asked.

"Right, Mom, everything is air-conditioned. And in the winter when you're shoveling snow, we're out in shorts. Anything else you want to know?"

I heard Kit heave a deep sigh. "I just want to know that you are all right. That you are happy. That you are making the right choice. Is that so bad?"

"Mom . . ." He didn't finish his thought.

I suspected he probably had Leslie's replacement lined up. And after a while he'd have another replacement in his sights. *Guys like him just can't be content*, I thought. And although she wasn't even there, I took a sip of wine and silently wished Leslie the best. And I felt certain her life *was* about to get better.

It all made me sick to my stomach, and so it was almost—*almost*—easy to decline when Kit offered dessert. "I have to get over to Buddy's hotel and say good-bye, and then I need to get home to bed." I knew I could have been talked into staying if it had been only my work schedule I was concerned with. But as compelling as the James family drama was, I couldn't get my mind off my brother.

"Val, are you sure you have to leave?" Kit asked one last time as I gathered my purse from their front closet.

"Yes."

"At least let me fix you some food to go," she extended her customary offer of leftovers.

"Not tonight. I have to get going so I can be fresh tomorrow. I'm meeting a new client in the morning, and I really think it's going to lead to a sale."

"Who is it? What are you showing?"

"The house on Glassmore. I think it might be perfect for this family. But I have a few other listings lined up too. They're doctors, just moving here. I met the wife at Target." I kissed her cheek at the front door and exited sans the chicken-in-wine dish. I heard her close the door and headed to my car parked at the end of their driveway, behind what I assumed was Sam's rental car.

"Val," I heard a male voice. "Auntie Val, can you wait a minute?"

I looked back to see Sam headed my way. I wasn't pleased, not only because I wanted to get to Buddy as soon as possible, but also because I thought there was nothing I could offer that would help Kit in any way.

When he reached me, he gave me an awkward hug. Or did I receive the hug awkwardly? "Sorry you were put on the spot in there," he said.

"I wasn't on the spot, Sam. I was being honest. If you no longer love Leslie, then—"

"That's the problem. I do love her. More than anything."

I took my key fob out of my purse and hit the button, wondering how many times David had said the very same thing to someone about me, not meaning a word of it. I turned my back to Sam and reached for the car door, but he put his hand on my shoulder. "Val, my parents have me tried and convicted. Without really saying it, they believe I've cheated on Leslie, but it's not true. I wouldn't. I love her."

I turned to face him, and maybe for the first time ever, his demeanor appeared earnest. But I still didn't trust him. "Sam, it's none of my business—"

Before I could finish, he whipped his phone out of his pocket and began flipping through pictures. When he found the one he wanted, he held it up to my face: a picture of Leslie locked in an intimate embrace with a man, a man who wasn't Sam. "She left me, Val. I've done all I can to show her I don't want her to leave, but she's filed for divorce."

"Who took this?"

"An investigator I hired. There are more; this is the PG version."

I grabbed the phone from him and zoomed in on the picture. "So *you* never . . ."

"Cheated on her? No. Never. I swear it. I love her. The last thing I want is a divorce, but I'm afraid it's too late."

"Have your parents seen this picture?"

"Not yet. I'll show them this evening. They are so convinced I screwed up, I had the pictures taken as some sort of proof."

He was right. For all Kit's posturing about what a saint her son was and how he was married to a shrew, deep in her heart I was sure she thought her son was the bad guy. But as I watched him shut off his phone and return it to his pocket, I was overwhelmed with sadness for him. In this matter, perhaps the most important matter of his young life, it seemed that Kit was wrong, and I was too.

***

"Val, am I glad to see you." Hearing my brother sound so relieved again made me more than nervous. It made me scared, especially when he grabbed me in a bear hug.

I extricated myself from his embrace. "Why—"

"I just wanted to see you, that's all. Is that so terrible?"

"No, of course not. But Buddy, what's going on? *Now*," I added for good measure. "Is it about Oxana Hutz— Kutz—"

"Oxana Kusnetsov. No, she's out of the picture," he said. He'd walked over to the bedside table and was fiddling with the clock. "I can never set these damn things."

"Here, let me do it. What time do you want it set for?"

"Six." He handed me the clock and then immediately walked across the room to a small circular table and two cozy armchairs by the window. "Val, come sit down for a minute. Please."

I put the clock back on the bedside table, noting the look of anguish that had suddenly appeared on his face. "What is it?" I asked, taking the seat across from him.

"There's something I need you to do." As he spoke, he took his phone out of his pocket and placed it on the table between us. "I need your help."

"Okay. What do you need?" I was smiling brightly, as if he were going to ask me to iron his shirt or trim the back of his hair, but I was terrified to learn just what it was he needed. If he was going to ask me to accompany him on some Secret Service mission to Timbuktu, I was going to be out of there in two seconds. But it was worse than that. So much worse.

"I have to call Mom, and William, and tell them there is no Autumn."

My fake bright smile widened and then morphed into a gale of laughter. He said nothing, just stared at me, waiting for my bout of hilarity to subside. "Oh," I said when it was finally over and I had transformed back from hyena to incredulous sister. "Oh, you're *serious*?"

He nodded, looking solemn.

"Maybe you should drive up to Door County and tell her in person."

He shook his head, focusing on the phone lying in the middle of the table.

"Then how about you call her when you get back home, with Elaine—"

He shook his head again. "I have to do it now, Val. The longer I wait, the worse it will be."

"Okay." I put my hands on the arms of the chair, about to get up.

"And I need you here."

I slumped back down. "No, Buddy. You don't need me. It'll be much better if I leave and—"

"Val, did you hear me? I *need* you here. She'll take it much better if she knows you're in the room."

I watched his fingers hover over the phone, and it was like waiting for him to pull the pin out of a grenade. "Buddy, please, think about it; she's probably asleep, anyway, and if you wake her—"

"She won't be asleep. And I have to do this now. I don't want to leave here with any loose ends."

"But—"

"I'm doing it, Val. Remember when you told me not to jump off the Carlsons' roof, and I did it anyway—"

"How is that remotely like—"

"Oh, hi, Mom. How are you?" he said. He'd not only pulled the damn pin, but now he hit the speaker button and turned the phone so that we could both enjoy the delightful conversation to come. "It's your son—Buddy."

A few seconds of silence ensued.

"Buddy? Well, I'm glad you clarified that. I was thinking I might have another son out there I didn't know anything about."

"I'm here too," I chirped, after a wave from my brother's hand indicated I should say something.

"Valerie? Or am I rushing to conclusions?"

216

"Look, Mom." Roof-jumping Brother had instantly switched to Navy Commander. "I have something to tell you. I'm sorry it's so late, but I need to come clean."

"Again?" Doubting Mother responded. "What is it this time? Have you stumbled across another of your offspring? Is there a tribe of Pygmies in Africa worshipping you as their chieftain?"

I slapped a hand across my mouth to keep from laughing. This was going much better than I'd thought it might. In fact, I was glad I'd come; it was downright entertaining.

"Autumn is not my daughter," he began slowly, and then relayed the story—as much of it as he could, anyway—while our mother listened in silence. As his fantastic tale poured out, he rose and paced around the table, stopping occasionally to grab the back of the armchair as if using it to prop himself up. When he had spilled everything he had already told me, he sat back down. We both stared at the phone.

The seconds of silence ticked by again.

"Mom, are you okay?" he asked at last. "Are you still there?"

"Yes, I'm still here. Where else would I be after learning that my son has been gallivanting around the world with a woman young enough to be his daughter, but not actually his daughter, just someone pretending to be his daughter, and meanwhile his sister is getting her nails done with this person and is oblivious to the murder going on right under her nose?"

I glanced across the table at Buddy, wondering if there was any point in explaining anything to her that she might have misconstrued. No, definitely no point. So I remained silent.

When I was about to ask if she'd hung up, our mother spoke again. "Are you safe? Is Valerie safe?"

We nodded, then realized she couldn't see us, and so we both practically yelled, "Yes, we're safe."

"Mom," Buddy said, "you know, because of my job, I can't go into details, and I'm sorry I had to . . . fool you for a while. But believe me, it was absolutely necessary."

"Because?" she asked in a soft voice.

"In order to be safe. And to help keep our country safe."

More silence and then, "Buddy, I'm proud of you. And your father would be too."

"Whew, that went well," I said when he'd turned his phone off. "And I don't mean that it *didn't* go well, which people normally mean when they say that. It really *did* go well."

"Yeah, it kinda did, didn't it?" He rose from the armchair and stretched. "Val, I've been thinking; why don't you come back to DC with me? Tomorrow. It's been too long since you've visited, and Elaine and the girls would love to see you, and—"

"I wish I could. That sounds so fun," I lied. "But I can't possibly leave right now. Tom would have kittens; he's already on my case—"

"I can handle Tom."

"Seriously, I can't, Buddy. I have an early—and important—meeting with a new client and a whole day of showings tomorrow. In fact, I really should get going now."

"Okay." The expression on his face was an older version of the one he wore as a kid on Christmas mornings when our parents told us it was too early to open presents yet. "Well, promise me you'll come visit soon. A long weekend, at least."

"Promise."

CHAPTER TWENTY-NINE

As I walked to my car (by now, all I could think of was crawling into bed and getting some much-needed rest), I remembered that I'd silenced my phone in the hotel room in order to give Buddy my full attention. I dug it out of my purse to turn the volume back on and noticed I'd missed several calls from Larry. Because I could count on one hand the number of phone calls I'd received from him, a tiny fear crept over me. And before I even reached my car, he called again.

"Larry?"

"Val! I've been trying you for the last thirty minutes; I was just about to give up."

"Is everything okay?"

"Yeah. I just wanted to have a quick word, without Kit—or Sam, for that matter—in earshot. Can you talk?"

"Yes, of course. What's up?"

"It's about Kit. You're her oldest friend, so I know there's not much I can tell you about her that you don't already know. But when it comes to divorce—"

"I get it, Larry. She hates the whole idea of it, especially for her son."

"Yeah, she does. There's not much Kit can't handle, but divorce is a tricky one for her. And you know why, right?"

"Well, I suppose no one wants to see their loved one's marriage come to an end."

"Yeah, but it's not just that. You remember when her parents split, right? It was really nasty. We were newly married, and it was very hard on her. I know your own divorce left you better off, but Kit's parents' divorce left her with a lot of scars."

I knew Larry was right. But the sad truth was, I didn't know a lot about Kit's parents' breakup. She had rarely spoken about it back then, and when she did, it was mainly in terms of how inconvenient it was for her and her sister, especially the holidays they were forced to split between their parents. I was a newlywed at the time, and I realized now, with a feeling of shame, that I hadn't paid my friend enough attention. I was caught up in my own new marriage, and it was too early to foresee what a disaster that would become. "We were in our twenties, right?" I didn't know what else to say.

"Yep, but I don't think it matters how old you are when your parents divorce. Still hurts like hell." His voice held a trace of bitterness, like he was still mad at Kit's parents for putting her through that pain.

"You're right, Larry. Of course." I stopped to think about Kit again, going through something traumatizing without my full support. "So, Larry, what do *you* really think about Sam divorcing? If it comes to that."

"I think he should do what makes him happy. He's my son; I love him no matter what." I assumed Sam hadn't shown his parents the pictures on his phone yet, and I felt some kind of relief knowing what was coming their way when he did. In this situation, at least, their son was not the bad guy.

"I won't keep you, Val. I know you've got a big day tomorrow. I just wanted to point out where Kit is coming from. Maybe we can both try not to be too hard on her."

"I get it. I totally get it."

"I knew you would. Now I have to get back. Sam says he has something to show us." He laughed a little bit as he added, "God help us all."

***

Early the next morning, after showering and washing my hair, I searched in my closet for something I hoped would impress Dr. Heathcote. I chose a pair of beige linen pants and a chocolate-colored summer blazer that was flattering. At least it was long enough to cover my rear end and boxy enough to give the appearance that there might be a waistline lurking somewhere beneath it. I had just turned my attention to selecting the right blouse when I heard my phone ring. I hurried to my bedside table to retrieve it.

"Val?" It was Kit, calling before seven.

"I really can't talk now," I said, knowing she was probably desperate to discuss Sam and Leslie. "I have to leave. But when I get done, I'll come right over."

"Did Sam show you the pictures?" she asked.

"Yes, he—"

"I just wanted to remind you that I was right all along. Sam is the innocent one in this mess; he's done nothing wrong. I just knew it."

I didn't point out that she would deem Sam innocent if she'd just learned he was a serial killer; she would have found a way to justify it. I didn't have time right now to point anything out. "Kit, we'll discuss it, I promise, but I can't be late. And I have a few things to do before I meet my new client."

"Okay, we'll talk when you get here. And good luck, Valley Girl. You could do with a big sale."

Well, thank you so much for pointing that out.

I returned to my closet, and my phone rang again. Seeing my mother's name appear on the screen, I didn't answer but waited for the ringing to stop—something that goes against my very nature. Then I put my phone on mute so I could finish dressing without interruption. I didn't have time to talk, and I figured everything that *had* to be said was said last night. I'd call her later, when I was finished with my client.

I felt excited as I stopped at the office before meeting Dr. Heathcote. Billie was at my desk before I sat down and handed me several sheets of paper with all the details printed out for the upcoming showings. "Thanks, Bill." I took the papers and the steaming cup of coffee she handed me.

"There's been a change," she said. "Dr. Heathcote called twenty minutes ago; she tried your cell but got no answer. She's found a house on her own that she wants to see and would like you to meet her there. Oh, and Kit called."

"Again? I just talked to her." I quickly checked my phone, noting a couple of missed calls that had come while I was getting dressed. *Damn*, I thought as I unmuted it, *I seriously need to stop this habit.* "Dr. Heathcote didn't sound like she was backing out, did she?"

"No. Not at all. She was very apologetic. She sounded nice. Is she British?"

"Yes."

"Her accent is so cool. I love a British accent."

"Yes, it's cool," I agreed, looking at my watch. I still had an hour before I needed to leave to meet Kendra Heathcote, and I had a few things to go over. "I'll call her now."

When she didn't answer her phone, I left a message asking her to call me as soon as she could. Then, as I looked over the listings I planned to show her, the door opened and

Tom breezed in, nodding to me as he passed my desk and indicating I should follow him. I grabbed the Target bag that held the purse for his girlfriend's kid and entered his office, laying the bag on his desk.

"What's this?"

"The gift you told me to pick up for Sophie."

"Sophia."

"Whatever, it's a cute purse."

"Take it back."

"What?"

"Yeah, take it back. Her mother and I broke up."

I sat down. "Well, that was quick. You just met her five minutes ago."

"She's an imbecile, Val. Can't tell a full house from a flush. Never heard of Sandy Koufax—"

"Who's she?"

He stared at me, incredulous. "Just return whatever it is I got her."

"She sounds pretty normal." *And young.*

"Normal, I don't need. She's gone. Now go sell me a house. I think you owe me one."

I rose and headed toward the office door, mumbling. "Well, maybe if I wasn't your personal shop—"

"Bye, Val. And by the way, you look very nice today."

***

When Kendra Heathcote returned my call, she asked me to meet her at the house she'd found. She couldn't remember the name of the realty company on the sign in the yard, or the actual address of the property, but she said she was on her way there now and she'd text me the information in a few minutes. If I just headed out toward her hotel, I'd be going in the right direction, she assured me. I suggested we visit her new find later in the day so I could have a chance to check it out. But she was adamant that we see it immediately. I kept any irritation out of my voice as I told her that would be fine, but I was forced to ask Billie to move all the appointments I had painstakingly set up to later in the day. I gulped down the remains of my second cup of coffee, which had by now grown cold, and headed out.

When I was halfway to her hotel, a text came with an address on Roland Circle. I was not familiar with the location, and my GPS seemed as lost as I was as I slowly drove up and down the streets in the vicinity.

Eventually, I reached a huge cul-de-sac with six three-story houses forming a horseshoe, and I spotted a sign outside the largest. A black SUV was parked in the driveway, and as I drove past the sign in the middle of the front lawn, I noticed it announced that the house was for sale by owner.

I parked in the street, and before I even stepped out of my car, the front door opened and Kendra Heathcoat appeared, waving at me.

"Hi, Val," she yelled. "Come in; it's perfect, don't you think?"

I made my way out of my Lexus and headed up the winding sidewalk that bisected the spacious lawn. "Dr. Heathcote," I called before I reached her, "are the owners okay with me coming? I mean, it's by owner—"

"Don't worry, Val. They're here, and they're very nice. Come in; they're dying to meet you." She waved me in, like a vendor at a sidewalk sale urging me inside a store.

By the time I arrived at the front door and entered the spacious foyer, I could feel my hefty commission shrinking. *Damn* owners who try to sell their houses themselves.

Kendra smiled as she reached around me and pushed the front door shut, and then I became aware of another person, standing behind me. Still facing Kendra, I felt a heavy forearm rapidly lodge itself against my throat and something soft and sweet-tasting cover my mouth and nose. I made no concerted effort to struggle free and instead could feel myself breathing deeply into the fabric. It even felt nice as I began to relax, like the first sniff of nitrous oxide the dentist gives you; and then I felt my eyes become heavy, and I just had to close them.

"Not too much" was the last thing I heard Kendra say as I drifted off to another place, thinking how beautiful the chandelier was that hung from the fifteen-foot ceiling.

CHAPTER THIRTY

I awoke on a concrete floor, leaning against a cold wall. My wrists were tied together with those white plastic things the police seem to use when they run out of real handcuffs.

In addition, there was a long piece of what appeared to be electrical tape binding me to a pole that stretched from the floor to the ceiling. My ankles were also bound in the same way, and yet, miraculously, my shoes were still on my feet. But the worst part, as if all that wasn't bad enough, was the strip of what I presumed was duct tape plastered across my mouth. I tried desperately to remain calm and breathe slowly through my nose. In and out. I forced myself into a state of composure I'd never experienced before. Since I hadn't suffocated, I assumed it was working.

The room appeared to be a basement, the kind found in many large homes, running the length of the entire first floor. The only light was coming from three small windows just below the ceiling, which I guessed was at ground level on the outside.

I had no idea how long I'd been asleep or sequestered in my basement prison. All I felt was terror, immediate and barely controllable. The horror of being restrained, alone, with no one knowing my whereabouts, was agonizing. I was desolate. I started to cry. What would have been large, howling sobs were instead deadened cries for help. At least I was getting the hang of the duct tape and discovered that if I stretched my cheeks by trying to grin, it loosened somewhat.

After five minutes or five hours—surely not five days?—I heard the door at the top of the long staircase squeak open and footsteps descending. I could see a woman's legs, which I assumed were Kendra's, and that was soon confirmed. I raised my eyebrows in hope and tried to speak. I wanted to warn her to be careful, that there was someone else in the house—maybe more than one person— but my words were unintelligible.

I soon realized it didn't matter, however.

She crossed the basement and stopped in front of me and then began a strange sort of striptease. First, she removed her large glasses, and then she rubbed her adorable freckles from her cheeks and ran the back of her hand across her mouth, removing her lipstick. In horror, I watched her pull her cute Kendra nose off her face, revealing another one not quite so cute—but no doubt the one she was born with. Finally, her pièce de résistance, the gorgeous auburn wig. She pulled it roughly from her head, and what we were left with was Autumn's—or rather Oxana's—shaved hair on the sides of her head. Worst of all, it was already growing out, and not in an attractive way. One of the big disadvantages of shaving one's head: you have to commit to it or wear a baseball cap.

"How are you feeling?" She knelt in front of me. As much as I feared her ripping off the tape, I was praying she would do so, and quickly. My prayers were answered when in a swift movement, she yanked the sucker off.

I noticed her Kendra accent was also gone, and she now spoke with a hint of something foreign that was definitely not British. "Who are you today?" I took a huge gulp of air. "Obviously not Kendra. Or Autumn. Oxana?"

"One out of three ain't bad. But don't worry about who I am."

"Well, weren't we related at one time?" I asked, feeling a little braver.

"You are funny, Valerie Pankowski," she said. "Your name is Polish?"

"I can neither confirm nor deny." Then, deciding it could do no harm, I nodded. "My husband's name, or rather my ex-husband's. And you are . . ."

"I think you know who I am."

"Okay, listen." I tried to sound even braver, or at least not as frightened as I felt. "You should know that my brother followed me here. He's going to show up any minute, if he isn't here already. It's going to take him two seconds to find me."

"I seriously doubt that," she said nonchalantly, standing and putting her hands on her hips. "But don't worry; you'll see him eventually, when we are ready."

I felt like I was chatting with a vicious dog that might bite me at any moment. "Look," I said calmly, "I'm not sure why I'm here or what your plan is, but please, please, I mean you no harm."

With that, she burst into loud laughter. "*You* mean *me* no harm? I think you've got it backwards."

"Okay, then just tell me what the hell it is you want. If it's my brother, he's back in DC and—"

"Really? You just told me he'd be here in two seconds to rescue you."

"Okay, obviously that wasn't true. But—"

"Valerie Pankowski, you talk too much. I think you should just be quiet for a while." And then the unthinkable happened. From her pocket, she removed a fresh roll of silver duct tape, and I watched her rip off a healthy chunk with her teeth. Before I even had a chance to recite the Geneva Convention rules of hostage taking, or the Warsaw

Pact of prisoner something or other, she pressed it across my mouth.

***

When clouds moved across the sun, the light from the windows faded. As the basement darkened, so did my spirits, my bravado, and my hope.

The duct tape across my mouth was itchy and uncomfortable. And even though I was sure it was still warm outside, the basement was cold. I could feel tears running down my cheeks as I wondered how long I could survive without food and water. I was already hungry and thirsty.

I closed my eyes for just a second, I thought, but when I opened them again, the clouds had passed and the basement was lighter.

I could hear a series of thumping sounds, and at first I chalked them up to the normal rumblings of pipes common in all houses. But the sound grew louder, closer, clomp, clomp, clomp, and turning my attention to the stairs, I identified the sound as footsteps. Heavy ones, possibly those of a man, heading my way. After a few seconds, I could make out his shape.

He walked slowly toward me, and when he became truly visible, I was actually relieved. I knew this man, I liked this man, and surely he was here to help me. The only confusing part was that I had never seen him upright, using his legs for their intended purpose.

"Andy!" I mouthed through the dreadful tape, but Oxana had done a good job, and I barely made a sound.

When he reached my feet, he squatted down in front of me. Apparently, his legs were now in good working order. Then he cocked his head to one side and gave me a crooked grin. "I'm going to remove this." He pointed to the duct tape. Then he leaned forward and almost tenderly dislodged my gag. But it still hurt.

"Andy!" I said again, and it felt so good to speak normally and hear my own voice. "Andy, where's your wheelchair? You can walk?"

He laughed a little, probably because I was foolishly clinging to the idea that maybe he had suddenly gained the use of his legs and his first outing was to rescue his neighbor. But his laugh soon ended and his face grew solemn. "Valerie. I am sorry about this. You are a very nice lady."

"This? You mean this kidnapping? Who are you? I presume not Andy."

He sat all the way down, stretching out his miracle legs and resting the palms of his hands on the ground, like he was sitting on a patch of grass and enjoying a sunny day. "You were a good neighbor," he said, and I noticed a slight tinge of an accent I'd never heard from him. It wasn't exactly Bela Lugosi, but it wasn't Mr. Rogers, either. "I'd go so far as to call you a friend. Not overly intrusive."

"Why did you pretend you couldn't walk, and what is your real name? And who the hell are you, really?"

He shook his head, the smile back on his face. "Suddenly you are inquisitive. One of the things I liked about you, Valerie, was you didn't ask me endless questions." He crossed his feet. "So, to answer your questions now, but maybe not in the right order, you don't need to know my name. It will mean nothing to you. The wheelchair? Well, as you can see, I don't need it, but it served my purpose. Americans are kind to people with disabilities; you can't do enough for us." Now he laughed, throwing his head back, proving he was clearly enjoying our little chat.

"And Hettie? Did she work for you?"

Now he laughed harder. "No, definitely not. She was nice, but annoying, and very nosy. We had no choice other than to get rid of her."

My mind raced as I recalled with shame the times I had literally shut the door in Hettie's face, leaving her standing in the hall in her Adidas getup. "Because she found out that Autumn was really Oxana?" I asked.

"Yes, you know about Oxana. Did your friend Kit figure that out?"

I felt offended that he was crediting Kit with the unveiling of his superspy. "Kit never even met her—well, not until the day she left town with my brother. I assume you were in cahoots with Oxana."

"Not in cahoots, as you so charmingly call it. Oxana works for me. I work for someone else. She was doing some contract work for our employer; my job was to keep an eye on her, keep her safe, if you like. But the unfortunate Hettie got too close. I believe the expression is too close for comfort. Or that other one: curiosity killed the cat. She just wouldn't stay out of it."

"So you killed Hettie . . . or Oxana did?"

"Neither one of us. I'm not sure of the person who did the actual killing."

"But it was done under your orders?"

He nodded, but had the good manners to look upset about it. "Unfortunate, because I really enjoyed her meat loaf."

"And it was you who brought Oxana to our—my—building?" I was relieved to think it had not been my brother's idea.

"Yes. Since you are a relative of Charles Caldwell, I was betting that he would visit you."

"But why? And how do you know my brother? And where—"

"Too many questions, Valerie. That's what got Hettie in trouble."

He reached for the tape, and I could see it headed back in my direction. "Are you going to kill me, Andy?" I said this calmly, without any fear. I might have been asking him if he wanted to stay for dinner.

"Not yet, but eventually we will probably have to. It will bring me no joy. But first, we need to get your brother back here. What he has to say might alter things dramatically."

Before I even had a chance to tell Andy that I'd been planning to buy him a flat-screen TV, not to mention all the fun chess games we were going to enjoy together, he returned the tape to my mouth. Then he rose from his crouching position and headed back up the stairs.

I sat perfectly still except for my shivering, hoping for another visitor and dreading it at the same time.

When I tried to comprehend the situation I now found myself in, I knew I had no one else to blame. How could I have been so easily manipulated by Andy? How did I not see that his nifty maneuvering of an ancient wheelchair hinted—if not screamed—*able-bodied man*?

Since no one knew where I was, except perhaps the entire Eastern Bloc, I was not expecting a rescue anytime soon.

But I should have known better.

When I heard the sound of something hitting the middle window on the other side of the basement, I thought maybe I was hallucinating. I seemed to have lost all sense of reality.

I stared at the window with a mixture of hope and disbelief, unable to move. The sound grew louder, and then one tap was accompanied by another, until finally it was clear that someone was using two hands to bang on the glass. Since it was obvious that my captors could simply just use the stairs to visit me, a glimmer of hope began to form.

"Val!" I heard a muffled scream, and I nodded my head vigorously. "Val? Val, are you in there?" I could see the outline of someone's face pressed up against the window, hands forming a visor above the eyes.

The tapping stopped momentarily, and the face disappeared; with it went my hope of ever seeing human life again.

I tried to yell, but the duct tape thwarted me. Then I heard the sound of breaking glass, and a large brick came hurtling through the window and landed on the basement floor. Then, through the broken glass, a face appeared. The dearest face in the world.

Kit.

CHAPTER THIRTY-ONE

My pal had another brick in her hand, and she used it to punch out the remaining glass of the window before she was able to poke her head fully through. "What the fuck, Valley Girl." She looked at me with surprise and then slowly surveyed my new living space.

Unable to answer, I merely nodded, my eyes wide.

I could see she was biting her bottom lip as she contemplated what to do. "I guess I'm going to have to come in and get you out," she said, like she'd just settled on her next move in a bizarre game of Parcheesi.

I nodded vigorously, hoping to convey that she better hurry in case my kidnappers returned. But even if that were to happen, I felt safer already, knowing Kit was just outside.

My eyes remained glued to the window as her face disappeared from view, and then her feet appeared, encased in silver flip-flops that complemented her perfectly manicured glossy-white toenails. When her legs, covered in black yoga pants, made it through the narrow space and she was able to get a firm hold on the window frame, she dropped all the way down, landing on the cement floor like an Olympic gymnast. A perfect ten.

"Kitty Kat, be careful." My voice was once again stifled by the duct tape.

She began kicking away the glass shards, wasting no time getting to me. I watched in awe as she took a Swiss Army knife from a side pocket in her pants (did she always carry a knife?) and picked the perfect tool to cut my shackles and the umbilical cord attached to the pole. "Rub your wrists to get the circulation going," she said.

I complied, dreading the removal of the duct tape and praying *this* would be the last time. She quickly and without ceremony ripped it from my mouth, and it was every bit as painful as before. But I was just so relieved that it was Kit and not my captors doing the ripping that I joyfully once again gulped in the stale air of the musty basement.

With my hands now free and my ability to speak restored, I put my index finger to my lips, indicating that we should be as quiet as possible. "There are people upstairs," I whispered.

Kit nodded. "So," she whispered back, sitting down on the floor and looking relaxed, "how'd this happen?"

I was unable to answer immediately and could feel tears forming again, only this time they were happy tears. Relief, awe, love. Love for my best friend, whom I should have known would rescue me. I merely nodded.

"Hey, you don't have Stockholm syndrome, do you?"

That made me laugh—very quietly—and after I wiped my tears away, I reached over to her and wrapped my arms around her. "Thank you, Kit. Thank you for coming to get me." Even whispering, my voice sounded hoarse, and my throat hurt a little.

She patted my leg. "No problem. Now let's get out of here."

By tacit agreement, we didn't ascend the stairs and try to exit that way. Nevertheless, it proved to be quite easy to escape. In fact, I wondered how Oxana Kusnetsov could have been so careless as to leave four dining room chairs stacked in a dark corner of the basement. Clearly, she didn't know Kit James. We easily moved one to the open window.

I stood on the chair first and hoisted myself up to the ledge of the window, with Kit pushing my rear end.

"I hope you have learned your lesson," she said.

"Er ... not to get myself kidnapped?" I huffed as I placed my elbows on the sill and managed to get my upper body out of the window.

"I was thinking more about wearing linen pants. They never really look good after about five minutes."

"Riiight," I agreed, as I pulled my legs through the window. "Next time I am taken hostage, I'll definitely consider Lycra." Once I was fully out of the window, I turned and reached for Kit's arms and pulled her to freedom. We both fell back on the grass.

Then, as if remembering that someone could come out of the house at any minute, Kit sat up and said, "That was fun, but it would probably be a good idea to get the hell out of here."

I glanced at the empty driveway and began to doubt that anyone else was still here. And then I noticed Kit's BMW parked in front of a house on the other side of the cul-de-sac. I stood and reached for her arms, helping her to her feet. "Kit, I think I'm too shaky to drive," I said.

"No worries. We'll take my car and come back for yours later."

"How did you know where I was?" I asked as she put her arm around my waist and led me to her car.

"I followed you."

"What? That's crazy."

"Not so crazy. I never really bought the idea that Shaved Head had left town as Frick and Frack seemed to think."

"You mean Buddy and Culotta?"

236

"Naturally. And I was very suspicious of this new client who appeared out of nowhere. Let's face it, Val, a genuine doctor doesn't shop for Realtors at Walmart—"

"It was Target, actually."

"Same difference. I didn't want to spook you, so I thought the best thing to do was just keep an eye on you. And when I called your office—before you got there—Billie mentioned your client had changed the place you were supposed to meet. And when she told me she didn't know where—"

"Right, that makes sense. How could I have been so stupid? One of Tom's rules is that we always let someone know where we're going."

"Yes, because Tom is such a master of security." Kit opened the car door on the passenger side and strapped me in with the seat belt as if I were a toddler. "You're okay now, honey."

"Kit, I can't thank you—"

"Save it. Nothing to thank me for."

"What about Buddy? Or Culotta? Do they know what happened?"

"I called Culotta when I realized you weren't in there with a legitimate client, when I saw Autumn come out. I'm guessing a million or so agents will show up here any minute and go over this place with a fine-tooth comb. I gave your boyfriend the license plate number of her car, so I suppose he's looking for Autumn . . . aka Kendra . . . aka Oxana— hey, what *are* we calling her?"

"How about bitch?"

Kit laughed as she started the car. "Bitch? That's the best you can do?"

I felt another wave of gratitude toward my friend wash over me. "Could we go to Starbucks?" I asked.

"Of course. Eventually, I have to deliver you to the police station, but I see no reason we can't stop for a latte first."

***

"How long were you watching the house? You must have been parked there for hours," I said as Kit placed two paper cups on the table.

"Forty-five minutes." She took a seat.

"*What?* I was in there for only forty-five minutes? Surely—"

"Forty-seven minutes, to be exact. I watched some dude come out and drive away, and soon after that, Aut— the bitch—came out and drove off. That's when I decided it was time to get you out."

"Forty-seven? Are you sure? And was it Andy you saw?"

"Andy?"

"OMG, Kit. Can you believe it? Andy—I don't even remember his last name, if I ever knew it—but Andy, who has lived in my building about three months, the guy who uses a wheelchair, is apparently working with Oxy. In fact, he's her boss." I took a sip of my latte.

I watched her scrunch up her face before responding. "I should have known."

"You? How would you have known that?"

"Because. Because I usually pick up on stuff like that. Because he never returned the plate I took him with my veal cannelloni, and it's been a week and a half. Remember? When you asked me to feed our local spy? Thank goodness the plate wasn't part of a set."

"Right," I agreed, although it hardly seemed important.

"And the son of a bitch can walk? The wheelchair was just part of . . . what? His disguise? That explains why I didn't recognize him when he came out of the house."

We both sipped in silence for a few seconds. "It must have been really terrifying, Val."

"Oh, it was." Once again, I was overcome with gratitude for my friend.

"So why do you think they left you there in that house?" Kit asked. "And what the hell did they even want with you, anyway?"

"It's Buddy they're after, obviously. Not me. He has something they want badly. But I'm not sure what. Something to do with his Navy stuff. So much for him being retired."

"Yeah, Buddy's too smart to just hang around the house and shell peas all day."

"Shell peas? Who the hell shells peas?"

"No one. But I don't know what a guy like Buddy would do all day if he was retired. So tell me what else this Andy person said."

I picked up my cup. "Okay, for starters, he's part of some kind of spy ring. They work for a foreign country, but he didn't say which one." I took a sip of coffee and put my cup back down. After a few seconds, I said in a soft voice, "They killed Hettie. And probably Rayjean Boxer too."

"They? The two of them? Wheelchair and Oxy?"

"Actually, neither. Someone in their organization. Hettie was getting too suspicious of Autumn, so they had to . . ."

We were both silent for a few seconds, in deference to the deceased women. My thoughts wandered to Bree and how—and if—she would learn the truth of Hettie's death.

Then Kit broke our silence. "Maybe this foreign country wants the keys to the USS Missouri."

That made me laugh a little, and I was thankful for Kit's sense of humor, even though it seemed inappropriate right now. "So, is our Buddy a spy too?" she asked.

"I don't think they call them spies. Do they? More like intelligence officers, maybe?" I liked the sound of that; it sounded much less dangerous.

"So whaddya know." Kit sat back in her chair, looking a little impressed. "Our Buddy is a spy. I can't wait to tell Larry."

"No, don't tell Larry; don't tell anyone. Promise me, please."

She nodded, but I wasn't convinced she'd keep quiet. "It's very important, Kit. I've told you all I know, but I shouldn't have said—"

"Relax. I won't breathe a word. It's our secret. Can I at least tell him how I rescued you?"

"No!"

"Humph. Ya know, I think I'd make a good spy."

"No doubt," I agreed. "So, with all your super-intelligence spy knowledge, what do you think will happen now?"

"Obviously, Culotta and I have taken care of the situation at hand. Oxy will be picked up, she'll be dealt with however those people are dealt with, and she won't be running around Chicagoland wreaking havoc and changing her hairstyle every five minutes. The only problem now is you explaining to your boss that you didn't make the sale."

I gulped my coffee. Yes, that was definitely going to be a problem.

CHAPTER THIRTY-TWO

Did you get that new listing up on the website?" Tom asked.

"Yes," I answered in surprise. It was only a temporary lie. I hadn't actually done it, but I planned to within the next hour. Not that I thought he'd look at the company website, anyway. I know he's not the Luddite he claims to be when it comes to using a computer, but in general, he leaves it to Billie or me. "So, anything else?" I asked, ready to end our Monday morning meeting.

"You tell me."

"No. I guess I'll hit the streets looking for houses we can sell."

"Yeah, that would be a first."

I closed my notebook and stood up, but Tom immediately waved at me to sit back down. "Before you go," he said, taking a cigar out of his breast pocket and rolling it between his fingers, "tell me what's going on with Buddy."

I sat back down immediately. Usually, Tom grows very weary, very quickly, listening to anything concerning my private life. But because my brother is a good friend of his, I believed Tom's interest contained genuine concern.

"Right now he's lounging on a cruise ship with his family. Somewhere close to The Bahamas, I believe."

"Before that." Tom's impatience was rearing its head.

"Well . . ." I wasn't sure where to begin. "As you know—"

"Buddy's a Naval Intelligence officer. He was targeted by a covert operative working for a foreign government with the aim of procuring classified information on upgrading our submarine and nuclear arms programs."

I stared at him with my mouth open and my eyes wide. He had rattled off the facts as casually as if he were ordering a sandwich at Subway. I had, so far, not learned what exactly it was that Oxana was after, so I was grateful to Tom for the information. I locked his words away as something to share with Kit to explain the whole mess, not to mention two murdered women.

"Am I right?" he asked when I didn't reply.

"Well . . . yes. I guess so. In a nutshell. But how did you—"

"I know people, Val."

"Okay, so now you also know everything."

"Probably not. Give me a few more details. A *few*."

"Oxana Kusnetsov is the name of the operative, as you call her—"

"What would *you* call her?"

"Same. But I'd add that she was—is—a nasty, dangerous woman with multiple disguises. She started out as my blond neighbor, then switched to k.d. lang—"

"Who's he?"

"He is a she, a singer, but that's not important. Oxana's last impersonation was Kendra Heathcote, a rich doctor looking to buy a house."

"So I hear, and by the way, you might want to upgrade where you recruit clients—"

"She recruited me, and—oh, never mind. That's not important, either. She sought Buddy out, posing as his never-before-seen daughter, supposedly one he didn't even know existed. Buddy went along with the ruse to help, eventually, expose the impostors and their operation."

"But he always knew this chick was not his kid, right?"

"Yes, but how did you know *that*?"

"It's obvious; Buddy's too smart. You didn't believe it, either, I'm sure."

"Not for a minute," I lied. "And Buddy was expecting her. His intelligence staff knew she was a fraud and what she was up to. And they'd been after her for a long time. So Buddy was on a mission to beat her at her own game. She moved into my building and—"

"Yeah, I wondered about that. If Buddy knew she was a spy, why did he move her into your place? There's plenty of homeless shelters in town with far better accommodations."

"Ha ha. But it wasn't Buddy's idea. And it wasn't even her decision alone."

"Who else, then?"

"Andy. You don't know him. But he is—was—a neighbor of mine. A nice guy, or so I thought, faking the need for a wheelchair, of all things. We got very friendly. I thought he needed my help occasionally, but now that I think about it, his involvement with me grew much greater after Oxana moved in. Turns out that this Andy was actually her boss. Another agent, only higher up."

"So you had two of them living over there at Spy Central."

"Yep. They probably wanted to get close to me, maybe for leverage against my brother, and he played along with it. But I was never in danger, not really. I was under surveillance the whole time—by the good guys, and maybe the bad, I suppose—and anyway, Oxy wasn't there very long."

"Where are they now, by the way?"

"Both of them are in federal custody. They'll most definitely wind up in prison."

"Good. And your neighbor guy is probably gonna need that wheelchair in there. What about your other neighbor, Hattie—"

"Hettie."

"Hettie. What's the story there? You know, finding a dead body two doors down from you isn't what I like to hear."

"Thank you for your concern. It was scary, and terrible, and Hettie was such a nice—"

"It's bad for *business*, Val. *My* business. If you, as a representative of Haskins Realty, can't find a decent place to live, how do you expect our clients to trust your judgment?"

"Well, I'm sorry you're so broken up about her death."

"Just tell me why she was killed."

"Oh, I would have thought you already had the answer since you *know people*," I said, using air quotes.

Tom began removing the cellophane from around his cigar. "Continue," he said.

And so I did. "She was suspicious of our neighbor, who at the time was claiming to be Autumn, Buddy's love child. Hettie may have confronted her; we'll never know. Her body was found in Autumn's apartment, and all indications are that she took an opportunity, when Autumn wasn't home, to snoop around and then got herself caught—and murdered. But it seems clear that Hettie was the catalyst that caused Autumn to change her appearance and run. She told Buddy she was afraid to stay there, and so he went along with it. But it's certain that members of this organization killed both women."

"Both women? Who else was killed?"

"Rayjean Boxer. She had worked with Naval Intelligence and was part of Buddy's team. She'd most recently worked as a PI; that's a private investigator."

"I know what a PI is, Val."

"Well, anyway, she's the one who drove Oxana here in the first place. But she was killed at her home in DC. Kit and I found her name on a piece of paper in Hettie's pocket, so we think Hettie might have also figured out who she was. We're afraid Hettie's interference might have inadvertently led to them killing Rayjean."

"Okay, so Buddy goes on the run with this Russian chick; then what?"

"I'm not sure she's Russian, but she was working for a cell in that general part of the world."

"She wasn't from Dubuque, Iowa, that's for sure. What next?"

"The police or maybe the CIA or FBI—or all of them—were after her and Buddy, but for different reasons. Probably Naval Intelligence was involved as well, although they were far more subtle about it. In any event, the government agencies were to protect Buddy, and obviously contain Oxana. It all came to a head when I was kidnapped—"

"Yeah, skip that part; we all know about your traumatic experience. What was it, a half hour or something?"

"Your concern for me is so touching. And it was forty-five minutes. Actually, forty-seven."

"And I understand Kit James rescued you?"

"Yes."

"Okay, then that proves my point. I don't think Kit could rescue her own big toe from one of her designer shoes."

I stood up, angry. I didn't understand what point he thought he was proving. "You have no idea how Kit saved my life. She was extremely brave."

He smiled. "Calm down. I'm glad she did. Sit, please. I'm not quite done."

Reluctantly, I sat down again. "Okay, what else do you want to know?"

He had the palms of his hands on the desk, his fingers splayed, and he was avoiding my eyes. An unusual position for him to take. The still-unlit cigar sat waiting in its heavy glass ashtray.

"Val," he said quietly. "It would kill me if anything happened to you. I mean it. If I ever hear of you running off to who knows where without telling me or Billie . . ." He looked at me now, and his face was stonelike with concern. "Promise me, Valerie; I can't—"

"I got it." I had to stop him. He was making me uncomfortable. "I was stupid. I won't do that again." I'd never seen Tom quite so serious, and it was a little terrifying. "So, now I've told you all I know. I'm going back to work." This time I stood up without any intention of sitting down again.

"One last thing." He picked up his cigar and took his eyes off me. "I hear your old pal Culotta was involved. What's he doing now?"

"I have no idea. I haven't seen or heard from him since all of this ended."

Now Tom began to light the end of his smoke, taking his time but returning his eyes to me. "Don't worry, Pankowski. You will. That guy is like a bad penny. He'll turn up."

***

Tom's mention of Culotta made me want to get my hair freshly highlighted and stop eating sugar. I took Tom at his word, certain I would see Culotta again.

And I did.

It took another week, but when I arrived at my apartment one night after a highly successful day at work—having sold three houses—I saw Culotta sitting outside my door. He was on the floor, his back leaning against the wall, with a bouquet of flowers in his hand. I didn't say a word as he got to his feet while I unlocked the door, and I wondered if he could hear how fast my heart was beating.

"Hello, beautiful," he said as I tried to discreetly smooth away the wrinkles in my linen skirt.

Why hadn't I taken Kit's advice to avoid the easily creased fabric? I smiled, but didn't speak, as Culotta followed me into my apartment.

Instead of sitting down on his favorite spot on the couch, he handed me the flowers. "Here, put these in water. And I'm taking you out to dinner. Spiaggia on Michigan. Reservations in forty-five minutes."

I stared at him in silence for a few seconds. "Then I better get changed."

"If you feel the need." I noticed then that he was wearing an expensive-looking gray suit with a crisp white shirt underneath, no tie, and his collar open at the neck.

I turned away from him to head to my bedroom, but he caught my hand. "First," he said, turning me around to face him, "let's say hello properly." I tossed the bouquet onto the couch, and he gently placed his hands on my cheeks and drew our faces together. When our lips touched, I could faintly smell Emporio Armani, which was familiar to me only because I smell it on Perry every day at work.

"Give me five minutes," I said as our lips parted, but he still held my face in his hands. Then he nodded and let me go. I hurried to my bedroom, peeking back to the living room just to be sure he was really there and I wasn't dreaming.

It was no dream. He had moved to the couch and was reading *Cosmopolitan.* I rushed to change clothes and put on my Rum Raisin lipstick. I had to get back out there before he came across the *Cosmo* quiz: "How to Tell If Your Man Is Really Into You."

I didn't want him to see my low score.

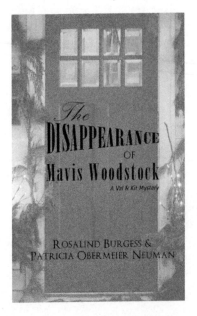

The Disappearance of Mavis Woodstock

Mavis Woodstock (a vaguely familiar name) calls Val and insists she has to sell her house as quickly as possible. Then she fails to keep her scheduled appointment. Kit remembers Mavis from their school days, an unattractive girl who was ignored when she was lucky, ridiculed when she was not. She also remembers Mavis being the only daughter in a large family that was as frugal as it was wealthy. When Val and Kit cannot locate Mavis, they begin an investigation, encountering along the way a little romance, a lot of deception, and more than one unsavory character.

FIVE STARS! "I highly recommend this novel and I'm looking forward to the next book in this series. I was kept guessing throughout the entire novel. The analogies throughout are priceless and often made me laugh. . . . I found myself on the edge of my seat. . . . The ending to this very well-written novel is brilliant!"

FIVE STARS! "I recommend this book if you like characters such as Kinsey Millhone or Stone Barrington . . . or those types. Excellent story with fun characters. Can't wait to read more of these."

FIVE STARS! "A cliff-hanger with an I-did-not-see-that-coming ending."

FIVE STARS! " . . . well written, humorous . . . a good plot and a bit of a surprise ending. An easy read that is paced well, with enough twists and turns to keep you reading to the end."

FIVE STARS! "Very enjoyable book and hard to put down. Well-written mystery with a great surprise ending. A must-read."

FIVE STARS! "This is a well-written mystery that reads along at a bright and cheerful pace with a surprisingly dark twist at the end."

FIVE STARS! "I really enjoyed this book: the characters, the story line, everything. It is well written, humorous, engaging."

FIVE STARS! "The perfect combo of sophisticated humor, fun and intriguing twists and turns!"

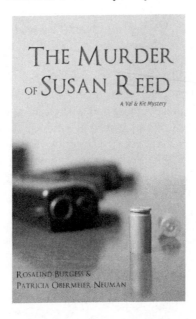

THE MURDER
OF SUSAN REED

A Val & Kit Mystery

ROSALIND BURGESS &
PATRICIA OBERMEIER NEUMAN

The Murder of Susan Reed

When Kit suspects Larry of having an affair with one of his employees, Susan Reed, she enlists Val's help in uncovering the truth. The morning after a little stalking expedition by the lifelong friends, Val reads in the newspaper that Susan Reed was found shot to death in her apartment the night before, right around the time Kit was so certain Larry and Susan were together. *Were* they having an affair? And did Larry murder her? The police, led by dishy Detective Dennis Culotta, conduct the investigation into Susan's murder, hampered at times by Val and Kit's insistent attempts to discover whether Larry is guilty of infidelity and/or murder. As the investigation heats up, so does Val's relationship with Detective Culotta.

FIVE STARS! "I couldn't wait to get this Val & Kit adventure after reading the authors' first book, and I was not disappointed. As a fan of this genre . . . I just have to write a few words praising the incredible talent of Roz and Patty. One thing I specifically want to point out is the character development. You can completely visualize the supporting actors (suspects?) so precisely that you do not waste time trying to recall details about the character. . . . Roz and Patty practically create an imprint in your mind of each character's looks/voice/mannerisms, etc."

FIVE STARS! "Even better than the first! Another page-turner! Take it to the beach or pool. You will love it!!! I did!!!"

FIVE STARS! "Great writing. Great plot."

FIVE STARS! "Once again Val & Kit star in a page-turner mystery!"

FIVE STARS! "I loved this book and these two best friends who tend to get in trouble together. Reminds me of my best friend and myself."

FIVE STARS! "Ms. Burgess and Ms. Neuman are fantastic writers and did a great job with their sophomore effort! I enjoy their writing style and they really capture the genre of cozy mystery well! I highly recommend their books!"

FIVE STARS! "Val and Kit's interactions and Val's thoughts about life in general were probably the best part of the book. I was given enough info to 'suspect' just about every character mentioned."

Death in Door County

Val embarks on a Mother's Day visit to her mom in Door County, Wisconsin, a peninsula filled with artists, lighthouses, and natural beauty. Her daughter, Emily, has arrived from LA to accompany her, and at the last minute her best friend, Kit, invites herself along. Val and Kit have barely unpacked their suitcases when trouble and tension greet them, in the form of death and a disturbing secret they unwittingly brought with them. As they get to know the locals, things take a sinister turn. And when they suspect someone close to them might be involved in blackmail—or worse—Val and Kit do what they do best: they take matters into their own hands in their obsessive, often zany, quest to uncover the truth.

What readers are saying about . . .
Death in Door County

FIVE STARS! "I really enjoyed this book. Not only was I in Door County at the time that I was reading it and Door County has always been one of my favorite places, I am also a homeowner in Downers Grove, IL, which is where Val and Kit also live. I did read the first two books in The Val & Kit Mystery Series which I also thoroughly enjoyed. Being from Downers Grove, I got quite a kick out of the real names of most of the streets being used in the stories because I could just picture where the events were taking place. Even though all three books were mysteries, they were lighthearted enough to hold my interest. I would love to see more stories in this series."

FIVE STARS! "Whether you are a mother, daughter, grandmother, great-grandmother or best friend . . . This is a heartwarming and hilarious read that would be a perfect part of your Mother's Day celebration!!! I loved getting to know Val and Kit better. Their relationships with their loved ones had me laughing and weeping all at the same time!!! I loved ending my day with Val and Kit; it just made it hard to start my day as I could not stop reading *Death in Door County*!"

FIVE STARS! "Another page-turner in the Val & Kit Series! What a great story! I loved learning about Val's family."

FIVE STARS! "Really enjoy the Val and Kit characters. They are a yin and yang of personalities that actually fit like a hand and glove. This is the third in the series and is just as much a fun read as the first two. The right amount of intrigue coupled with laughter. I am looking forward to the next in the series."

FIVE STARS! "*Death in Door County* is the third installment in the series, and each book just gets better than the last."

FIVE STARS! "The girls have done it again . . . and by girls, do I mean Val and Kit, or Roz and Patty? The amazingly talented authors, Roz and Patty, of course. Although Val and Kit have landed themselves right smack dab in the middle of yet another mystery. This is their third adventure, but don't feel as though you have to (albeit you SHOULD if you haven't done so already) read *The Disappearance of Mavis Woodstock* and *The Murder of Susan Reed* in order. This book and all the other(s) . . . are wonderful stand-alones, but read all . . . to enjoy all of the main and supporting characters' quirks . . . I can't seem to express how much I love these books . . . Speaking of characters . . . This is what sets the Val & Kit series apart from the others in this genre. The authors always give us a big cast of suspects, and each are described so incredibly . . . It's like playing a game of Clue, but way more fun. . . . the authors make the characters so memorable that you don't waste time trying to 'think back' to whom they are referring. In fact, it's hard to believe that there are only two authors writing such vivid casts for these books. So come on, ladies, confess . . . no, wait, don't. I don't want to know how you do it, just please keep it up."

FIVE STARS! "Great read! I love this series and this particular book kept me intrigued until the very end. I found myself rooting for certain characters and against others."

FIVE STARS! "Just the right mix of a page-turner mystery and humor with a modern edge. I have read all three books and am waiting impatiently for more."

FIVE STARS! "Love, love these two writers! I'm these authors' best fan, and I can't wait for these lovely ladies to write more!"

Lethal Property

In this fourth book of The Val & Kit Mystery Series (a stand-alone, like the others), our ladies are back home in Downers Grove. Val is busy selling real estate, eager to take a potential buyer to visit the home of a widow living alone. He turns out not to be all that he claimed, and a string of grisly events follows, culminating in a perilous situation for Val. Her lifelong BFF Kit is ready to do whatever necessary to ensure Val's safety and clear her name of any wrongdoing. The dishy Detective Dennis Culotta also returns to help, and with the added assistance of Val's boss, Tom Haskins, and a *Downton Abbey*–loving Rottweiler named Roscoe, the ladies become embroiled in a murder investigation extraordinaire. As always, we are introduced to a new cast of shady characters as we welcome back the old circle of friends.

FIVE STARS! "OK . . . so I thought I knew whodunit early in the book, then after changing my mind at least 8-10 times, I was still wrong. (I want to say so much more, but I really don't want to give anything away.) Just one of the many, many things I love about the Val & Kit books. I love the characters/suspects, I love the believable dialogue between characters and also Valley Girl's inner dialogue (when thinking about Tina . . . hehe). I'd like to also add that (these books) are just good, clean fun. A series of books that you would/could/should recommend to anyone. (My boss is a nun, so that's a little something I worry about . . . lol) Thanks again, ladies. I agree with another reviewer . . . it IS like catching up with old friends, and I can't wait for the next one."

FIVE STARS! "Reading *Lethal Property* was like catching up with old friends, and a few new characters, but another fun ride! I love these characters and I adore these writers. Would recommend to anyone who appreciates a good story and a sharp wit. Well done, ladies; you did it again!"

FIVE STARS! "As with the other books in this series, this can be read as a stand-alone. However, I've read all of them to date in order and that's probably the best way to do it. I'm to the point where I don't even read the cover blurb for these books . . . because I know that I'll enjoy them. This book certainly didn't disappoint. Plenty of Val and Kit and their crazy antics, a cast of new colorful characters and a mystery that wasn't predictable."

Palm Desert Killing

When one of them receives a mysterious letter, BFFs Val and Kit begin to unravel a sordid story that spans a continent and reaches back decades. It also takes them to Palm Desert, California, a paradise of palm trees, mountains, blue skies . . . and now murder. The men in their lives— Val's favorite detective, Dennis Culotta; her boss, Tom Haskins; and Kit's husband, Larry—play their (un)usual parts in this adventure that introduces a fresh batch of suspicious characters, including Kit's New York–attorney sister, Nora, and their mother. Val faces an additional challenge when her daughter, Emily, reveals her own startling news. Val and Kit bring to this story their (a)typical humor, banter, and unorthodox detective skills.

Foreign Relations

After sightseeing in London, Val and Kit move on to a rented cottage in the bucolic village of Little Dipping, where Val's actress daughter, Emily, and son-in-law are temporarily living and where Emily has become involved in community theater. Val and Kit revel in the English countryside, despite Val's ex-husband showing up and some troubling news from home. The harmony of the village is soon broken, however, by the vicious murder of one of their new friends. The shocking events that follow are only slightly more horrific than one from the past that continues to confound authorities. The crimes threaten to involve Emily, so Val and Kit return to their roles as amateur sleuths, employing their own inimitable ways.

What readers are saying about . . .
Foreign Relations

FIVE STARS! "Blimey! What fun! . . . These girls bring a sense of humor and a lot of fun to their search for who dunnit. I so enjoyed traveling with them across the pond for their latest adventure. They always keep me guessing until the end—not only about the who but the why. I especially liked the thoughtful way this book navigates the delicate challenges experienced by older children and their parents after divorce. Well done."

FIVE STARS! "Loved this fun book and a chance to catch up with my two favorite girl authors (and detectives). I particularly enjoyed that it was set in England as I am an Anglophile and some of the observations were so 'spot on' . . . a really great story that captured my attention from beginning to end. Just waiting to see what comes next and if Val will ever find a 'friend' and settle down? Please keep the books coming, Val and Kit!"

FIVE STARS! "Better than bangers and mash! These two ladies in England . . . what can possibly go wrong? A marvelous adventure punctuated with enough wit, humor and suspense to keep me a fan of Val & Kit for a long time."

FIVE STARS! "Fun series. . . . just finished reading all . . . and am already missing the stories. The characters were fun to follow as they solved the murders."

FIVE STARS! "This is my favorite series. I know I could be BFFs with Val and Kit. Characters are real. Writing is smart and funny . . . who could ask for more?? Well, I could . . . more books, please!!!"

FIVE STARS! "My husband and I enjoyed the book. It was entertaining and light reading."

FIVE STARS! "Patty and Rosalind wrote a funny, awesome book! Well done! And no royals were harmed in the process . . ."

FIVE STARS! "A wonderful book that will keep you on the edge of your seat! The mixing of the suspense with the fact that they were on vacation balanced the book perfectly. The touch of being in England was the perfect touch."

FIVE STARS! "I love the Val and Kit books because they combine a quirky friendship, distinctive personalities and humor with a mystery. This one has the added charm of being set in a quaint English village replete with tangled family relationships and unique characters. A worthy addition to the Val and Kit series."

And if you want to read about the mystery of marriage, here's a **NON–Val & Kit** book for you . . .

Rosalind Burgess & Patricia Obermeier Neuman

Dressing Myself

Meet Jessie Harleman in this contemporary women's novel about love, lust, friends, and family. Jessie and Kevin have been happily married for twenty-eight years. With their two grown kids now out of the house and living their own lives, Jessie and Kevin have reached the point they thought they longed for, yet slightly dreaded. But the house that used to burst at the seams now has too many empty rooms. Still, Jessie is a glass-half-full kind of woman, eager for this next period of her life to take hold. The problem is, nothing goes the way she planned. This novel explores growth and change and new beginnings.

FIVE STARS! "Love these writers!! So refreshing to have writers who really create such characters you truly understand and relate to. Looking forward to the next one. Definitely my favorites!"

FIVE STARS! "This book is about a woman's life torn apart. . . . A lot of detail as to how she would feel . . . very well-written. I have to agree with the other readers, 5 stars."

FIVE STARS! "What a fun read *Dressing Myself* was! . . . I have to admit I didn't expect the ending. . . . It was hard to put this book down."

FIVE STARS! "Great, easy, captivating read!! The characters seem so real! I don't read a lot, but I was really into this one! Read it for sure!"

FIVE STARS! "Loved it! Read this in one day. Enjoyed every page and had a real feeling for all of the characters. I was rooting for Jessie all the way. . . . Hope there's another story like this down the road."

FIVE STARS! "*Dressing Myself* deals with an all-too-common problem of today in a realistic manner that is sometimes sad, sometimes hopeful, as befits the subject. My expectation of the ending seesawed back and forth as the book progressed. I found it an interesting, engaging read with fully developed characters."

FIVE STARS! "Great book! It has been a long time since I have read a book cover to cover in one day . . . fantastic read . . . real page-turner that was hard to put down . . . Thanks, Ladies!"